PRETTY LITTLE LIARS

Pretty Little Liars

SARA SHEPARD

HarperTempest
An Imprint of HarperCollins*Publishers*

Produced by Alloy Entertainment
151 West 26th Street, New York, NY 10001

Library of Congress Cataloging-in-Publication Data is available.
ISBN-10: 0-06-088730-3 (trade bdg.) — ISBN-13: 978-0-06-088730-8 (trade bdg.)
ISBN-10: 0-06-088731-1 (lib. bdg.) — ISBN-13: 978-0-06-088731-5 (lib. bdg.)

Design by Amy Trombat
1 2 3 4 5 6 7 8 9 10

First Edition

For JSW

Three may keep a secret, if two of them are dead.

—BENJAMIN FRANKLIN

HOW IT ALL STARTED

Imagine it's a couple of years ago, the summer between seventh and eighth grade. You're tan from lying out next to your rock-lined pool, you've got on your new Juicy sweats (remember when everybody wore those?), and your mind's on your crush, the boy who goes to that other prep school whose name we won't mention and who folds jeans at Abercrombie in the mall. You're eating your Cocoa Krispies just how you like 'em—doused in skim milk—and you see this girl's face on the side of the milk carton. MISSING. She's cute—probably cuter than you—and has a feisty look in her eyes. You think, *Hmm, maybe* she *likes soggy Cocoa Krispies too.* And you bet she'd think Abercrombie boy was a hottie as well. You wonder how someone so . . . well, so much like you went missing. You thought only girls who entered beauty pageants ended up on the sides of milk cartons.

Well, think again.

Aria Montgomery burrowed her face in her best friend Alison DiLaurentis's lawn. "Delicious," she murmured.

"Are you smelling the grass?" Emily Fields called from behind her, pushing the door of her mom's Volvo wagon closed with her long, freckly arm.

"It smells good." Aria brushed away her pink-striped hair and breathed in the warm early-evening air. "Like summer."

Emily waved 'bye to her mom and pulled up the blah jeans that were hanging on her skinny hips. Emily had been a competitive swimmer since Tadpole League, and even though she looked great in a Speedo, she never wore anything tight or remotely cute like the rest of the girls in her seventh-grade class. That was because Emily's parents insisted that one built character from the inside out. (Although Emily was pretty certain that being forced to hide her IRISH GIRLS DO IT BETTER baby tee at the back of her underwear drawer wasn't exactly character enhancing.)

"You guys!" Alison pirouetted through the front yard. Her hair was bunched up in a messy ponytail, and she was still wearing her rolled-up field hockey kilt from the team's end-of-the-year party that afternoon. Alison was the only seventh grader to make the JV team and got rides home with the older Rosewood Day School girls, who blasted Jay-Z from their Cherokees and sprayed Alison with perfume before dropping her off so that she wouldn't smell like the cigarettes they'd all been smoking.

"What am I missing?" called Spencer Hastings, sliding through a gap in Ali's hedges to join the others. Spencer lived next door. She flipped her long, sleek dark-blond ponytail over her shoulder and took a swig from her purple Nalgene bottle. Spencer hadn't made the JV cut with Ali in the fall, and had to play on the seventh-grade team. She'd been on a year-long field hockey binge to perfect her game, and the girls *knew* she'd been practicing dribbling in the backyard before they arrived. Spencer hated when anyone was better at anything than she was. Especially Alison.

"Wait for me!"

They turned to see Hanna Marin climbing out of her mom's Mercedes. She stumbled over her tote bag and waved her chubby arms wildly. Ever since Hanna's parents had gotten a divorce last year, she'd been steadily putting on weight and outgrowing her old clothes. Even though Ali rolled her eyes, the rest of the girls pretended not to notice. That's just what best friends do.

Alison, Aria, Spencer, Emily, and Hanna bonded last year when their parents volunteered them to work Saturday afternoons at Rosewood Day School's charity drive—well, all except for Spencer, who volunteered herself. Whether or not Alison knew about the other four, the four knew about Alison. She was perfect. Beautiful, witty, smart. Popular. Boys wanted to kiss Alison, and girls—even older ones—wanted to *be* her. So the first time Ali laughed at one of Aria's jokes, asked Emily a question about swimming, told Hanna her shirt was adorable, or commented that Spencer's penmanship was *way* neater than her own, they couldn't help but be, well . . . dazzled. Before Ali, the girls had felt like pleated, high-waisted mom jeans—awkward and noticeable for all the wrong reasons—but then Ali made them feel like the most perfect-fitting Stella McCartneys that no one could afford.

Now, more than a year later, on the last day of seventh grade, they weren't just best friends, they were *the* girls of Rosewood Day. A lot had happened to make it that way. Every sleepover they had, every field trip, had been a new adventure. Even homeroom had been memorable when they were together. (Reading a steamy note from the varsity crew captain to his math tutor over the PA system was now a Rosewood Day legend.) But there were other things they all wanted to forget. And there was *one* secret they couldn't even bear to talk about. Ali said that secrets were what bonded their five-way best-friendship together for eternity. If that was true, they were going to be friends for life.

"I'm so glad this day is over." Alison moaned before gently pushing Spencer back through the gap in the hedges. "Your barn."

"I'm so glad seventh *grade* is over," Aria said as she, Emily, and Hanna followed Alison and Spencer toward the renovated barn-turned-guesthouse where Spencer's older sister, Melissa, had lived for her junior and senior years of high school. Fortunately, she'd just graduated

and was headed to Prague this summer, so it was all theirs
for the night.

Suddenly they heard a very squeaky voice. "Alison!
Hey, Alison! Hey, Spencer!"

Alison turned to the street. "Not it," she whispered.

"Not it," Spencer, Emily, and Aria quickly followed.

Hanna frowned. "Shit."

It was this game Ali had stolen from her brother,
Jason, who was a senior at Rosewood Day. Jason and his
friends played it at inter-prep school field parties when
scoping out girls. Being the last to call out "not it"
meant you had to entertain the ugly girl for the night
while your friends got to hook up with her hot friends—
meaning, essentially, that you were as lame and
unattractive as she was. In Ali's version, the girls called
"not it" whenever there was anyone ugly, uncool, or
unfortunate near them.

This time, "not it" was for Mona Vanderwaal—a dork
from down the street whose favorite pastime was trying
to befriend Spencer and Alison—and her two freaky
friends, Chassey Bledsoe and Phi Templeton. Chassey
was the girl who'd hacked into the school's computer system and then *told* the principal how to better secure it,
and Phi Templeton went everywhere with a yo-yo—
enough said. The three stared at the girls from the middle of the quiet, suburban road. Mona was perched on
her Razor scooter, Chassey was on a black mountain
bike, and Phi was on foot—with her yo-yo, of course.

"You guys want to come over and watch *Fear Factor?*"
Mona called.

"Sorry," Alison simpered. "We're kind of busy."

Chassey frowned. "Don't you want to see when they
eat the bugs?"

"Gross!" Spencer whispered to Aria, who then started
pretending to eat invisible lice off Hanna's scalp like a
monkey.

"Yeah, I wish we could." Alison tilted her head.
"We've planned this sleepover for a while now. But
maybe next time?"

Mona looked at the sidewalk. "Yeah, okay."

"See ya." Alison turned around, rolling her eyes, and
the other girls did the same.

They crossed through Spencer's back gate. To their
left was Ali's neighboring backyard, where her parents
were building a twenty-seat gazebo for their lavish out-
door picnics. "Thank *God* the workers aren't here," Ali
said, glancing at a yellow bulldozer.

Emily stiffened. "Have they been saying stuff to you
again?"

"Easy there, Killer," Alison said. The others giggled.
Sometimes they called Emily "Killer," as in Ali's person-
al pit bull. Emily used to find it funny, too, but lately she
wasn't laughing along.

The barn was just ahead. It was small and cozy and
had a big window that looked out on Spencer's large,
rambling farm, which had its very own windmill. Here

in Rosewood, Pennsylvania, a little suburb about twenty miles from Philadelphia, you were more likely to live in a twenty-five-room farmhouse with a mosaic-tiled pool and hot tub, like Spencer's house, than in a prefab McMansion. Rosewood smelled like lilacs and mown grass in the summer and clean snow and wood stoves in the winter. It was full of lush, tall pines, acres of rustic family-run farms, and the cutest foxes and bunnies. It had fabulous shopping and Colonial-era estates and parks for birthday, graduation, and just-'cause-we-feel-like-it fêtes. And Rosewood boys were gorgeous in that glowing, healthy, just-stepped-out-of-an-Abercrombie-catalog way. This was Philadelphia's Main Line. It was full of old, noble bloodlines, older money, and practically ancient scandals.

As they reached the barn, the girls heard giggles coming from inside. Someone squealed, "I said, *stop* it!"

"Oh God," Spencer moaned. "What is she doing here?"

As Spencer peeked through the keyhole, she could see Melissa, her prim and proper, excellent-at-everything older sister, and Ian Thomas, her tasty boyfriend, wrestling on the couch. Spencer kicked at the door with the heel of her shoe, forcing it open. The barn smelled like moss and slightly burned popcorn. Melissa turned around.

"What the fu–?" she asked. Then she noticed the others and smiled. "Oh, hey guys."

The girls eyed Spencer. She constantly complained that Melissa was a venomous super-bitch, so they were always taken aback when Melissa seemed friendly and sweet.

Ian stood up, stretched, and grinned at Spencer. "Hey."

"Hi, Ian," Spencer replied in a much brighter voice. "I didn't know you were here."

"Yeah you did." Ian smiled flirtatiously. "You were spying on us."

Melissa readjusted her long blond hair and black silk headband, staring at her sister. "So, what's up?" she asked, a little accusingly.

"It's just . . . I didn't mean to barge in . . . ," Spencer sputtered. "But we were supposed to have this place tonight."

Ian playfully hit Spencer on the arm. "I was just messing with you," he teased.

A patch of red crept up her neck. Ian had messy blond hair, sleepy-looking hazelnut-colored eyes, and totally gropeworthy stomach muscles.

"Wow," Ali said in a too-loud voice. All heads turned to her. "Melissa, you and Ian make the kuh-*yoo*-test couple. I've never told you, but I've always thought it. Don't you agree, Spence?"

Spencer blinked. "Um," she said quietly.

Melissa stared at Ali for a second, perplexed, and then turned back to Ian. "Can I talk to you outside?"

Ian downed his Corona as the girls watched. They only ever drank super-secretively from the bottles in their parents' liquor cabinets. He set the empty bottle down and offered them a parting grin as he followed Melissa outside. "Adieu, ladies." He winked before closing the door behind him.

Alison dusted her hands together. "Another problem solved by Ali D. Are you going to thank me now, Spence?"

Spencer didn't answer. She was too busy looking out the barn's front window. Lightning bugs had begun to light up the purplish sky.

Hanna walked over to the abandoned popcorn bowl and took a big handful. "Ian's *so* hot. He's, like, hotter than Sean." Sean Ackard was one of the cutest guys in their grade and the subject of Hanna's constant fantasies.

"You know what I heard?" Ali asked, flopping down on the couch. "Sean really likes girls who have good appetites."

Hanna brightened. "Really?"

"*No.*" Alison snorted.

Hanna slowly dropped the handful of popcorn back into the bowl.

"So, girls," Ali said. "I know the perfect thing we can do."

"I hope we're not streaking again." Emily giggled. They'd done that a month earlier—in the freezing frickin' cold—and although Hanna had refused to strip down to less than her undershirt and day-of-the-week panties, the rest of them had run through a nearby barren cornfield without a lick on.

"*You* loved that a little too much," Ali murmured. The smile faded from Emily's lips. "But no—I was leaving this for the last day of school. I learned how to hypnotize people."

"Hypnotize?" Spencer repeated.

"Matt's sister taught me," Ali answered, looking at the framed photos of Melissa and Ian on the mantel. Her boyfriend of the week, Matt, had the same sandy-colored hair as Ian.

"How do you do it?" Hanna asked.

"Sorry, she swore me to secrecy," Ali said, turning back around. "You want to see if it works?"

Aria frowned, taking a seat on a lavender floor pillow. "I don't know. . . ."

"Why not?" Ali's eyes flickered to a stuffed pig puppet that was peeking out of Aria's purple sweater-knit tote bag. Aria was always carrying around weird things—stuffed animals, random pages torn out of old novels, postcards of places she'd never visited.

"Doesn't hypnosis make you say stuff you don't want to say?" Aria asked.

"Is there something you can't tell us?" Ali responded. "And why do you still bring that pig puppet every-where?" She pointed at it.

Aria shrugged and pulled the stuffed pig out of her bag. "My dad got me Pigtunia in Germany. She advises me on my love life." She stuck her hand into the puppet.

"You're shoving your hand up its butt!" Ali squealed and Emily started to giggle. "Besides, why do you want to carry around something your *dad* gave you?"

"It's not funny," Aria snapped, whipping her head around to face Emily.

Everyone was quiet for a few seconds, and the girls looked blankly at one another. This had been happening a lot lately: Someone—usually Ali—mentioned something, and someone else got upset, but everyone was too shy to ask what in the world was going on.

Spencer broke the silence. "Being hypnotized, um, does sound sort of sketch."

"*You* don't know anything about it," Alison said quickly. "C'mon. I could do it to you all at once."

Spencer picked at the waistband of her skirt. Emily blew air through her teeth. Aria and Hanna exchanged a look. Ali was always coming up with stuff for them to try—last summer, it was smoking dandelion seeds to see if they'd hallucinate, and this past fall they'd gone swimming in Pecks Pond, even though a dead body was once discovered there—but the thing was, they often didn't *want* to do the things that Alison made them do. They all loved Ali to death, but they sometimes hated her too—for bossing them around and for the spell she'd cast on them. Sometimes in Ali's presence, they didn't feel real, exactly. They felt kind of like dolls, with Ali arranging their every move. Each of them wished that, just once, she had the strength to tell Ali no.

"Puh-*leeeeeze?*" Ali asked. "Emily, you want to do it, right?"

"Um . . . " Emily's voice quivered. "Well . . . "

"I'll do it," Hanna butted in.

"Me too," Emily said quickly after.

Spencer and Aria reluctantly nodded. Satisfied, Alison shut off all the lights with a snap and lit several sweetly scented vanilla votive candles that were on the coffee table. Then she stood back and hummed.

"Okay, everyone, just relax," she chanted, and the girls arranged themselves in a circle on the rug. "Your heartbeat's slowing down. Think calm thoughts. I'm going to count down from one hundred, and as soon as I touch all of you, you'll be in my power."

"Spooky." Emily laughed shakily.

Alison began. "One hundred . . . ninety-nine . . . ninety-eight . . ."

Twenty-two . . .

Eleven . . .

Five . . .

Four . . .

Three . . .

She touched Aria's forehead with the fleshiest part of

her thumb. Spencer uncrossed her legs. Aria twitched her left foot.

"Two . . ." She slowly touched Hanna, then Emily, and then moved toward Spencer. "One."

Spencer's eyes sprang open before Alison could reach her. She jumped up and ran to the window.

"What're you doing?" Ali whispered. "You're ruining the moment."

"It's too dark in here." Spencer reached up and opened the curtains.

"No." Alison lowered her shoulders. "It's got to be dark. That's how it works."

"C'mon, no it doesn't." The blind stuck; Spencer grunted to wrench it free.

"No. It does."

Spencer put her hands on her hips. "I want it lighter. Maybe everyone does."

Alison looked at the others. They all still had their eyes closed.

Spencer put her hands on her hips. "It doesn't always have to be the way you want it, you know."

Alison barked out a laugh. "*Close* them!"

Spencer rolled her eyes. "God, take a pill."

"You think *I* should take a pill?" Alison demanded.

Spencer and Alison stared at each other for a few moments. It was one of those ridiculous fights that could have been about who saw the new Lacoste polo dress at Neiman Marcus first or whether honey-colored high-lights looked too brassy, but it was really about something else entirely. Something way bigger.

Finally, Spencer pointed at the door. "Leave."

"Fine." Alison strode outside.

"Good!" But after a few seconds passed, Spencer followed her. The bluish evening air was still, and there weren't any lights on in her family's main house. It was quiet, too—even the crickets were quiet—and Spencer could hear herself breathing. "Wait a second!" she cried after a moment, slamming the door behind her. "Alison!"

But Alison was gone.

When she heard the door slam, Aria opened her eyes. "Ali?" she called. "Guys?" No answer.

She looked around. Hanna and Emily sat like lumps on the carpet, and the door was open. Aria moved out to the porch. No one was there. She tiptoed to the edge of Ali's property. The woods spread out in front of her and everything was silent.

"Ali?" she whispered. Nothing. "Spencer?"

Inside, Hanna and Emily rubbed their eyes. "I just had the weirdest dream," Emily said. "I mean, I guess it was a dream. It was really quick. Alison fell down this really deep well, and there were all these giant plants."

"That was my dream too!" Hanna said.

"It *was*?" Emily asked.

Hanna nodded. "Well, kind of. There was a big plant in it. And I think I saw Alison too. It might've been her shadow—but it was definitely *her*."

"Whoa," Emily whispered. They stared at each other, their eyes wide.

"Guys?" Aria stepped back through the door. She looked very pale.

"Are you okay?" Emily asked.

"Where's Alison?" Aria creased her forehead. "And Spencer?"

"We don't know," Hanna said.

Just then, Spencer burst back into the house. All the girls jumped. "What?" she asked.

"Where's Ali?" Hanna asked quietly.

"I don't know," Spencer whispered. "I thought . . . I don't know."

The girls fell silent. All they could hear were the tree branches sliding across the windows. It sounded like someone scraping her long fingernails against a plate.

"I think I want to go home," Emily said.

The next morning, they still hadn't heard from Alison. The girls called one another to talk, a four-way call this time instead of five.

"Do you think she's mad at us?" Hanna asked. "She seemed weird all night."

"She's probably at Katy's," Spencer said. Katy was one of Ali's field hockey friends.

"Or maybe she's with Tiffany—that girl from camp?" Aria offered.

"I'm sure she's somewhere having fun," Emily said quietly.

One by one, they got calls from Mrs. DiLaurentis, asking if they'd heard from Ali. At first, the girls all covered for her. It was the unwritten rule: They'd covered for Emily when she snuck in after her 11 P.M. weekend curfew; they'd fudged the truth for Spencer when she borrowed Melissa's Ralph Lauren duffel coat and then accidentally left it on the seat of a SEPTA train; and so on. But as each one hung up with Mrs. DiLaurentis, a sour feeling swelled in her stomach. Something felt horribly wrong.

That afternoon, Mrs. DiLaurentis called again, this time in a panic. By that evening, the DiLaurentises had called the police, and the next morning there were cop cars and news vans camped out on the DiLaurentises' normally pristine front lawn. It was a local news channel's wet dream: a pretty rich girl, lost in one of the safest upper-class towns in the country.

Hanna called Emily after watching the first nightly Ali news report. "Did the police interview you today?"

"Yeah," Emily whispered.

"Me too. You didn't tell them about . . . " She paused. "About *The Jenna Thing*, did you?"

"No!" Emily gasped. "Why? Do you think they know something?"

"No . . . they couldn't," Hanna whispered after a second. "We're the only ones who know. The four of us . . . and Alison."

The police questioned the girls—along with practically everybody from Rosewood, from Ali's second-grade gymnastics instructor to the guy who'd once sold her Marlboros at Wawa. It was the summer before eighth grade and the girls were supposed to be flirting with older boys at pool parties, eating corn on the cob in one another's backyards, and shopping all day at the King James Mall. Instead they were crying alone in their canopied beds or staring blankly at their photo-covered walls. Spencer went on a room-cleaning binge, reviewing what her fight with Ali had *really* been about, and thinking of things she knew about Ali that none of the others did. Hanna spent hours on her bedroom floor, hiding emptied Cheetos bags under her mattress. Emily couldn't stop obsessing over a letter she'd sent to Ali before she disappeared. Had Ali ever gotten it? Aria sat at her desk with Pigtunia. Slowly, the girls began calling one another less frequently. The same thoughts haunted all four of them, but there wasn't anything left to say to one another.

The summer turned into the school year, which turned into the next summer. Still no Ali. The police continued to search—but quietly. The media lost interest, heading off to obsess over a Center City triple homicide. Even the DiLaurentises moved out of Rosewood almost two and a half years after Alison disappeared. As for Spencer, Aria, Emily, and Hanna, something shifted in them, too. Now if they passed Ali's old street and glanced at her house, they didn't go into insta-cry mode. Instead, they started to feel something else.

Relief.

Sure, Alison was *Alison*. She was the shoulder to cry on, the only one you'd ever want calling up your crush to find out how he felt about you, and the final word on whether your new jeans made your butt look big. But the girls were also afraid of her. Ali knew more about them than anyone else did, including the bad stuff they wanted to bury—just like a body. It was horrible to think Ali might be dead, but . . . if she was, at least their secrets were safe.

And they were. For three years, anyway.

1

ORANGES, PEACHES, AND LIMES, OH MY!

"Someone finally bought the DiLaurentises' old house," Emily Fields's mother said. It was Saturday afternoon, and Mrs. Fields sat at the kitchen table, bifocals perched on her nose, calmly doing her bills.

Emily felt the Vanilla Coke she was drinking fizz up her nose.

"I think another girl your age moved in," Mrs. Fields continued. "I was going to drop off that basket today. Maybe you want to do it instead?" She pointed to the cellophaned monstrosity on the counter.

"God, Mom, *no,*" Emily replied. Since she'd retired from teaching elementary school last year, Emily's mom had become the unofficial Rosewood, Pennsylvania, Welcome Wagon lady. She assembled a million random things—dried fruit, those flat rubber thingies you use to get jars open, ceramic chickens (Emily's mom was chicken-obsessed), a guide to Rosewood inns, whatever—into a big wicker welcome basket. She was a prototypical suburban mom, minus the SUV. She thought they were ostentatious and gas-guzzling, so she drove an oh-so-practical Volvo wagon instead.

Mrs. Fields stood and ran her fingers through Emily's chlorine-damaged hair. "Would it upset you too much to go there, sweetie? Maybe I should send Carolyn?"

Emily glanced at her sister Carolyn, who was a year older and lounging comfortably on the La-Z-Boy in the den watching *Dr. Phil*. Emily shook her head. "No, it's fine. I'll do it."

Sure, Emily whined sometimes and occasionally rolled her eyes. But the truth was, if her mom asked, Emily would do whatever she was supposed to do. She was a nearly straight-A, four-time state champion butter-flyer and hyper-obedient daughter. Following rules and requests came easily to her.

Plus, deep down she kind of *wanted* a reason to see Alison's house again. While it seemed the rest of Rosewood had started to move on from Ali's disappearance three years, two months, and twelve days ago, Emily hadn't. Even now, she couldn't glance at her seventh-grade yearbook without wanting to curl up in a ball. Sometimes on rainy days, Emily still reread Ali's old notes, which she stored in a shell-top Adidas shoe box under her bed. She even kept a pair of Citizens corduroys Ali had let her borrow on a wooden hanger in her closet, even though they were now way too small on her. She'd spent the last few lonely years in Rosewood longing for another friend like Ali, but that probably wasn't going to happen. She hadn't been a perfect friend, but for all her flaws, Ali was pretty tough to replace.

Emily straightened up and grabbed the Volvo's keys from the hook next to the phone. "I'll be back in a little while," she called as she closed the front door behind her.

The first thing she saw when she pulled up to Alison's old Victorian home at the top of the leafy street was a huge pile of trash on the curb and a big sign marked, FREE! Squinting, she realized that some of it was Alison's stuff—she recognized Ali's old, overstuffed white corduroy bedroom chair. The DiLaurentises had moved away almost nine months ago. Apparently they'd left some things behind.

She parked behind a giant Bekins moving van and got out of the Volvo. "Whoa," she whispered, trying to keep her bottom lip from trembling. Under the chair, there were several piles of grimy books. Emily reached down and looked at the spines. *The Red Badge of Courage. The Prince and the Pauper.* She remembered reading them in Mr. Pierce's seventh-grade English class, talking about symbolism, metaphors, and denouement. There were more books underneath, including some that just looked like old notebooks. Boxes sat next to the books; they were marked ALISON'S CLOTHES and ALISON'S OLD PAPERS. Peeking out of a crate was a blue and red ribbon. Emily pulled at it a little. It was a sixth-grade swimming medal she'd left at Alison's house one day when they'd made up a game called Olympian Sex Goddesses.

"You want that?"

Emily shot up. She faced a tall, skinny girl with tawny-colored skin and wild, black-brown curly hair. The girl wore a yellow tank top whose strap had slid off her shoulder to reveal an orange and green bra strap. Emily wasn't certain, but she thought she had the same bra at home. It was from Victoria's Secret and had little oranges, peaches, and limes all over the, er, boob parts.

The swimming medal slid out of her hands and clattered to the ground. "Um, no," she said, scrambling to pick it up.

"You can take any of it. See the sign?"

"No, really, it's okay."

The girl stuck out her hand. "Maya St. Germain. Just moved here."

"I . . ." Emily's words clogged up in her throat. "I'm Emily," she finally managed, taking Maya's hand and shaking it. It felt really formal to shake a girl's hand— Emily wasn't sure she'd ever done that before. She felt a little fuzzy. Maybe she hadn't eaten enough Honey Nut Cheerios for breakfast?

Maya gestured to the stuff on the ground. "Can you

believe all this crap was in my new room? I had to move it all out myself. It sucked."

"Yeah, this all belonged to Alison," Emily practically whispered.

Maya stooped down to inspect some of the paperbacks. She shoved her tank top strap back onto her shoulder. "Is she a friend of yours?"

Emily paused. *Is?* Maybe Maya hadn't heard about Ali's disappearance? "Um, she *was*. A long time ago. Along with a bunch of other girls who live around here," Emily explained, leaving out the part about the kidnapping or murder or whatever might have happened that she couldn't bear to imagine. "In seventh grade. I'm going into eleventh now at Rosewood Day." School started after this weekend. So did fall swim practice, which meant three hours of lap swimming daily. Emily didn't even want to think about it.

"I'm going to Rosewood too!" Maya grinned. She sank down on Alison's old corduroy chair, and the springs squeaked. "All my parents talked about on the flight here was how lucky I am to have gotten into Rosewood and how different it will be from my school in California. Like, I bet you guys don't have Mexican food, right? Or, like, really *good* Mexican food, like Cali-Mexican food. We used to have it in our cafeteria and *mmm*, it was so good. I'm going to have to get used to Taco Bell. Their gorditas make me want to vomit."

"Oh." Emily smiled. This girl sure talked a lot. "Yeah, the food kind of sucks."

Maya sprang up from the chair. "This might be a weird question since I just met you, but would you mind helping me carry the rest of these boxes up to my room?" She motioned to a few Crate & Barrel boxes sitting at the base of the truck.

Emily's eyes widened. Go into Alison's old room? But it would be totally rude if she refused, wouldn't it? "Um, sure," she said shakily.

The foyer still smelled like Dove soap and potpourri—just as it had when the DiLaurentises lived here. Emily paused at the door and waited for Maya to give her instructions, even though she knew she could find Ali's old room at the end of the upstairs hall blindfolded. Moving boxes were everywhere, and two spindly Italian greyhounds yapped from behind a gate in the kitchen.

"Ignore them," Maya said, climbing the stairs to her room and shoving the door open with her terry-covered hip.

Wow, it looks the same, Emily thought as she entered the bedroom. But the thing was, it didn't: Maya had put her queen-size bed in a different corner, she had a huge, flat-screen computer monitor on her desk, and she'd put up posters everywhere, covering Alison's old flowered wallpaper. But *something* felt the same, as if Alison's presence was still floating here. Emily felt woozy and leaned against the wall for support.

"Put it anywhere," Maya said. Emily rallied herself to stand, set her box down at the foot of the bed, and looked around.

"I like your posters," she said. They were mostly of bands: M.I.A., Black Eyed Peas, Gwen Stefani in a cheerleading uniform. "I love Gwen," she added.

"Yeah," Maya said. "My boyfriend's totally obsessed with her. His name's Justin. He's from San Fran, where I'm from."

"Oh. I've got a boyfriend too," Emily said. "His name's Ben."

"Yeah?" Maya sat down on her bed. "What's he like?"

Emily tried to conjure up Ben, her boyfriend of four months. She'd seen him two days ago—they'd watched the *Doom* DVD at her house. Emily's mom was in the other room, of course, randomly popping in, asking if they needed anything. They'd been good friends for a while, on the same year-round swim teams. All their teammates told them they should go out, so they did. "He's cool."

"So why aren't you friends with the girl who lived here anymore?" Maya asked.

Emily pushed her reddish-blond hair behind her ears. Wow. So Maya really *didn't* know about Alison. If Emily started talking about Ali, though, she might start crying—which would be weird. She hardly knew this Maya girl. "I grew apart from all my old seventh-grade friends. Everyone changed a lot, I guess."

That was an understatement. Of Emily's other best

friends, Spencer had become a more exaggerated version of her already hyper-perfect self; Aria's family had suddenly moved to Iceland the fall after Ali went missing; and dorky-but-lovable Hanna had become totally *un*dorky and *un*lovable and was now a total bitch. Hanna and her now best friend, Mona Vanderwaal, had completely transformed themselves the summer between eighth and ninth grade. Emily's mom had recently seen Hanna going into Wawa, the local convenience store, and told Emily that Hanna looked "sluttier than that Paris Hilton girl." Emily had never heard her mom use the word *slutty*.

"I know how growing apart is," Maya said, bouncing up and down on her bed as she sat. "Like my boyfriend? He's so scared I'm going to ditch him now that we're on different coasts. He's such a big baby."

"My boyfriend and I are on the swim team, so we see each other all the time," Emily replied, looking for a place to sit down too. *Maybe* too *much of the time*, she thought.

"You swim?" Maya asked. She looked Emily up and down, which made Emily feel a little weird. "I bet you're really good. You totally have the shoulders."

"Oh, I don't know." Emily blushed and leaned against Maya's white wooden desk.

"You do!" Maya smiled. "But . . . if you're a big jock, does that mean you'd kill me if I smoked a little weed?"

"What, right now?" Emily's eyes widened. "What about your parents?"

"They're at the grocery store. And my brother—he's here somewhere, but he won't care." Maya reached under her mattress for an Altoids tin. She hefted up the window, which was right next to her bed, pulled out a joint, and lit it. The smoke curled into the yard and made a hazy cloud around a large oak tree.

Maya brought the joint back inside. "Want a hit?"

Emily had never tried pot in her entire life—she always thought her parents would somehow *know*, like by smelling her hair or forcing her to pee in a cup or something. But as Maya pulled the joint gracefully from her cherry-frosted lips, it looked sexy. Emily wanted to look sexy like that too.

"Um, okay." Emily slid closer to Maya and took the joint from her. Their hands brushed and their eyes met. Maya's were green and a little yellow, like a cat's. Emily's hand trembled. She felt nervous, but she put the joint to her mouth and took a tiny drag, like she was sipping Vanilla Coke through a straw.

But it didn't taste like Vanilla Coke. It felt like she'd just inhaled a whole jar of rotten spices. She hacked an old man–ish cough.

"Whoa," Maya said, taking back the joint. "First time?"

Emily couldn't breathe and just shook her head, gasping. She wheezed some more, trying to get air into her chest. Finally she could feel air hitting her lungs again. As Maya turned her arm, Emily saw a long, white scar running lengthwise down her wrist. *Whoa*. It looked a little like an albino snake on her tan skin. God, she was probably high already.

Suddenly there was a loud clank. Emily jumped. Then she heard the clank again. "What is that?" she wheezed.

Maya took another drag and shook her head. "The workers. We're here for one day and my parents have already started on the renovations." She grinned. "You just totally freaked, like you thought the cops were coming. You been busted before?"

"No!" Emily burst out laughing; it was such a ridiculous thought.

Maya smiled and exhaled.

"I should go," Emily rasped.

Maya's face fell. "Why?"

Emily shuffled off the bed. "I told my mom I'd only stop over for a minute. But I'll see you in school Tuesday."

"Cool," Maya said. "Maybe you could show me around?"

Emily smiled. "Sure."

Maya grinned and waved good-bye with three fingers. "You know how to find your way out?"

"I think so." Emily took one more look around Ali's— er, *Maya's*—room, and then stomped down the all-too-familiar stairs.

It wasn't until Emily shook her head out in the open air, passed all of Alison's old stuff on the curb, and climbed back into her parents' car, that she saw the Welcome Wagon basket on the backseat. *Screw it*, she thought, wedging the basket between Alison's old chair and her boxes of books. *Who needs a guide to Rosewood's inns, anyway? Maya already lives here.*

And Emily was suddenly glad she did.

2

ICELANDIC (AND FINNISH) GIRLS ARE EASY

"Omigod, *trees*. I'm so happy to see big fat *trees*."

Aria Montgomery's fifteen-year-old brother, Michelangelo, wagged his head out of the family's Outback window like a golden retriever. Aria; her parents, Ella and Byron—they wanted their kids to call them by their first names—and Mike were all driving back from Philadelphia International Airport. They'd just gotten off a flight from Reykjavík, Iceland. Aria's dad was an art history professor, and the family had spent the last two years in Iceland while he helped do research for a TV documentary on Scandinavian art. Now that they were back, Mike was marveling at the Pennsylvania cow-country scenery. And that meant . . . Every. Single. Thing. The 1700s-era stone inn that sold ornate ceramic vases; the black cows staring dumbly at their car from behind a wooden roadside fence; the New England village–style mall that had sprung up since they'd been gone. Even the dingy twenty-five-year-old Dunkin' Donuts.

"Man, I can't *wait* to get a Coolata!" Mike gushed.

Aria groaned. Mike had spent a lonely couple of years in Iceland—he claimed that all Icelandic boys were "pussies who rode small, gay horses"—but Aria had blossomed. A new start had been just what she needed at the time, so she was happy when her dad made the announcement that her family was moving. It was the fall after Alison went missing, and her girls had grown far apart, leaving her with no real friends, just a school full of people she'd known forever.

Before she left for Europe, Aria would sometimes see boys look at her from afar, intrigued, but then look away. With her coltish, ballet-dancer frame, straight black hair, and pouty lips, Aria knew she was pretty. People were always saying so, but why didn't she have a date to the seventh-grade spring social, then? One of the last times she and Spencer had hung out—one of the awkward get-togethers that summer after Ali disappeared—Spencer told Aria she'd probably get a lot of dates if she just tried to fit in a little bit more.

But Aria didn't know how to fit in. Her parents had drilled it into her head that she was an individual, not a follower of the herd, and should be herself. Trouble was Aria wasn't sure who Aria was. Since turning eleven, she'd tried out punk Aria, artsy Aria, documentary film Aria, and, right before they moved, she'd even tried ideal

Rosewood girl Aria, the horse-riding, polo-shirt-wearing, Coach-satchel-toting girl who was everything Rosewood boys loved but everything Aria wasn't. Thankfully, they moved to Iceland two weeks into that disaster, and in Iceland, everything, everything, *everything* changed.

Her father got the job offer in Iceland just after Aria had started eighth grade, and the family packed up. She suspected they'd left so quickly because of a secret about her dad that only she—and Alison DiLaurentis—knew about. She'd vowed not to think about that again the minute the Icelandair plane took off, and after living in Reykjavík for a few months, Rosewood became a distant memory. Her parents seemed to fall back in love and even her totally provincial brother learned both Icelandic *and* French. And Aria fell in love . . . a few times, actually.

So what if Rosewood boys didn't get kooky Aria? Icelandic boys—rich, worldly, fascinating Icelandic boys— sure did. As soon as they moved there, she met a boy named Hallbjorn. He was seventeen, a DJ, and had three ponies and the most beautiful bone structure she'd ever seen. He offered to take her to Iceland's geysers, and then, when they saw one burble up and leave a big cloud of steam, he kissed her. After Hallbjorn was Lars, who liked to play with her old pig puppet, Pigtunia—the one who advised Aria on her love life—and took her to the best all-night dance parties by the harbor. She felt adorable and sexy in Iceland. There, she became Icelandic Aria, the best Aria yet. She found her style—a sort of bohemian-hipster-girl thing, with lots of layers, lace-up boots, and APC jeans, which she bought on a trip to Paris—read French philosophers, and traveled on the Eurail with just an outdated map and a change of underwear.

But now, every Rosewood sight outside the car window reminded her of the past she wanted to forget. There was Ferra's Cheesesteaks, where she spent hours with her friends in middle school. There was the stone-gated country club—her parents didn't belong, but she'd gone with Spencer, and once, feeling bold, Aria had walked up to her crush, Noel Kahn, and asked him if he wanted to share an ice-cream sandwich with her. He turned her down cold, of course.

And there was the sunny, tree-lined road where Alison DiLaurentis used to live. As the car paused at the four-way stop sign, Aria stared; she could see it, second house from the corner. There was a bunch of trash on the curb, but otherwise, the house was quiet and still. She could look for only so long before covering her eyes. In Iceland, days could go by when she could almost forget about Ali, their secrets, and what had happened. She'd been back in Rosewood for less than ten minutes, and Aria could practically hear Ali's voice at every bend in the road and see her reflection in every house's oversize bay window. She slumped down in her seat, trying not to cry.

Her father continued a few streets down and pulled up to their old house, a postmodern angry brown box with only one square window, right in the center—a huge letdown after their waterfront faded-blue Icelandic row house. Aria followed her parents inside and they bustled off into separate rooms. She heard Mike answer his cell phone outside and she swished her hands through the sparkly floating dust in the air.

"Mom!" Mike ran through the front door. "I just talked to Chad, and he said the first lacrosse tryouts are today."

"Lacrosse?" Ella emerged from the dining room. "Right now?"

"Yeah," Mike said. "I'm going!" He tore up the wrought-iron staircase to his old bedroom.

"Aria, honey?" Her mother's voice made her turn. "Can you drive him to practice?"

Aria let out a small laugh. "Um, Mom? I don't have my license."

"So? You drove all the time in Reykjavík. The lacrosse field's only a couple of miles away, isn't it? Worst thing, you'll hit a cow. Just wait for him until he's done."

Aria paused. Her mother already sounded frazzled. She heard her dad in the kitchen opening and closing cabinets and muttering under his breath. Would her parents love each other here like they had in Iceland? Or would things go back to the way they used to be?

"All right," she mumbled. She plopped her bags on the landing, grabbed the car keys, and slid into the wagon's front seat.

Her brother climbed in next to her, amazingly already dressed in his gear. He punched the netting on his stick enthusiastically and gave her an evil, knowing smile. "Happy to be back?"

Aria only sighed in response. The entire drive, Mike had his hands pressed up against the car's window, shouting things like, "There's Caleb's house! They tore down the skate ramp!" and "Cow poop still smells the same!" At the vast, well-mown practice field, she'd barely stopped the car when Mike opened the door and immediately bolted.

She slid back into the seat, stared up through the sunroof, and sighed. "*Thrilled* to be back," she murmured. A hot air balloon floated serenely through the clouds. It used to be such a delight to see them, but today she focused in on it, closed one eye, and pretended to crush the balloon between her thumb and pointer finger.

A bunch of boys in white Nike T-shirts, baggy shorts, and backward white baseball caps walked slowly past her car toward the field house. *See?* Every Rosewood boy was a carbon copy. Aria blinked. One of them was even wearing the same Nike University of Pennsylvania T-shirt that Noel Kahn, the ice-cream sandwich boy she loved in eighth grade, used to wear. She squinted at the boy's black wavy hair. Wait. Was that . . . *him*? Oh God. It was. Aria couldn't believe he was wearing the same T-shirt he wore when he was thirteen. He probably did it for luck or some other queer jock superstition.

Noel looked quizzically at her, then walked toward her car and knocked on her window. She rolled it down.

"You're that girl that went to the North Pole. Aria, right? You were Ali D's friend?" Noel continued.

Aria's stomach plummeted. "Um," she said.

"No, dude." James Freed, the second-hottest boy at Rosewood, came up behind Noel. "She didn't go to the North Pole, she went to Finland. You know, like where that model Svetlana is from. The one who looks like Hanna?"

Aria scratched the back of her head. Hanna? As in, Hanna *Marin*?

A whistle blew, and Noel reached into the car to touch Aria's arm. "You're going to stay and watch practice, aren't you, Finland?"

"Uh . . . *ja*," Aria said.

"What's that, a Finnish sex grunt?" James grinned.

Aria rolled her eyes. She was pretty sure *ja* was Finnish for *yes*, but of course these guys wouldn't know that. "Have fun playing with your balls." She smiled wearily.

The boys nudged each other, then ran off, flicking their lacrosse sticks to and fro even before they hit the field. Aria stared out the window. How ironic. This was the first time she'd ever been flirty with a boy in Rosewood—*especially* Noel—and she didn't even care.

Through the trees, she could just make out the spire that belonged to the chapel at Hollis College, the small liberal arts school where her dad taught. On Hollis's main street there was a bar, Snookers. She sat up straighter and checked her watch. Two-thirty. It might be open. She could go have a beer or two and find her own fun.

And hey, maybe beer goggles could make even Rosewood boys look good.

Where Reykjavík's bars smelled like freshly brewed lager, old wood, and French cigarettes, Snookers smelled like a mixture of dead bodies, festering hot dogs, and sweat. And Snookers, like everything else in Rosewood, carried memories: One Friday night, Alison DiLaurentis had dared Aria to go into Snookers and order a screaming orgasm. Aria had waited in line behind a bunch of preppie college boys, and when the bouncer at the door wouldn't let her in, she cried, "But my screaming orgasm is in there!" Then she realized what she'd said and fled back to her friends, who were crouching behind a car in the parking lot. They all laughed so hard they got the hiccups.

"Amstel," she said to the bartender after crossing through the glass-paneled front doors—apparently there was no need for bouncers at two-thirty on a Saturday. The bartender looked at her questioningly but then set a pint in front of her and turned away. Aria took a big sip. It tasted bland and watery. She spit it back into the glass.

"You all right there?"

Aria turned. Three stools down was a guy with messy, blondish hair and ice-blue, Siberian husky eyes. He was nursing something in a little tumbler.

Aria frowned. "Yeah, I forgot how beer tastes here. I've been in Europe for two years. Beer's better there."

"Europe?" The guy smiled. He had a very cute smile. "Where?"

Aria smiled back. "Iceland."

His eyes brightened. "I once spent a few nights in Reykjavík on my way to Amsterdam. There was this huge, awesome party in the harbor."

Aria cupped her hands around her pint glass. "Yeah," she said, smiling, "they have the best parties there."

"Were you there for the northern lights?"

"Of course," Aria replied. "And the midnight sun. We had these awesome raves in the summer . . . with the best music." She looked at his glass. "What are you drinking?"

"Scotch," he said, already signaling to the bartender. "Want one?"

She nodded. The guy moved three stools down next to her. He had nice hands with long fingers and slightly ragged fingernails. He wore a small button on his corduroy jacket that said, SMART WOMEN VOTE!

"So you lived in Iceland?" He smiled again. "Like for a junior year abroad?"

"Well, no," Aria said. The bartender set the Scotch down in front of her. She took a big, beer-size gulp. Her throat and chest immediately sizzled. "I was in Iceland because . . ."

She stopped herself. "Yeah, it was my, uh, year abroad." Let him think what he wanted.

"Cool." He nodded. "Where were you before that?"

She shrugged. "Um . . . back here in Rosewood." She smiled and quickly added, "But I liked it over there so much better."

He nodded. "I was really depressed to come back to the States after Amsterdam."

"I cried the whole way home," Aria admitted, feeling like herself—her new, improved Icelandic Aria self—for the first time since she'd been back. Not only was she talking to a cute, smart guy about Europe, but this might be the only guy in Rosewood who didn't know her as Rosewood Aria—the weirdo friend of the pretty girl who vanished. "So, do you go to school here?" she asked.

"Just graduated." He wiped his mouth off with a napkin and lit a Camel. He offered her one from the pack, but she shook her head. "I'm gonna do some teaching."

Aria took another sip of the Scotch and realized she'd finished it. Wow. "I'd like to teach, I think. Once I finish school. Either that or write plays."

"Yeah? Plays? What's your major?"

"Um, English?" The bartender set another Scotch in front of her.

"That's what I'm teaching!" the guy said. As he said it, he put his hand on Aria's knee. Aria was so surprised she flinched and nearly knocked over her drink. He pulled his hand away. She blushed.

"Sorry," he said, a little sheepishly. "I'm Ezra, by the way."

"Aria." Suddenly her name sounded hilarious. She giggled, off balance.

"Whoa." Ezra grabbed her arm to steady her.

Three Scotches later, Aria and Ezra had established that they'd both met the same old sailor bartender at the Borg bar in Reykjavík, loved the way bathing in the mineral-rich blue lagoon hot springs made them feel sleepy, and actually *liked* the rotten-egg sulfur smell of the geothermal hot spring water. Ezra's eyes were getting bluer by the second. Aria wanted to ask if he had a girl-friend. She felt warm inside, and she was pretty sure it wasn't just from the Scotch.

"I kind of have to go to the bathroom," Aria said woozily.

Ezra smiled. "Can I come?"

Well, that answered the girlfriend question.

"I mean, uh . . ." He rubbed the back of his neck. "Was that too forward of me?" he asked, looking up from under his knitted eyebrows.

Her brain buzzed. Hooking up with strangers wasn't really her thing, at least not in America. But hadn't she said she wanted to be Icelandic Aria?

She stood up and took his hand. They stared at each other the whole way to Snookers' women's bathroom. There was toilet paper all over the floor and it smelled even worse than the rest of the bar, but Aria didn't care. As Ezra hoisted her onto the sink and she wrapped her

legs around his waist, all she could smell was his scent—
a combination of Scotch, cinnamon, and sweat—and
nothing had ever smelled sweeter.

As they said in Finland or wherever, *ja.*

3

HANNA'S FIRST TOGGLE

"And apparently they were having sex in Bethany's parents' bedroom!"

Hanna Marin stared at her best friend, Mona Vanderwaal, across the table. It was two days before school started and they were sitting in the King James Mall's terraced French-inspired café, Rive Gauche, drinking red wine, comparing *Vogue* to *Teen Vogue*, and gossiping. Mona always knew the best dirt on people. Hanna took another sip of wine and noticed a fortysomething guy staring lecherously at them. *A regular Humbert Humbert,* Hanna thought, but didn't say out loud. Mona wouldn't get the literary reference, but just because Hanna was the most sought-after girl at Rosewood Day didn't mean she was above sampling the books on Rosewood Day's recommended summer reading list now and then, especially when she was lying out next to her pool with nothing to do. Besides *Lolita* looked deliciously dirty.

Mona swiveled around to see who Hanna was looking at. Her lips twisted up into a naughty smile. "We should flash him."

"Count of three?" Hanna's amber eyes widened.

Mona nodded. On three, the girls slowly pulled up the hems of their already sky-high minis, revealing their panties. Humbert's eyes boggled and he knocked his glass of pinot noir into the crotch of his khakis. "Shit!" he yelled before he shot off to the bathroom.

"Nice," Mona said. They threw their napkins on their uneaten salads and stood to leave.

They'd become friends the summer between eighth and ninth grade, when they both got cut from Rosewood's freshman cheerleading tryouts. Vowing to make the squad the following year, they decided to lose tons of weight—so they could be the cute, perky girls that the boys tossed in the air. But once they got skinny and gorgeous, they decided cheerleading was passé and the cheerleaders were losers, so they never bothered trying out for the team again.

Since then, Hanna and Mona shared everything—well, almost everything. Hanna hadn't told Mona how she'd lost weight so quickly—it was too gross to talk about. While hard-core dieting was sexy and admirable, there was nothing, *nothing* glamorous about eating a ton of fatty, greasy, preferably cheese-filled crap and then puking it all up. But Hanna was over that bad little habit by now, so it didn't really matter.

"You know that guy had a boner," Mona whispered, gathering the magazines into a pile. "What's Sean gonna think?"

"He'll laugh," Hanna said.

"Uh, I don't think so."

Hanna shrugged. "He might."

Mona snorted. "Yeah, flashing strangers goes well with a virginity pledge."

Hanna looked down at her Michael Kors purple wedges. The virginity pledge. Hanna's incredibly popular, extraordinarily hot boyfriend, Sean Ackard—the boy she'd lusted over since seventh grade—was behaving a little strangely lately. He'd always been Mr. All-American Boy Scout—as in volunteering at the old-age home and serving turkey to the homeless on Thanksgiving—but last night, when Hanna, Sean, Mona, and a bunch of other kids were hanging out in Jim Freed's cedar hot tub, covertly drinking Coronas, Sean had taken All-American Boy Scout up a notch. He'd announced, a little proudly, that he'd signed a virginity "promise" and vowed not to have sex before marriage. Everyone, Hanna included, had been too stunned to respond.

"He's not serious," Hanna said confidently. How could he be? A bunch of kids signed the promise; Hanna figured it was just a passing trend, like those Lance Armstrong bracelets or Yogalates.

"You think?" Mona smirked, brushing her long bangs

out of her eyes. "Let's see what happens at Noel's party next Friday."

Hanna gritted her teeth. It seemed like Mona was laughing at her. "I want to go shopping," she said, standing up.

"How about Tiffany's?" Mona asked.

"Awesome."

They strolled through the brand-new luxe section of the King James Mall, which had a Burberry, a Tiffany's, a Gucci, and a Coach; smelled of the latest Michael Kors perfume; and was packed full of pretty back-to-prep-school girls with their beautiful moms. On a solo shopping trip a few weeks ago, Hanna had noticed her old friend Spencer Hastings slipping into the new Kate Spade, and remembered how she used to special-order an entire season's worth of nylon shoulder bags from New York.

Hanna felt funny knowing those sorts of details about someone she wasn't friends with anymore. And as she watched Spencer peruse Kate Spade's leather luggage, Hanna wondered if Spencer was thinking what she was thinking: that the mall's new wing was just the sort of place Ali DiLaurentis would have loved. Hanna often thought of all the things Ali had missed—last year's homecoming bonfire, Lauren Ryan's sweet sixteen karaoke party in her family's mansion, the return of round-toed shoes, Chanel's leather iPod nano holders . . . iPod nanos, in general. But the biggest thing Ali had missed? Hanna's makeover, of course—and it was *such* a bummer she had. Sometimes, when Hanna twirled around in front of her full-length mirror, she pretended that Ali was sitting behind her, critiquing her outfits the way she used to. Hanna had wasted so many years being a chubby, clingy loser, but things were *so* different now.

She and Mona strode into Tiffany's; it was full of glass, chrome, and white lights that made the flawless diamonds extra shimmery. Mona prowled around the cases and then raised her eyebrows at Hanna. "Maybe a necklace?"

"What about a charm bracelet?" Hanna whispered.

"Perfect."

They walked to the case and eyed the silver charm bracelet with the heart-shaped toggle. "So pretty," Mona breathed.

"Interested?" an elegant older saleswoman asked them.

"Oh, I don't know," Hanna said.

"It suits you." The woman unlocked the case and felt around for the bracelet. "It's in all the magazines."

Hanna nudged Mona. "You try it."

Mona slid it onto her wrist. "It's really beautiful." Then the woman turned to another customer. When she did, Mona slid the bracelet off her wrist and into her pocket. Just like that.

Hanna mashed her lips together and flagged down another saleswoman, a honey-blond girl who wore coral lipstick. "Can I try that bracelet there, with the round charm?"

"Sure!" The girl unlocked the case. "I have one of these myself."

"How about the matching earrings, too?" Hanna pointed to them.

"Of course."

Mona had moved over to the diamonds. Hanna held the earrings and the bracelet in her hands. Together, they were $350. Suddenly, a swarm of Japanese girls crowded around the counter, all pointing at another round-charm bracelet in the glass case. Hanna scanned the ceilings for cameras and the doors for detectors.

"Oh, Hanna, come look at the Lucida!" Mona called.

Hanna paused. Time slowed down. She slid the bracelet onto her wrist and then shoved it farther up her sleeve. She stuck the earrings in her Louis Vuitton cherry-monogrammed coin purse. Hanna's heart pounded. This was the best part of taking stuff: the feeling beforehand. She felt all buzzy and alive.

Mona waved a diamond ring at her. "Doesn't this look good on me?"

"C'mon." Hanna grabbed her arm. "Let's go to Coach."

"You don't want to try any on?" Mona pouted. She always stalled after she knew Hanna had done the job.

"Nah," Hanna said. "Purses are calling our names." She felt the bracelet's silver chain press gently into her arm. She had to get out of here while the Japanese girls were still bustling around the counter. The salesgirl hadn't even looked back in her direction.

"All right," Mona said dramatically. She handed the ring–holding it by its diamond, which even Hanna knew you weren't supposed to do–back to the saleswoman. "These diamonds are all too small," she said. "Sorry."

"We have others," the woman tried.

"Come on," Hanna said, grabbing Mona's arm.

Her heart hammered as they wove their way through Tiffany's. The charm tinkled on her wrist, but she kept her sleeve pulled down. Hanna was a seasoned pro at this–first it had been loose candy at the Wawa convenience store, then CDs from Tower, then baby tees from Ralph Lauren–and she felt bigger and more badass every time. She shut her eyes and crossed the threshold, bracing herself for the alarms to blare.

But nothing did. They were out.

Mona squeezed her hand. "Did you get one too?"

"Of course." She flashed the bracelet around her wrist. "And these." She opened the coin purse and showed Mona the earrings.

"Shit." Mona's eyes widened.

Hanna smiled. Sometimes it felt so good to one-up your best friend. Not wanting to jinx it, she walked quickly away from Tiffany's and listened for someone to come chasing after them. The only noise, though, was the burbling of the fountain and a Muzak version of "Oops! I Did It Again."

Oh yes, I did, Hanna thought.

4

SPENCER WALKS THE PLANK

"Honey, you're not supposed to eat mussels with your hands. It's not polite."

Spencer Hastings looked across the table at her mother, Veronica, who nervously ran her hands through her perfectly highlighted ash-blond hair. "Sorry," Spencer said, picking up the ridiculously small mussel-eating fork.

"I really don't think Melissa should be living in the town house with all that dust," Mrs. Hastings said to her husband, ignoring Spencer's apology.

Peter Hastings rolled his neck around. When he wasn't practicing law, he was furiously cycling all the back roads of Rosewood in tight, colorful spandex shirts and bike pants, shaking his fist at speeding cars. All that cycling gave him chronically sore shoulders.

"All that hammering! I don't know how she'll get *any* studying done," Mrs. Hastings went on.

Spencer and her parents were sitting at Moshulu, a restaurant aboard a clipper ship in the Philadelphia harbor, waiting for Spencer's sister, Melissa, to meet them for dinner. It was a big celebratory dinner because Melissa had graduated from U Penn undergrad a year early and had gotten into Penn's Wharton School of Business. The downtown Philly town house was being renovated as a gift from their parents to Melissa.

In just two days, Spencer was starting her junior year at Rosewood and would have to surrender herself to this year's jam-packed schedule: five APs, leadership training, charity drive organizing, yearbook editing, drama try-outs, hockey practice, and sending in summer program applications ASAP, since everyone knew that the best way to get into an Ivy was to get into one of their pre-college summer camps. But there was one thing Spencer had to look forward to this year: moving into the converted barn that sat at the back of her family's property. According to her parents, it was the perfect way to prepare for college—just look how well it had worked for Melissa! Barf. But Spencer was happy to follow in her sister's footsteps in this case, since they led out to the tranquil, light-flooded guesthouse where Spencer could escape her parents and their constantly barking labradoodles.

The sisters had a quiet yet long-standing rivalry and Spencer was always losing: Spencer had won the Presidential Physical Fitness Award four times in elementary school; Melissa had won it five. Spencer got second place in the seventh-grade geography bee; Melissa got first. Spencer was on the yearbook staff, in all of the school plays, and was taking five AP classes this year; Melissa did all those things her junior year plus worked at their mother's horse farm and trained for the Philadelphia marathon for leukemia research. No matter how high Spencer's GPA was or how many extra-curriculars she smashed into her schedule, she never quite reached Melissa's level of perfection.

Spencer picked up another mussel with her fingers and popped it into her mouth. Her dad loved this restau-rant, with its dark wood paneling, thick oriental rugs, and the heady smells of butter, red wine, and salty air. Sitting among the masts and sails, it felt like you could jump right overboard into the harbor. Spencer gazed out across the Schuylkill River to the big bubbly aquarium in Camden, New Jersey. A giant party boat decorated with Christmas lights floated past them. Someone shot a yel-low firework off the front deck. That boat was having way more fun than this one was having.

"What's Melissa's friend's name again?" her mother murmured.

"I think it's Wren," Spencer said. In her head she added, *As in scrawny bird.*

"She told me he's studying to be a doctor," her mother swooned. "At U Penn."

"Of course he is," Spencer quietly singsonged. She bit down hard on a piece of mussel shell and winced. Melissa was bringing her boyfriend of two months to dinner. The family hadn't met him yet—he'd been away visiting family or something—but Melissa's boyfriends were all the same: textbook handsome, well mannered, played golf. Melissa didn't have an ounce of creativity in her body and clearly looked for the same predictability in her boyfriends.

"Mom!" a familiar voice called from behind Spencer.

Melissa swooped to the other side of the table and gave each of her parents a huge kiss. Her look hadn't changed since high school: her ash-blond hair was cut bluntly to her chin, she wore no makeup except for a little foundation, and she wore a dowdy square-necked yellow dress, a pearl-buttoned pink cardigan, and semi-cute kitten-heeled shoes.

"Darling!" her mother cried.

"Mom, Dad, here's Wren." Melissa pulled in someone next to her.

Spencer tried to keep her mouth from dropping open. There was nothing scrawny, birdlike, or textbook about Wren. He was tall and lanky and wore a beautifully cut Thomas Pink shirt. His black hair was cut in a long, shaggy, messy style. He had beautiful skin, high cheekbones, and almond-shaped eyes.

Wren shook her parents' hands and sat down at the table. Melissa asked her mom a question about where to have the plumber's bill sent, while Spencer waited to be introduced. Wren pretended to be really interested in an oversize wineglass.

"I'm Spencer," she said finally. She wondered if her breath smelled like mussels. "The other daughter." Spencer nodded toward the other side of the table. "The one they keep in the basement."

"Oh." Wren grinned. "Cool."

Was that a British accent she heard? "Isn't it strange they haven't asked you a single thing about yourself?" Spencer gestured at her parents. Now they were talking about contractors and the best wood to use for the living room floor.

Wren shrugged, and then whispered, "Kinda." He winked.

Suddenly Melissa grabbed Wren's hand. "Oh, I see you've met her," she cooed.

"Yeah." He smiled. "You didn't tell me you had a sister."

Of course she hadn't.

"So Melissa," Mrs. Hastings said. "Daddy and I were talking about where you might be staying while all the renovations are happening. And I just thought of something. Why not just come back to Rosewood to live with us for a few months? You can commute to Penn; you know how easy it is."

Melissa wrinkled her nose. *Please say no, please say no,* Spencer willed.

"Well." Melissa adjusted the strap of her yellow dress. The more Spencer stared at it, the more the color made Melissa look like she had the flu. Melissa glanced at Wren. "The thing is . . . Wren and I are going to be moving into the town house . . . together."

"Oh!" Her mother smiled at both of them. "Well . . . I suppose Wren could stay with us too . . . what do you think, Peter?"

Spencer had to clutch her boobs to keep her heart from exploding out of her chest. They were moving *in* together? Her sister really had some balls. She could just imagine what would happen if *she* dropped a bomb like that. Mom really *would* make Spencer live in the basement—or maybe in the stable. She could set up shop next to the horses' companion goat.

"Well, I suppose that's all right," her father said. *Unbelievable!* "It'll certainly be quiet. Mom's in the stable most of the day, and of course Spencer will be in school."

"You're in school?" Wren asked. "Where?"

"She's in high school," Melissa butted in. She stared long at Spencer, as if she were sizing her up. From Spencer's tight ecru Lacoste tennis dress to her long, dark blond wavy hair to her two-carat diamond earrings. "Same high school I went to. I never asked, Spence—are you president of the class this year?"

"VP," Spencer mumbled. There was *no way* Melissa hadn't already known that.

"Oh, aren't you *so* happy it worked out that way?" Melissa asked.

"No," Spencer said flatly. She'd run for the spot last spring but had been beaten out and had to take the VP slot. She hated losing at anything.

Melissa shook her head. "You don't understand,

Spence—it's *soooooo* much work. When I was president, I barely had time for anything else!"

"You do have quite a few activities, Spencer," Mrs. Hastings murmured. "There's yearbook, and all those hockey games. . . . "

"Besides, Spence, you'll take over if the president, you know . . . dies." Melissa winked at her as if they were sharing this joke, which they weren't.

Melissa turned back to her parents. "Mom. I just got the best idea. What if Wren and I stayed in the barn? Then we'd be out of your hair."

Spencer felt as if someone had just kicked her in the ovaries. The *barn*?

Mrs. Hastings put her French-manicured finger to her perfectly lipsticked mouth. "Hmm," she started. She turned tentatively to Spencer. "Would you be able to wait a few months, honey? Then the barn will be all yours."

"Oh!" Melissa laid down her fork. "I didn't know you were going to move in there, Spence! I don't want to cause problems—"

"It's fine," Spencer interrupted, grabbing her glass of ice water and taking a hearty swallow. She willed herself not to throw a tantrum in front of her parents and Perfect Melissa. "I can wait."

"Seriously?" Melissa asked. "That's so sweet of you!"

Her mother pressed her cold, thin hand against Spencer's and beamed. "I *knew* you'd understand."

"Can you excuse me?" Spencer dizzily shoved her

seat back from the table and stood up. "I'll be right back." She walked across the boat's wooden floor, down the carpeted main stairs, and out the front entrance. She needed to get to dry land.

Out on the Penn's Landing walkway, the Philadelphia skyline glittered. Spencer sat down on a bench and breathed yoga fire breaths. Then she pulled out her wallet and started to organize her money. She turned all the ones, fives, and twenties in the same direction and alphabetized them according to the long letter-number combination printed in green in the corners. Doing this always made her feel better. When she finished, she gazed up at the ship's dining deck. Her parents faced the river, so they couldn't see her. She dug through her tan Hogan bag for her emergency pack of Marlboros and lit one.

She took drag after angry drag. Stealing the barn was evil enough, but doing it in such a polite way was *just* Melissa's style—Melissa had always been outwardly nice but inwardly horrid. And no one could see it but Spencer.

She'd gotten revenge on Melissa just once, a few weeks before the end of seventh grade. One evening, Melissa and her then-boyfriend, Ian Thomas, were studying for finals. When Ian left, Spencer cornered him outside by his SUV, which he'd parked behind her family's row of pine trees. She'd merely wanted to flirt—Ian was wasting all his hotness on her plain vanilla, goody-two-shoes sister—so she gave Ian a peck good-bye on the cheek. But when he pressed her up against his passenger door, she didn't try to run away. They only stopped kissing when his car alarm started to blare.

When Spencer told Alison about it, Ali said it was a pretty foul thing to do and that she should confess to Melissa. Spencer suspected Ali was just pissed because they'd had a running competition all year over who could hook up with the most older boys, and kissing Ian put Spencer in the lead.

Spencer inhaled sharply. She hated being reminded of that period of her life. But the DiLaurentises' old house was right next door to hers, and one of Ali's bedroom windows faced one of Spencer's—it was like Ali haunted her 24/7. All Spencer had to do was look out her window and there was seventh-grade Ali, hanging her JV hockey uniform right where Spencer could see it or strolling around her bedroom gossiping into her cell phone.

Spencer wanted to think she'd changed a lot since seventh grade. They'd all been so mean—especially Alison—but not *just* Alison. And the worst memory of all was *the thing* . . . The Jenna Thing. Thinking of that made Spencer feel so horrible, she wished she could erase it from her brain like they did in that movie *Eternal Sunshine of the Spotless Mind*.

"You shouldn't be smoking, you know."

She turned, and there was Wren, standing right next to her. Spencer looked at him, surprised. "What are you doing down here?"

"They were . . ." He opened and closed his hands at each other, like mouths yapping. "And I have a page." He pulled out a BlackBerry.

"Oh," Spencer said. "Is that from the hospital? I hear you're a big-time doctor."

"Well, no, actually, I'm only a first-year med student," Wren said, and then pointed at her cigarette. "You mind if I have a bit of that?"

Spencer twisted the corners of her mouth up wryly. "You just told me not to smoke," she said, handing it over to him.

"Yeah, well." Wren took a deep drag off the cigarette. "You all right?"

"Whatever." Spencer wasn't about to talk things over with her sister's new live-in boyfriend who'd just stolen her barn. "So where are you from?"

"North London. My Dad's Korean, though. He moved to England to go to Oxford and ended up staying. Everyone asks."

"Oh. I wasn't going to," Spencer replied, even though she *had* thought about it. "How'd you and my sister meet?"

"At Starbucks," he answered. "She was in line in front of me."

"Oh," Spencer said. How incredibly lame.

"She was buying a latte," Wren added, kicking at the stone curb.

"That's nice." Spencer fiddled with her pack of cigarettes.

"This was a few months ago." He raggedly took another drag, his hand shaking a little and his eyes darting around. "I fancied her before she got the town house."

"Right," Spencer said, realizing he seemed a little nervous. Maybe he was tense about meeting her parents. Or was it moving in with Melissa that had him on edge? If Spencer were a boy and had to move in with Melissa, she'd throw herself off Moshulu's crow's nest into the Schuylkill River.

He handed the cigarette back to her. "I hope it's okay that I'm going to be staying in your house."

"Um, yeah. Whatever."

Wren licked his lips. "Maybe I can get you to kick your smoking addiction."

Spencer stiffened. "I'm not addicted."

"Sure you're not," Wren answered, smiling.

Spencer shook her head emphatically. "No, I'd never let that happen." And it was true: Spencer hated feeling out of control.

Wren smiled. "Well, you certainly sound like you know what you're doing."

"I do."

"Are you that way with everything?" Wren asked, his eyes shining.

There was something about the light, teasing way he said it that made Spencer pause. Were they . . . flirting? They stared at each other for a few seconds until a big group of people came whooshing off the boat onto the street. Spencer lowered her eyes.

"So, do you think it's time we go back?" Wren asked.

Spencer hesitated and looked at the street, full of taxis, ready to take her wherever she wanted. She almost wanted to ask Wren to get in one of the cabs with her and go to a baseball game at Citizens Bank Park, where they could eat hot dogs, yell at the players, and count how many strikeouts the Phillies' starting pitcher racked up. She could use her dad's box seats—they mostly just went to waste, anyway—and she bet Wren would be into that. Why go back in, when her family was just going to continue to ignore them? A cab paused at the light, just a few feet from them. She looked at it, then back at Wren.

But no, that'd be wrong. And who would fill the vice president's post if he died and she was murdered by her own sister? "After you," Spencer said, and held the door open for him so they could climb back aboard.

5

STARTS AND FITZ

"Hey! Finland!"

On Tuesday, the first day of school, Aria walked quickly to her first-period English class. She turned to see Noel Kahn, in his Rosewood Day sweater vest and tie, jogging toward her. "Hey." Aria nodded. She kept going.

"You bolted from our practice the other day," Noel said, sidling up next to her.

"You expected me to watch?" Aria looked at him out of the corner of her eye. He looked flushed.

"Yeah. We scrimmaged. I scored three goals."

"Good for you," Aria deadpanned. Was she supposed to be impressed?

She continued down the Rosewood Day hallway, which she'd unfortunately dreamed about way too many times in Iceland. Above her were the same eggshell-white, vaulted ceilings. Below her were the same farm-house-cozy wood floors. To her right and left were the usual framed photos of stuffy alums, and to her left, incongruous rows of dented metal lockers. Even the very same song, the *1812 Overture*, hummed through the PA speakers—Rosewood played between-classes music because it was "mentally stimulating." Sweeping by her were the exact same people Aria had known for a gazillion years . . . and all of them were staring.

Aria ducked her head. Since she'd moved to Iceland at the beginning of eighth grade, the last time everyone had seen her she was part of the grief-stricken group of girls whose best friend freakishly vanished. Back then, wherever she went, people were whispering about her.

Now, it felt like she'd never left. And it almost felt like Ali was still here. Aria's breath caught in her chest when she saw a flash of blond ponytail swishing around the corner to the gym. And when Aria rounded the corner past the pottery studio, where she and Ali used to meet between classes to trade gossip, she could almost hear Ali yelling, "Hey, wait up!" She pressed her hand to her forehead to see if she had a fever.

"So what class do you have first?" Noel asked, still keeping pace with her.

She looked at him, surprised, and then down at her schedule. "English."

"Me too. Mr. Fitz?"

"Yeah," she mumbled. "He any good?"

"Dunno. He's new. Heard he was a Fulbright Scholar, though."

Aria eyed him suspiciously. Since when did Noel Kahn care about a teacher's credentials? She turned around a corner and saw a girl standing in the English room doorway. She looked familiar and foreign all at the same time. This girl was model-thin, had long, red-brown hair, and wore a rolled-up blue plaid Rosewood uniform skirt, purple platform wedge-heels, and a Tiffany charm bracelet.

Aria's heart started to pound. She'd worried about how she might react when she saw her old friends again, and here was Hanna. What had *happened* to Hanna?

"Hey," Aria said softly.

Hanna turned and looked Aria up and down, from her long, shaggy haircut to her Rosewood Day white shirt and chunky Bakelite bracelets to her brown scuffed lace-up boots. A blank expression crossed her face, but then she smiled.

"Omigod!" Hanna said. At least it was still Hanna's same high-pitched voice. "How was . . . where were you? Czechoslovakia?"

"Um, yeah," Aria answered. Close enough.

"Cool!" Hanna gave Aria a tight smile.

"Kirsten looks like she's gone off South Beach," interrupted a girl next to Hanna. Aria turned her head sideways, trying to place her. Mona Vanderwaal? The last time Aria saw her, Mona had put a billion teensy braids in her hair and was riding her Razor scooter. Now, she looked even more glamorous than Hanna.

"Doesn't she?" Hanna agreed. She then gave Aria and Noel—who was *still* standing there—an apologetic shrug. "Sorry, guys, can you excuse us?"

Aria headed into the classroom and fell into the first desk she saw. She put her head down and took heaving, emotional breaths.

"*Hell is other people*," she chanted. It was her favorite quote by the French philosopher Jean-Paul Sartre and a perfect mantra for Rosewood.

She rocked back and forth for a few seconds, in full freak-out mode. The only thing that made her feel better was the memory of Ezra, that guy she'd met at Snookers. At the bar, Ezra had followed her into the bathroom, grabbed her face, and kissed her. Their mouths fit perfectly together—they didn't bang teeth once. His hands floated all over the small of her back, her stomach, her legs. They'd had such a *connection*. And okay, fine, some might say it was just a . . . a tongue connection . . . but Aria knew it was more.

She'd felt so overcome thinking about it last night, she'd written a haiku about Ezra to express her feelings—haikus were her favorite kind of poem. Then, pleased with how it turned out, she'd keyed it into her phone and texted it to the number Ezra had given her.

Aria let out a tortured sigh and looked around the classroom. It smelled like books and Mop & Glo. The oversize, four-paned windows faced the south lawn and beyond that, green rolling hills. A few trees had started to turn yellow and orange. There was a great Shakespearean sayings poster next to the blackboard, and a MEAN PEOPLE SUCK sticker someone had stuck to the wall. It looked like the janitor had tried to scrape off the sticker but gave up halfway through.

Was it desperate to text Ezra at 2:30 A.M.? She still hadn't heard back from him. Aria felt for her phone in her bag and pulled it out. The screen read, NEW TEXT MESSAGE. Her stomach swooped, relieved and excited and nervous all at once. But as she clicked READ, a voice interrupted her.

"Excuse me. Um, you can't use your cell in school."

Aria covered her phone with her hands and looked up. Whoever had said it—the new teacher, she guessed—stood with his back to the rest of the room and was writing on the chalkboard. *Mr. Fitz* was all he'd written so far. He was holding a memo with Rosewood's insignia on the top. From the back, he looked young. A few of the other girls in the class gave him an appreciative once-over as they found seats. The now-fabulous Hanna even whistled.

"I know I'm the new guy," he went on, writing, *AP English,* under his name, "but I have this handout from the front office. Some stuff about no cell phones in school." Then he turned. The handout fluttered out of his hand and onto the linoleum floor.

Aria's mouth instantly went dry. Standing in front of the classroom was Ezra from the bar. Ezra, the recipient of her haiku. *Her* Ezra, looking lanky and adorable in a

Rosewood jacket and tie, his hair combed, his buttons buttoned correctly, and a leather-bound lesson planner under his left arm. Standing at the blackboard and writing . . . *Mr. Fitz, AP English.*

He stared at her, his face draining of color. "Holy shit."

The entire class turned around to see who he was looking at. Aria didn't want to stare back at them, so she looked down at her text message.

Aria: Surprise! I wonder what your pig puppet will have to say about this . . . —A

Holy shit, indeed.

6

EMILY'S FRENCH TOO!

Tuesday afternoon, Emily stood in front of her green metal locker after the final bell of the day had rung. The locker still had her old stickers from last year—USA Swimming, Liv Tyler as Arwen the elf, and a magnet that said, COED NAKED BUTTERFLY. Her boyfriend, Ben, hovered next to her.

"You want to hit Wawa?" he asked. His Rosewood swimming jacket hung loosely off his lanky, muscular body, and his blond hair was a little messy.

"Nah, I'm good," Emily answered. Because they had practice at three-thirty after school, the swimmers usually just stayed at Rosewood and sent someone off to Wawa so they could get their hoagie/iced tea/Cheats/Reese's Pieces fix before swimming a billion laps.

A bunch of boys stopped to slap Ben's hand as they headed toward the parking lot. Spencer Hastings, who was in Ben's history class last year, waved. Emily waved back before realizing Spencer was looking at Ben, not her. It was hard to believe that after everything they'd been through together and all the secrets they shared, they now acted like strangers.

After everyone passed, Ben turned back to her and frowned. "You've got your jacket on. You're not practicing?"

"Um." Emily shut her locker and gave the combination a spin. "You know that girl I've been showing around today? I'm walking her to her house 'cause this is her first day and all."

He smirked. "Well, aren't *you* sweet? Parents of prospective students pay for tours, but you're doing it for free."

"Come on." Emily smiled uneasily. "It's like a ten-minute walk."

Ben looked at her, vaguely nodding for a little while.

"What? I'm just trying to be nice!"

"That's cool," he said, and smiled. He took his eyes off her to wave at Casey Kirschner, the captain of the boys' varsity wrestling team.

Maya appeared a minute after Ben loped down the side stairs out to the student parking lot. She wore a white denim jacket over her Rosewood oxford shirt and Oakley flip-flops on her feet. Her toenails weren't painted. "Hey," she said.

"Hey." Emily tried to sound bright, but she felt uneasy. Maybe she should've just gone to practice with Ben. Was it weird to walk Maya home and walk right back?

"Ready?" Maya asked.

The girls walked through campus, which was basically a bunch of very old brick buildings off a twisty back road in Rosewood. There was even a Gothic clock tower that chimed out the hours. Earlier, Emily had shown Maya all the standard stuff that every private school has. She'd also shown her the cool things about Rosewood Day that you usually had to discover on your own, like the dangerous toilet in the girls' first-floor bathroom that sometimes spewed up geyser-style, the secret spot on the hill kids went when they cut gym class (not that Emily ever would), and the school's only vending machine that sold Vanilla Coke, her favorite. They'd even developed an inside joke about the prim, stick-up-her-butt model on the anti-smoking posters that hung outside the nurse's office. It felt good to have an inside joke again.

Now, as they cut through an unused cornfield to Maya's neighborhood, Emily took in every detail of her face, from her turned-up nose to her coffee-colored skin to the way her collar couldn't settle right around her neck. Their hands kept bumping against each other when they swung their arms.

"It's so different here," Maya said, sniffing the air. "It smells like Pine-Sol!" She took off her denim jacket and rolled up the sleeves of her button-down. Emily pulled at her hair, wishing it was dark and wavy, like Maya's, instead of chlorine-damaged and a slightly greenish shade of reddish blond. Emily also felt a little self-conscious about her body, which was strong, muscular, and not as slender as it used to be. She didn't usually feel so aware of herself, even when she was in her swimsuit, which was practically naked.

"Everyone has stuff they're really *into*," Maya continued. "Like this girl Sarah in my physics class. She's trying to form a band, and she asked me to be in it!"

"Really? What do you play?"

"Guitar," Maya said. "My dad taught me. My brother's actually a lot better, but whatever."

"Wow," Emily said. "That's cool."

"Omigod!" Maya grabbed Emily's arm. Emily flinched at first but then relaxed. "You should join the band too! How fun would that be? Sarah said we'd practice three days a week after school. She plays bass."

"But all I play is the flute," Emily said, realizing she sounded like Eeyore from *Winnie-the-Pooh*.

"The flute would be awesome!" Maya clapped her hands. "And drums!"

Emily sighed. "I really couldn't. I have swimming, like, every day after school."

"Hmm," Maya said. "Can't you skip a day? I bet you'd be so good at the drums."

"My parents would murder me." Emily tilted her head and stared at the old iron railroad bridge above them. Trains didn't use the bridge anymore, so now it was mostly a place for kids to go and get drunk without their parents knowing.

"Why?" Maya asked. "What's the big deal?"

Emily paused. What was she supposed to say? That her parents expected her to keep swimming because scouts from Stanford were already watching Carolyn's progress? That her older brother, Jake, and oldest sister, Beth, were now both at the University of Arizona on full swimming rides? That anything less than a swimming scholarship to somewhere top-notch would be a family failure? Maya wasn't afraid to smoke pot when her parents were buying groceries. Emily's parents, by comparison, seemed like old, conservative, controlling East Coast suburbanites. Which they were. But still.

"This is a shorter way home." Emily gestured across the street, to the large colonial house's lawn she and her friends used to cut through on winter days to get to Ali's house faster.

They started up through the grass, avoiding a sprinkler spraying the hydrangea bushes. As they pushed through the brambly tree branches to Maya's backyard, Emily stopped short. A small, guttural noise escaped her throat.

She hadn't been in this backyard—*Ali's* old backyard—in ages. There, across the lawn, was the teak deck where she and Ali had played countless games of Spit. There was the worn patch of grass where they'd hooked up Ali's thick white iPod to speakers and had dance parties. To her left was the familiar knotty oak tree. The tree house was gone, but carved in the bark on the trunk were the initials: *EF + AD*—Emily Fields + Alison DiLaurentis. Her face flushed. At the time, Emily hadn't known why she carved their names into the bark; she'd just wanted to show Ali how happy she was that they were friends.

Maya, who had walked on ahead of her, looked over her shoulder. "You okay?"

Emily shoved her hands into her jacket pockets. For a second, she considered telling Maya about Ali. But a hummingbird swept past her and she lost her nerve. "I'm fine," she said.

"Do you wanna come in?" Maya asked.

"No . . . I . . . I have to go back to school," Emily answered. "Swimming."

"Oh." Maya crinkled up her eyes. "You didn't have to walk me home, silly."

"Yeah, but I didn't want you to get lost."

"You're so cute." Maya looped her hands behind her back and swung her hips back and forth. Emily wondered what she meant by *cute*. Was that a California thing?

"So, well, have fun at swimming," Maya said. "And thanks for showing me around today."

"Sure." Emily stepped forward, and their bodies smushed together in a hug.

"*Mmm,*" Maya said, squeezing tighter. The girls stepped back and grinned at each other for a second. Then Maya leaned forward and kissed Emily on both cheeks. "Mwah, mwah!" she said. "Like the French."

"Well, then, I'll be French too." Emily giggled,

forgetting about Ali and the tree for a second. "Mwah!" She kissed Maya's smooth left cheek.

Then Maya kissed her again, on her right cheek, except now just a teensy bit closer to her mouth. There was no *mwah* this time.

Maya's mouth smelled like banana bubble gum. Emily jerked back and caught her swimming bag before it slid off her shoulder. When she looked up, Maya was grinning.

"I'll see ya," Maya said. "Be good."

Emily folded her towel into her swim bag after practice. The whole afternoon had been a blur. After Maya skipped into her house, Emily jogged back to school—as if running would untangle the jumble of feelings inside her. As she slipped into the water and swam lap after lap, she saw those haunting initials on the tree. When Coach blew her whistle and they practiced starts and turns, she smelled Maya's banana gum and heard her fun, easy laugh. Standing at her locker, she was pretty sure she'd shampooed her hair twice. Most of the other girls had stayed in the communal showers for longer, gossiping, but Emily was too spaced out to join them.

As she reached for her T-shirt and jeans, folded neatly on the shelf in her locker, a note came fluttering out. Emily's name was written on the front in plain, unfamiliar handwriting, and she didn't recognize the graph notebook paper. She picked it up off the cold, wet floor.

Hey Em,

Sob! I've been replaced! You found another friend to kiss!

—A

Emily curled her toes around the rubber locker room mat and stopped breathing for a second. She looked around. No one was looking at her.

Was this for real?

She stared at the note and tried to think rationally. She and Maya were out in the open, but no one was around.

And . . . *I've been replaced? Another friend to kiss?* Emily's hands trembled. She looked at the signature again. Laughter from the other swimmers echoed off the walls.

Emily had kissed just one other friend. It was two days after she carved their initials into that oak tree and just a week and a half before the end of seventh grade.

Alison.

7

SPENCER'S GOT A TIGHT POSTERIOR (DELTOID)

"Look at his butt!"

"Shut up!" Spencer knocked her friend Kirsten Cullen in the shin guard with her field hockey stick. They were supposed to be running defense drills, but they—along with the rest of the team—were too busy sizing up this year's new assistant coach. He was none other than Ian Thomas.

Spencer's skin prickled with adrenaline. Talk about weird; she remembered Melissa mentioning that Ian had moved to California. But then, a lot of people who you wouldn't expect ended up back in Rosewood.

"Your sister was so stupid to break up with him," Kirsten said. "He's so *hot*."

"*Shhh*," Spencer answered, giggling. "And anyway, my sister didn't break up with him. He broke up with her."

The whistle blew. "Get moving!" Ian called to them, jogging over. Spencer leaned over to tie her shoe, as if she didn't care. She felt his eyes on her.

"*Spencer?* Spencer Hastings?"

Spencer stood up slowly. "Oh. Ian, right?"

Ian's smile was so wide, Spencer was surprised his cheeks didn't rip. He still had that All-American, I'm-going-to-take-over-my-father's-company-at-twenty-five look, but now his curly hair was a little longer and messier. "You're all grown up!" he cried.

"I guess." Spencer shrugged.

Ian ran his hand against the back of his neck. "How's your sister these days?"

"Um, she's good. Graduated early. Going to Wharton."

Ian bent his head down. "And are her boyfriends still hitting on you?"

Spencer's mouth dropped open. Before she could answer, the head coach, Ms. Campbell, blew her whistle and called Ian over.

Kirsten grabbed Spencer's arm once his back was turned. "You *totally* hooked up with him, didn't you?"

"Shut *up!*" Spencer shot back.

As Ian jogged to center field, he glanced back at her over his shoulder. Spencer drew in her breath and leaned over to examine her cleat. She didn't want him to know she'd been staring.

By the time she got home from practice, every part of Spencer's body hurt, from her ass to her shoulders to her little toes. She'd spent the whole summer organizing committees, boning up on SAT words, and playing the lead in three different plays at Muesli, Rosewood's community theater—Miss Jean Brodie in *The Prime of Miss Jean Brodie*, Emily in *Our Town*, and Ophelia in *Hamlet*. With all that, she hadn't had time to keep in top shape for field hockey, and she was feeling it now.

All she wanted to do was go upstairs, crawl into bed, and not think about tomorrow and what another over-achieving day would hold: French club breakfast, reading the morning announcements, five AP classes, drama tryouts, a quick appearance at yearbook committee, and another grueling field hockey practice with Ian.

She opened the mailbox at the bottom of their private drive, hoping to find the scores for her PSATs. They were supposed to be in any day now, and she'd had a good feeling about them—a better feeling, in fact, than she'd ever had about any other test. Unfortunately, there were just a pile of bills, info from her dad's many investment accounts, and a brochure addressed to Ms. Spencer J (for *Jill*) Hastings from Appleboro College in Lancaster, Pennsylvania. Yeah, as if she'd go *there*.

Inside the house, she put the mail on the marble-topped kitchen island, rubbed her shoulder, and had a thought: *The backyard hot tub. A relaxing soak. Awww, yeah.*

She greeted Rufus and Beatrice, the family's two labradoodles, and threw a couple of King Kong toys out into the yard for them to chase. Then she dragged herself along the flagstone path toward the pool's changing room. Pausing at the door, ready to shower and change into her bikini, she realized, *Who cares?* She was too tired to change, and nobody was home. And the hot tub was surrounded by rose bushes. As she approached, it burbled, as if anticipating her arrival. She stripped down to her bra, undies, and tall field hockey socks, did a deep forward bend to loosen up her back, and climbed into the steaming tub. Now *that* was more like it.

"Oh."

Spencer turned. Wren stood next to the roses, naked to the waist, wearing the sexiest boxer brief Polo underwear she'd ever seen.

"Oops," he said, covering himself with a towel. "Sorry."

"You don't get here until tomorrow," she blurted, even though he was very clearly here, right now, which was obviously *today* and not tomorrow at all.

"We don't. But your sister and I were at Frou," Wren said, making a little face. Frou was this haughty store a few towns over that sold single pillowcases for about a thousand dollars. "She had to run another errand and told me to play with myself here."

Spencer hoped that was just some bizarre English expression. "Oh," she said.

"Did you just get home?"

"I was at field hockey," Spencer said, leaning back and relaxing a little. "First practice of the year."

Spencer glanced at her blurry body under the water. Oh God, she was still wearing her socks. And her high-waisted, sweaty panties and Champion sports bra! She kicked herself for not changing into the yellow Eres bikini she'd just bought but then realized how absurd that was.

"So, I was just planning to have a soak, but if you want to be alone, that's okay too," Wren said. "I'll just go inside and watch TV." He started to turn.

Spencer felt a tiny twinge of disappointment. "Um, no," she said. He stopped. "You can come in. I don't care." Quickly, while his back was turned, she yanked off her socks and threw them into the bushes. They landed with a soggy slap.

"If you're sure, Spencer," Wren said. Spencer loved the way he said her name with his British accent—Spen-*saah*.

He shyly slid into the tub. Spencer stayed very far on her side, curling her legs under her. Wren leaned his head back on the concrete deck and sighed. Spencer did the same and tried not to think about how her legs were getting really cramped and sore in this position. She stretched one tentatively and touched Wren's sinewy calf.

She jerked her leg away. "Sorry."

"No worries," Wren said. "So field hockey, huh? I rowed for Oxford."

"Really?" Spencer said, hoping she didn't sound too

gushy. Her favorite driving-into-Philadelphia sight was of the Penn and Temple men's crew teams rowing on the Schuylkill River.

"Yeah," he said. "I loved it. Do you love field hockey?"

"Um, not really." Spencer took her hair out of its ponytail and shook her head around but then wondered if Wren would find this really skanky and ridiculous. She'd probably imagined the spark between them outside Moshulu.

But then, Wren *had* gotten into the hot tub with her.

"So if you don't like field hockey, why do you play?" Wren asked.

"Because it looks good on a college application."

Now Wren sat up a little, making the water ripple. "It does?"

"Uh, *yeah*."

Spencer shifted and winced when her shoulder muscle cramped into her neck.

"You okay?" Wren asked.

"Yeah, it's nothing," Spencer said, and inexplicably felt an overwhelming wave of despair. It was only the first day of school, and she was already burned out. She thought of all the homework she had to do, lists she had to make, and lines she had to memorize. She was too busy to freak out, but that was the only thing keeping her from freaking out.

"Is it your shoulder?"

"I think," Spencer said, trying to rotate it. "In field hockey, you spend so much time bending over, and I don't know if I pulled it or what. . . ."

"I bet I could fix it for you."

Spencer stared at him. She suddenly had an urge to run her fingers through his shaggy hair. "That's okay. Thanks, though."

"Really," he said. "I'm not going to bite you."

Spencer hated when people said that.

"I'm a doctor," Wren continued. "I bet it's your posterior deltoid."

"Um, okay . . . "

"Your shoulder muscle." He motioned for her to come closer. "C'mere. Seriously. We just need to soften the muscle."

Spencer tried not to read into that. He was a doctor, after all. He was being doctorly. She drifted to him, and he pressed his hands into the middle of her back. His thumbs dug into the little muscles around her spine. Spencer closed her eyes.

"Wow. That's awesome," she murmured.

"You just have some fluid buildup in your bursa sac," he said. Spencer tried not to giggle at the word *sac*. When he reached under her sports bra strap to dig deeper, she swallowed hard. She tried to think about nonsexual things—her uncle Daniel's nose hair, the constipated look her mom got on her face when she rode a horse, the time her cat, Kitten, carried a dead mole from the creek out back and left it in her bedroom. *He's a doctor*, she told herself. *This is just what doctors do.*

"Your pectorals are a little tight too," Wren said, and, horrifyingly, moved his hand to the front of her body. He slid his fingers under her bra again, rubbing just above her chest, and suddenly the bra strap fell off her shoulder. Spencer breathed in but he didn't move away. *This is a doctor thing*, she reminded herself again. But then she realized: Wren was a first-year med student. *He* will *be a doctor*, she corrected herself. *One day. In about ten years.*

"Um, where's my sister?" she asked quietly.

"The store, I think? Wawa?"

"Wawa?" Spencer jerked away from Wren and pulled her bra strap back on her shoulder. "Wawa's only a mile away! If she's going there, she's just picking up cigarettes or something. She'll be back any minute!"

"I don't think she smokes," Wren said, tilting his head questioningly.

"You know what I mean!" Spencer stood up in the tub, grabbed her Ralph Lauren towel, and began violently drying her hair. She felt so hot. Her skin, bones—even her organs and nerves—felt like they'd been braised in the hot tub. She climbed out and fled to the house, in search of a giant glass of water.

"Spencer," Wren called after her. "I didn't mean to . . . I was just trying to help."

But Spencer didn't listen. She ran up to her room and

looked around. Her stuff was still in boxes, still packed up to move to the barn. Suddenly she wanted everything organized. Her jewelry box needed to be sorted by gemstone. Her computer was clogged with old English papers from two years ago, and even though they'd gotten A's back then they were probably embarrassingly bad and should be deleted. She stared at the books in the boxes. They needed to be arranged by subject matter, not by author. Obviously. She pulled them out and started shelving, starting with Adultery and *The Scarlet Letter*.

But by the time she got to Utopias Gone Wrong, she still didn't feel any better. So she switched on her computer and pressed her wireless mouse, which was comfortingly cool, to the back of her neck.

She clicked on her e-mail and saw an unopened letter. The subject line read, *SAT vocab*. Curious, she clicked on it.

Spencer,
Covet is an easy one. When someone covets something, they desire and lust after it. Usually it's something they can't have. You've always had that problem, though, haven't you? —A

Spencer's stomach seized. She looked around.
Who. The. Fuck. Could. Have. Seen?
She threw open her bedroom's biggest window, but the Hastingses' circular driveway was empty. Spencer looked around. A few cars swished past. The neighbors'

lawn service guy was trimming a hedge by their front gate. Her dogs were chasing each other around the side yard. Some birds flew to the top of a telephone pole.

Then, something caught her eye in the neighbor's upstairs window: a flash of blondish hair. But wasn't the new family black? An icy shiver crept up Spencer's spine. That was Ali's old window.

8

WHERE ARE THE DAMN GIRL SCOUTS WHEN YOU NEED THEM?

Hanna sank farther into the squishy cushions of her couch and tried to unbutton Sean's Paper Denim jeans.

"Whoa," Sean said. "We can't. . . . "

Hanna smiled mysteriously and put a finger to her lips. She started kissing Sean's neck. He smelled like Lever 2000 and, strangely, chocolate, and she loved how his recently buzzed haircut showed off all the sexy angles of his face. She'd loved him since sixth grade and he'd only gotten handsomer with each passing year.

As they kissed, Hanna's mother, Ashley, unlocked the front door and walked inside, chatting on her teensy LG flip phone.

Sean recoiled against the couch cushions. "She'll see!" he whispered, quickly tucking in his pale blue Lacoste polo.

Hanna shrugged. Her mom waved at them blankly and walked into the other room. Her mom paid more attention to her BlackBerry than she did to Hanna. Because of her work schedule, she and Hanna didn't bond much, aside from periodic checkups on homework, notes on which shops were running the best sales, and reminders that she should clean her room in case any of the execs coming to her cocktail party needed to use the upstairs bathroom. But Hanna was mostly okay with that. After all, her mom's job was what paid Hanna's AmEx bill—she wasn't *always* taking things—and her pricey tuition at Rosewood Day.

"I have to go," Sean murmured.

"You should come over on Saturday," Hanna purred. "My mom's going to be at the spa all day."

"I'll see you at Noel's party on Friday," Sean said. "And you know this is hard enough."

Hanna groaned. "It doesn't *have* to be so hard," she whined.

He leaned down to kiss her. "See you tomorrow."

After Sean let himself out, she buried her face in the couch pillow. Dating Sean still felt like a dream. Back when Hanna was chubby and lame, she'd adored how tall and athletic he was, how he was always really nice to teachers and kids who were less cool, and how he dressed well, not like a color-blind slob. She never stopped liking him, even after she shed her last few stubborn inches and discovered defrizzing hair products. So last school year, she casually whispered to James Freed in study hall that she liked Sean, and Colleen Rink told her three periods later that Sean was going to call Hanna on her cell that night after soccer. It was yet another moment Hanna was pissed Ali wasn't here to witness.

They'd been a couple for seven months and Hanna felt more in love with him than ever. She hadn't told him yet—she'd kept *that* to herself for years—but now, she was pretty sure he loved her too. And wasn't sex the best way to express love?

That was why the virginity pledge thing made no sense. It wasn't as if Sean's parents were overly religious, and it went against every preconceived notion Hanna had about guys. Despite how she used to look, Hanna had to hand it to herself: With her deep brown hair, curvy body, and flawless—we're talking no pimples, ever—skin, she was hot. Who wouldn't fall madly in love with her? Sometimes she wondered if Sean was gay—he *did* have a lot of nice clothes—or if he had a fear of vaginas.

Hanna called for her miniature pinscher, Dot, to hop up on the couch. "Did you miss me today?" she squealed as Dot licked her hand. Hanna had petitioned to let Dot come to school in her oversize Prada handbag—all the girls in Beverly Hills did it, after all—but Rosewood Day said no. So to prevent separation anxiety, Hanna had bought Dot the snuggliest Gucci bed money could buy and left QVC on her bedroom TV during the day.

Her mother strode into the living room, still in her

tailored tweed suit and brown kitten-heel slingbacks. "There's sushi," Ms. Marin said.

Hanna looked up. "Toro rolls?"

"I don't know. I got a bunch of things."

Hanna strode into the kitchen, taking in her mom's laptop and buzzing LG.

"What now?" Ms. Marin barked into the phone.

Dot's little claws *tick-ticked* behind Hanna. After searching through the bag, she settled on one piece of yellowtail sashimi, one eel roll, and a small bowl of miso soup.

"Well, I talked to the client this morning," her mom went on. "They were happy *then*."

Hanna daintily dipped her yellowtail roll into some soy sauce and flipped breezily through a J. Crew catalog. Her mom was second-in-command at the Philly advertising firm McManus & Tate, and her goal was to be the firm's first woman president.

Besides being extremely successful and ambitious, Ms. Marin was what most guys at Rosewood Day would call a MILF—she had long, red-gold hair, smooth skin, and an incredibly supple body, thanks to her daily Vinyasa yoga ritual.

Hanna knew her mom wasn't perfect, but she still didn't get why her parents had divorced four years ago, or why her father quickly began dating an average-looking ER nurse from Annapolis, Maryland, named Isabel. Talk about trading down.

Isabel had a teenage daughter, Kate, and Mr. Marin had said Hanna would just *love* her. A few months after the divorce, he'd invited Hanna to Annapolis for the weekend. Nervous about meeting her quasi-stepsister, Hanna begged Ali to come along.

"Don't worry, Han," Ali assured her. "We'll outclass whoever this Kate girl is." When Hanna looked at her, unconvinced, she reminded Hanna of her signature phrase: "I'm Ali and I'm fabulous!" It sounded almost silly now, but back then Hanna could only imagine what it would feel like to be so confident. Having Ali there was like a security blanket—proof she wasn't a loser her dad just wanted to get away from.

The day had been a train wreck, anyway. Kate was the prettiest girl Hanna had ever met and her dad had basically called her a pig right in front of Kate. He'd quickly backpedaled and said it was only a joke, but that was the very last time she'd seen him . . . and the very first time she ever made herself throw up.

But Hanna hated thinking about stuff in the past, so she rarely did. Besides, now Hanna got to ogle her mom's dates in a not so will-you-be-my-new-father? way. And would her father let Hanna have a 2 A.M. curfew and drink wine, like her mom did? Doubtful.

Her mom snapped her phone shut and fastened her emerald green eyes on Hanna. "Those are your back-to-school shoes?"

Hanna stopped chewing. "Yeah."

Ms. Marin nodded. "Did you get a lot of compliments?"

Hanna turned her ankle to inspect her purple wedges. Too afraid to face the Saks security, she'd actually paid for them. "Yeah. I did."

"Mind if I borrow them?"

"Um, sure. If you wa—"

Her mom's phone rang again. She pounced on it. "Carson? Yes. I've been looking for you all night. . . . What the hell is going on there?"

Hanna blew at her side-swept bangs and fed Dot a tiny piece of eel. As Dot spit it out on the floor, the door-bell rang.

Her mother didn't even flinch. "They need it *tonight*," she said to the phone. "It's your project. Do I have to come down and hold your hand?"

The doorbell rang again. Dot started barking and her mother stood to get it. "It's probably those Girl Scouts again."

The Girl Scouts had come over three days in a row, trying to sell them cookies at dinnertime. They were rabid in this neighborhood.

Within seconds, she was back in the kitchen with a young, brown-haired, green-eyed police officer behind her. "This gentleman says he wants to speak with you." A gold pin on the breast pocket of his uniform read WILDEN.

"Me?" Hanna pointed at herself.

"You're Hanna Marin?" Wilden asked. The walkie-talkie on his belt made a noise.

Suddenly Hanna realized who this guy was: Darren Wilden. He'd been a senior at Rosewood when she was in seventh grade. The Darren Wilden she remembered allegedly slept with the whole girls' diving team and was almost kicked out of school for stealing the principal's vintage Ducati motorcycle. But this cop was definitely the same guy—those green eyes were hard to forget, even if it had been four years since she'd seen them. Hanna hoped he was a stripper that Mona had sent over as a joke.

"What's this all about?" Ms. Marin asked, looking longingly back at her cell phone. "Why are you interrupting us at dinner?"

"We received a call from Tiffany's," Wilden said. "They have you on tape shoplifting some items from their store. Tapes from various other mall security cameras tracked you out of the mall and to your car. We traced the license plate."

Hanna started pinching the inside of her palm with her fingernails, something she always did when she felt out of control.

"Hanna wouldn't do that," Ms. Marin barked. "Would you, Hanna?"

Hanna opened her mouth to respond but no words came out. Her heart was banging against her ribs.

"Look." Wilden crossed his arms over his chest.

Hanna noticed the gun on his belt. It looked like a toy. "I just need you to come to the station. Maybe it's nothing."

"I'm sure it's nothing!" Ms. Marin said. Then she took her Fendi wallet out of its matching purse. "What will it take for you to leave us alone to have our dinner?"

"Ma'am." Wilden sounded exasperated. "You should just come down with me. All right? It won't take all night. I promise." He smiled that sexy Darren Wilden smile that had probably kept him from getting expelled from Rosewood.

"Well," Hanna's mother said. She and Wilden looked at each other for a long moment. "Let me get my bag."

Wilden turned to Hanna. "I'm gonna have to cuff you."

Hanna gasped. "Cuff me?" Okay, now that was silly. It sounded fake, like something the six-year-old twins next door would say to each other. But Wilden pulled out real steel handcuffs and gently put them around her wrists. Hanna hoped he didn't notice that her hands were shaking.

If only this were the moment when Wilden tied her to a chair, put on that old '70s song "Hot Stuff," and stripped off all his clothes. Unfortunately, it wasn't.

The police station smelled like burned coffee and very old wood, because, like most of Rosewood's municipal build-ings, it was a former railroad baron's mansion. Cops flut-tered around her, taking phone calls, filling out forms, and sliding around on their little castor-wheel chairs. Hanna half expected to see Mona here, too, with her mom's Dior stole thrown over her wrists. But from the look of the empty bench, it seemed Mona hadn't been caught.

Ms. Marin sat very stiffly next to her. Hanna felt squirmy; her mom was usually really lenient, but then, Hanna had never been taken downtown and had the book thrown at her or whatever.

And then, very quietly, her mom leaned over. "What was it that you took?"

"Huh?" Hanna asked.

"That bracelet you're wearing?"

Hanna looked down. *Perfect.* She'd forgotten to take it off; the bracelet was circling her wrist in full view. She shoved it farther up her sleeve. She felt her ears for the earrings; yep, she'd worn them today too. Talk about stupid!

"Give it to me," her mother whispered.

"Huh?" Hanna squeaked.

Ms. Marin held out her palm. "Give it here. I can handle this."

Reluctantly, Hanna let her mom unfasten the bracelet from her wrist. Then, Hanna reached up and took off the earrings and handed them over too. Ms. Marin didn't even flinch. She simply dropped the jewelry in her purse and folded her hands over the metal clasp.

The blond Tiffany's girl who'd helped Hanna with the charm bracelet strode into the room. As soon as she saw Hanna, sitting dejectedly on the bench with the cuffs still on her hands, she nodded. "Yeah. That's her."

Darren Wilden glared at Hanna, and her mom stood up. "I think there's been a mistake." She walked over to Wilden's desk. "I misunderstood you at the house. I was with Hanna that day. We bought that stuff. I have a receipt for it at home."

The Tiffany's girl narrowed her eyes in disbelief. "Are you suggesting I'm lying?"

"No," Ms. Marin said sweetly, "I just think you're confused."

What was she *doing*? A gooey, uncomfortable, almost-guilty feeling washed over Hanna.

"How do you explain the surveillance tapes?" Wilden asked.

Her mom paused. Hanna saw a tiny muscle in her neck quiver. Then, before Hanna could stop her, she reached into her purse and took out the loot. "This was all my fault," she said. "Not Hanna's."

Ms. Marin turned back to Wilden. "Hanna and I had a fight about these items. I said she couldn't have them—I drove her to this. She'll never do it again. I'll make sure of it."

Hanna stared, stunned. She and her mom had never once discussed Tiffany's, let alone something she could or couldn't have.

Wilden shook his head. "Ma'am, I think your daughter may need to do some community service. That's usually the penalty."

Ms. Marin blinked, innocently. "Can't we let this slide? Please?"

Wilden looked at her for a long time, one corner of his mouth turned up almost devilishly. "Sit down," he said finally. "Let me see what I can do."

Hanna looked everywhere but in her mom's direction. Wilden hunched over his desk. He had a Chief Wiggum figurine from *The Simpsons* and a metal Slinky. He licked his pointer finger to turn the pages of the papers he was filling out. Hanna flinched. What sort of papers were they? Didn't the local newspapers report crimes? This was bad. Very bad.

Hanna jiggled her foot nervously, having a sudden urge for some Junior Mints. Or maybe cashews. Even the Slim Jims on Wilden's desk would do.

She could just see it: Everyone would find out, and she'd be instantaneously friendless and boyfriendless. From there, she'd recede back to dorky, seventh-grade Hanna in reverse evolution. She'd wake up and her hair would be a yucky, washed-out brown again. Then her teeth would go crooked and she'd get her braces back on. She wouldn't be able to fit into any of her jeans. The rest would happen spontaneously. She'd spend her life chubby, ugly, miserable, and overlooked, just the way she used to be.

"I have some lotion if those are chafing your wrists," Ms. Marin said, gesturing to the cuffs and rooting around in her purse.

"I'm okay," Hanna replied, brought back to the present. Sighing, she pulled out her BlackBerry. It was tough because her hands were cuffed, but she wanted to convince Sean that he had to come over to her house this Saturday. She suddenly *really* wanted to know he would. As she stared blankly at the screen, an e-mail popped up in her inbox. She opened it.

Hey Hanna,

Since prison food makes you fat, you know what Sean's gonna say? Not it! —A

She was so startled that she stood up, thinking someone might be across the room, watching her. But there was no one. She closed her eyes, trying to think who might have seen the police car at her house.

Wilden looked up from his writing. "You all right?"

"Um," Hanna said. "Yeah." She slowly sat back down. *Not it?* What the hell? She checked the note's return address again, but it was just a mess of letters and numbers.

"Hanna," Ms. Marin murmured after a few moments. "No one needs to know about this."

Hanna blinked. "Oh. Yeah. I agree."

"Good."

Hanna swallowed hard. Except . . . someone *did* know.

9

NOT YOUR TYPICAL STUDENT-TEACHER CONFERENCE

Wednesday morning, Aria's father, Byron, rubbed his bushy black hair and hand-signaled out the Subaru window that he was making a left-hand turn. The turn signals had stopped working last night, so he was driving Aria and Mike to their second day of school and taking the car to the shop.

"You guys happy to be back in America?" Byron asked.

Mike, who sat next to Aria in the backseat, grinned. "America rocks." He went back to maniacally punching the tiny buttons of his PSP. It made a farting noise and Mike pumped one fist in the air.

Aria's father smiled and navigated across the single-lane stone bridge, waving to a neighbor as he passed. "Well, good. Now, *why* does it rock?"

"America rocks because it has lacrosse," Mike said, not

taking his eyes off his PSP. "And hotter chicks. And a Hooters in King of Prussia."

Aria laughed. Like Mike had been inside Hooters. Unless . . . Oh God, *had* he?

She shivered in her kelly green alpaca shrug and stared out the window at the thick fog. A woman wearing a long, red hooded stadium jacket that said, UPPER MAIN LINE SOCCER MOM, tried to stop her German shepherd from chasing a squirrel across the street. At the corner, two blondes with high-tech baby carriages stood together gossiping.

There was one word to describe yesterday's English class: *brutal*. After Ezra blurted out, "Holy shit," the whole class turned and stared at her. Hanna Marin, who sat in front of her, whispered in a not-so-quiet voice, "Did you sleep with the teacher?" Aria considered, for a half second, that maybe *Hanna* had written her the text message about Ezra—Hanna was one of the few people who knew about Pigtunia. But why would Hanna care?

Ezra—er, Mr. Fitz—had dispelled the laughing quickly, and come up with the lamest excuse for swearing in class. He said, and Aria quoted in her head, "I was afraid that a bee had flown into my pants, and I thought the bee was going to sting me, and so I yelled out in terror."

As Ezra then started talking about five-paragraph themes and the class's syllabus, Aria couldn't concentrate. *She* was the bee that had flown into his pants. She couldn't stop looking at his wolfish eyes and his sumptuous pink mouth. When he peeked in her direction out of the corner of his eye, her heart did two and a half somersaults off the high dive and landed in her stomach.

Ezra was the guy for her, and she was the girl for him—she just *knew* it. So what if he was her teacher? There *had* to be a way to make it work.

Her father pulled up to Rosewood's stone-gated entrance. In the distance, Aria noticed a vintage powder-blue Volkswagen beetle parked in the teacher's lot. She knew that car from Snooker's—it was Ezra's. She checked her watch. Fifteen minutes until homeroom.

Mike shot out of the car. Aria opened her door as well, but her father touched her forearm. "Hang on a sec," he said.

"But I have to . . . " She glanced longingly at Ezra's bug.

"Just for a minute." Her father turned down the radio volume. Aria slumped back in her seat. "You've seemed a little . . . " He flicked his wrist back and forth uncertainly. "You okay?"

Aria shrugged. "About what?"

Her father sighed. "Well . . . I don't know. Being back. And we haven't talked about . . . you know . . . in a while."

Aria fidgeted with her jacket's zipper. "What's there to talk about?"

Byron stuck a cigarette he'd rolled before they left into his mouth. "I can't imagine how hard it's been. Keeping quiet. But I love you. You know that, right?"

Aria looked out at the parking lot again. "Yeah, I know," she said. "I have to go. I'll see you at three."

Before he could answer, Aria shot out of the car, blood rushing in her ears. How was she supposed to be Icelandic Aria, who left her past behind, if one of her worst memories of Rosewood kept bubbling to the surface?

It had happened in May of seventh grade. Rosewood Day had dismissed the students early for teacher conferences, so Aria and Ali headed to Sparrow, Hollis campus's music store, to search for new CDs. As they cut through a back alley, Aria noticed her father's familiar beat-up brown Honda Civic in a far-off space in an empty parking lot. As Aria and Ali walked toward the car to leave a note, they realized there was someone inside. Actually, two someones: Aria's father, Byron, and a girl, about twenty years old, kissing his neck.

That's when Byron looked up and saw Aria. She sprinted away before she had to see any more and before he could stop her. Ali followed Aria all the way back to her house but didn't try to stop her when Aria said she wanted to be alone.

Later that night, Byron came up to Aria's room to explain. It wasn't what it looked like, he said. But Aria wasn't stupid. Every year her father invited his students over to their house for get-to-know-you cocktails, and Aria had seen that girl walk through her very door. Her name was Meredith, Aria remembered, because Meredith had gotten tipsy and spelled out her name on the refrigerator in plastic letter magnets. When Meredith left, instead of shaking her dad's hand as the other kids had, she gave him a lingering kiss on his cheek.

Byron begged Aria not to tell her mom. He promised her it would never happen again. She decided to believe him, and so she kept his secret. He'd never said so, but Aria believed Meredith was the reason her dad took his sabbatical when he did.

You promised yourself you wouldn't think about it, Aria thought, glancing back over her shoulder. Her father hand-signaled out of the Rosewood parking lot.

Aria walked into the narrow hallway of the faculty wing. Ezra's office was at the end of the hall, next to a small, cozy window seat. She stopped in the doorway and watched him as he typed something into his computer.

Finally, she knocked. Ezra's blue eyes widened when he saw her. He looked adorable in his button-down white shirt, blue Rosewood blazer, green cords, and beat-up black loafers. The corners of his mouth curled up into the tiniest, shyest smile.

"Hey," he said.

Aria hovered in the doorway. "Can I talk to you?" Aria asked. Her voice squeaked a little.

Ezra hesitated, pushing a lock of hair out of his eyes. Aria noticed a Snoopy Band-Aid wrapped around his left pinkie finger. "Sure," he said softly. "Come in."

She walked into his office and shut the door. It was empty, except for a wide, heavy wood desk, two folding chairs, and a computer. She sat down on the empty folding chair.

"So, um," Aria said. "Hey."

"Hey again," Ezra answered, grinning. He lowered his eyes and took a gulp from his Rosewood Day crest coffee mug. "Listen," he started.

"About yesterday," Aria said at the same time. They both laughed.

"Ladies first." Ezra smiled.

Aria scratched the back of her neck where her straight black hair was drawn up in a ponytail. "I, um, wanted to talk about . . . us."

Ezra nodded, but didn't say anything.

Aria wiggled in her chair. "Well, I guess it's shocking that I'm . . . um . . . your student, after, you know . . . Snooker's. But if you don't mind, I don't."

Ezra cupped his hand around his mug. Aria listened to the school-issued wall clock ticking off the seconds. "I . . . I don't think it's a good idea," he said softly. "You said you were older."

Aria laughed, not sure how serious he was. "I never told you how old I was." She lowered her eyes. "You just assumed."

"Yeah, but you shouldn't have implied it," Ezra responded.

"Everybody lies about their age," Aria said quietly.

Ezra ran his hand through his hair. "But . . . you're . . . " He met her eyes and sighed. "Look, I . . . I think you're amazing, Aria. I do. I met you in that bar, and I was like . . . wow, who *is* this? She's so unlike any other girl I've ever met."

Aria looked down, feeling both pleased and a little queasy.

Ezra reached across the desk and touched his hand to hers—it was warm, dry, and soothing—but then quickly pulled away. "But this isn't meant to be, you know? 'Cause, well, you're my student. I could get in a lot of trouble. You don't want me to get in trouble, do you?"

"No one would know," Aria said faintly, although she couldn't help but think about that bizarre text from yesterday, and that maybe someone *already* knew.

It took Ezra a long time to respond. It seemed to Aria that he was trying to make up his mind. She looked at him hopefully.

"I'm sorry, Aria," he finally mumbled. "But I think you should go."

Aria stood up, feeling her cheeks burn. "Of course." Aria wrapped her hands around the top of the chair. It felt like hot coals were bouncing around her insides.

"I'll see you in class," Ezra whispered.

She shut the door carefully. In the hall, teachers swarmed around her, rushing off to their homerooms. She decided to get to her locker by cutting through the commons—she needed some fresh air.

Outside, Aria heard a familiar girl's laugh. She froze for a second. When would she stop thinking she heard

Alison *everywhere*? She trudged not on the commons' winding stone path, like you were supposed to, but through the grass. The morning fog was so dense that Aria could barely see her legs below her. Her footprints vanished in the squishy grass as quickly as she made them.

Good. This seemed like an appropriate time to disappear completely.

10

SINGLE GIRLS HAVE
WAY MORE FUN

That afternoon, Emily was standing in the student parking lot, lost in thought, when someone threw their hands over her eyes. Emily jumped, startled.

"Whoa, chill! It's just me!"

Emily turned and sighed with relief. It was only Maya. Emily had been so distracted and paranoid since getting that bizarre note yesterday. She'd been about to unlock her car—her mom let her and Carolyn take it to school on the condition they *drive carefully and call when they got there*—and grab her swimming bag for practice.

"Sorry," Emily said. "I thought . . . never mind."

"I missed you today." Maya smiled.

"Me too." Emily smiled back. She'd tried calling Maya this morning to offer her a ride to school, but Maya's mom said she'd already left. "So, how are you?"

"Well, I could be better." Today, Maya had secured

her wild dark hair off her face with adorable iridescent pink butterfly clips.

"Oh yeah?" Emily tilted her head.

Maya pursed her lips together and slid one of her feet out of her Oakley sandals. Her second toe was longer than her big toe, just like Emily's. "I'd be better if you came somewhere with me. Right now."

"But I have swimming," Emily said, hearing Eeyore in her voice again.

Maya took her hand and swung it. "What if I told you that where we're going sort of *involves* swimming?"

Emily narrowed her eyes. "What do you mean?"

"You have to trust me."

Even though she'd been close to Hanna and Spencer and Aria, all of Emily's favorite memories were of hanging out alone with Ali. Like when they dressed up in bulky snow pants to sled down Bayberry Hill, talked about their ideal boyfriends, or cried about The Jenna Thing from sixth grade and comforted each other. When it was just the two of them, Emily saw a slightly less perfect Ali—which somehow made her seem even more perfect—and Emily felt she could be herself. It seemed like days, weeks, *years* had gone by where Emily hadn't been herself. And she thought that now, she could have something like that with Maya. She missed having a best friend.

Right now, Ben and all the other boys were probably changing into their suits, slapping one another's bare butts with wet towels. Coach Lauren was writing the practice sets on the big marker board and carrying out the appropriate fins, buoys, and paddles. And the girls on the team were complaining because they all had their periods at the same time. Did she dare miss the second day of practice?

Emily squeezed her plastic fish keychain. "I suppose I could tell Carolyn I had to tutor somebody in Spanish," she murmured. Emily knew Carolyn wouldn't buy that, but she probably wouldn't squeal on Emily, either.

Triple-checking the parking lot to see if anyone was watching, Emily smiled and unlocked the car.

"All right. Let's go."

"My brother and I checked out this spot this weekend," Maya said as Emily pulled into the gravel parking lot.

Emily stepped out of the car and stretched. "I forgot about this place." They were at the Marwyn trail, which was about five miles long and bordered a deep creek. She and her friends used to ride their bikes here all the time—Ali and Spencer would pedal furiously at the end and usually tie—and stop at the little snack bar by the swimming area for Butterfingers and Diet Cokes.

As she followed Maya up a muddy slope, Maya grabbed her arm. "Oh! I forgot to tell you. My mom said your mom stopped over yesterday while we were in school. She brought over brownies."

"Really?" Emily responded, confused. She wondered why her mother hadn't mentioned anything to her at dinner.

"The brownies were dee*lish*. My brother and I polished them off last night!"

They came to the dirt trail. A canopy of oaks sheltered them. The air had that fresh, woodsy smell and it felt about twenty degrees cooler.

"We're not there yet." Maya took her hand and led her down the path to a small stone bridge. Twenty feet beneath it, the stream widened. The calm water glittered in the late-afternoon sun.

Maya walked right up to the edge of the bridge and stripped down to her matching pale pink bra and undies. She threw her clothes in a pile, stuck her tongue out at Emily, and jumped off.

"Wait!" Emily rushed to the edge. Did Maya know how deep this was? A full *one-Mississippi, two-Mississippi* later, Emily heard a splash.

Maya's head popped back up out of the water. "Told you it involved swimming! C'mon, strip!"

Emily glanced at Maya's pile of clothes. She *really* hated undressing in front of people—even the swim team girls, who saw her every day. She slowly took off her pleated Rosewood skirt, crossing her legs over each other so Maya couldn't see her bare, muscular thighs, and then pulled at the tank top she wore under her uniform blouse. She decided to keep it on. She looked over the edge to the creek and, steeling herself, she jumped. A moment later, the water hugged her body. It was pleasantly warm and thick with mud, not cold and clean like the pool. The built-in shelf bra of her tank top puffed out with water.

"It's like a sauna in here," Maya said.

"Yeah." Emily paddled over to the shallower area, where Maya was standing. Emily realized she could see Maya's nipples straight through her bra, and cut her eyes away.

"I used to go cliff diving with Justin all the time back in Cali," Maya said. "He'd stand up at the top and, like, *think* about it for ten minutes before jumping. I like how you didn't even hesitate."

Emily floated on her back and smiled. She couldn't help it: she gobbled up Maya's compliments like cheesecake.

Maya squirted Emily with water through her cupped hands. Some of it squirted right into her mouth. The creek water tasted gooey and almost metallic, nothing like chlorinated pool water. "I think me and Justin are going to break up," Maya said.

Emily swam closer to the edge and stood up. "Really? Why?"

"Yeah. The long-distance thing is too stressful. He calls me, like, *all* the time. I've only been gone for a few days, and he's already sent me two letters!"

"Huh," Emily answered, sifting her fingers through the murky water. Then something occurred to her. She turned to Maya. "Did you, um, put a note in my swim locker yesterday?"

Maya frowned. "What, after school? No . . . you walked me home, remember?"

"Right." She didn't really think Maya had written the note, but things would've been so much simpler if she had.

"What did the note say?"

Emily shook her head. "Never mind. It was nothing." She cleared her throat. "You know, I think I might break up with my boyfriend too."

Whoa. Emily wouldn't have been any more surprised if a bluebird had just flown out of her mouth.

"Really?" Maya said.

Emily blinked water out of her eyes. "I don't know. Maybe."

Maya stretched her arms over her head, and Emily caught sight of that scar on her wrist again. She looked away. "Well, fuck a moose," Maya said.

Emily smiled. "Huh?"

"It's this thing I say sometimes," Maya said. "It means . . . *screw it!*" She turned away and shrugged. "I guess it's silly."

"No, I like it," Emily said. "Fuck a moose." She giggled. She always felt funny swearing—as if her mom could hear her from their kitchen, ten miles away.

"You totally should break up with your boyfriend, though," Maya said. "Know why?"

"Why?"

"That would mean we'd both be single."

"And that means what?" Emily asked. The forest was very quiet and still.

Maya moved closer to her. "And that means . . . we . . . can . . . *have fun!*" She grabbed Emily by the shoulder and dunked her under the water.

"Hey!" Emily squealed. She splashed Maya back, ripping her whole arm through the water, creating a giant wave. Then she grabbed Maya by the leg and started tickling underneath her toes.

"Help!" Maya screamed. "Not my feet! I'm so ticklish!"

"I've found your weakness!" Emily crowed, maniacally dragging Maya over to the waterfall. Maya managed to wrench her foot away and pounced on Emily's shoulders from behind. Maya's hands drifted up Emily's sides, then down to her stomach, where she tickled her. Emily squealed. She finally pushed Maya into a small cave in the rocks.

"I hope there are no bats in here!" Maya squealed. Beams of sunlight pierced through the cave's tiny openings, making a halo around the top of Maya's sopping wet head.

"You have to come in here," Maya said. She held out her hand.

Emily stood next to her, feeling the cave's smooth, cool sides. The sounds of her breathing echoed off the narrow walls. They looked at each other and grinned.

Emily bit her lip. This was such a perfect friend moment, it made her feel kind of melancholy and nostalgic.

Maya's eyes turned down in concern. "What's wrong?"

Emily took a deep breath. "Well . . . you know that girl who lived in your house? Alison?"

"Yeah."

"She went missing. Right after seventh grade. She was never found."

Maya shivered slightly. "I heard something about that."

Emily hugged herself; she was getting cold, too. "We were really close."

Maya moved closer to Emily and put her arm around her. "I didn't realize."

"Yeah." Emily's chin wobbled. "I just wanted you to know."

"Thanks."

A few long moments passed; Emily and Maya continued to hug. Then, Maya backed off. "I kind of lied earlier. About why I want to break up with Justin."

Emily raised an eyebrow, curious.

"I'm . . . I'm not sure if I like guys," Maya said quietly. "It's weird. I think they're cute, but when I get alone with them, I don't want to be with them. I'd rather be with, like, someone more like me." She smiled crookedly. "You know?"

Emily ran her hands over her face and hair. Maya's gaze felt too close all of a sudden. "I . . . ," she started. No, she *didn't* know.

The bushes above them moved. Emily flinched. Her mom used to hate when she came to this trail—you never knew what kind of kidnappers or murderers hid in places like this. The woods were still for a moment, but then a flock of birds scattered wildly into the sky. Emily flattened herself up against the rock. Was someone watching them? Who was that laughing? The laugh sounded familiar. Then Emily heard heavy breathing. Goose bumps rose up on her arms and she peered out of the cave.

It was only a group of boys. Suddenly, they burst into the creek, wielding sticks like swords. Emily backed away from Maya and out of the waterfall.

"Where are you going?" Maya called.

Emily looked at Maya, and then at the boys, who had abandoned the sticks and were now throwing rocks at each other. One of them was Mike Montgomery, her old friend Aria's little brother. He'd grown up quite a bit since she last saw him. And wait—Mike went to Rosewood. Would he recognize her? Emily climbed out of the water and started scurrying up the hill.

She turned back to Maya. "I have to get back to school before Carolyn's done with swimming." She pulled on her skirt. "Do you want me to throw down your clothes?"

"Whatev." At that, she stepped out of the waterfall and waded through the water, her sheer underwear clinging to her butt. Maya climbed up the slope slowly, not once covering up her stomach or boobs with her hands. The freshmen boys stopped what they were doing and stared.

And even though Emily didn't want to, she couldn't help but stare too.

11

AT LEAST SWEET POTATOES
HAVE LOTS OF VITAMIN A

"Her. Definitely her," Hanna whispered, pointing.

"Nah. They're too small!" Mona whispered back.

"But look at the way they puff up at the top! Totally fake," Hanna countered.

"I think that woman over there has had her butt done."

"Gross." Hanna wrinkled her nose and ran her hands over the sides of her own toned, perfectly round butt to make sure it was still perfectly perfect. It was late afternoon on Wednesday, just two days until Noel Kahn's annual field party, and she and Mona were lounging on the outside terrace at Yam, the organic café at Mona's parents' country club. Below them, a bunch of Rosewood boys played a quick round of golf before dinner, but Hanna and Mona were playing another type of game: Spot the Fake Boobs. Or fake anything else, as there was lots of fake stuff around here.

"Yeah, it looks like her surgeon messed up," Mona murmured. "I think my mom plays tennis with her. I'll ask."

Hanna looked again at the pixieish, thirtysomething woman by the bar whose butt did look suspiciously extra-luscious for the rest of her toothpick-skinny figure. "I'd die before I got plastic surgery."

Mona played with the charm on her Tiffany bracelet—the one she, evidently, didn't have to give back. "Do you think Aria Montgomery had hers done?"

Hanna looked up, startled. "Why?"

"She's really thin, and they're like, too perfect," Mona said. "She went to Finland or wherever, right? I hear in Europe they can do your boobs for really cheap."

"I don't think they're fake," Hanna murmured.

"How do *you* know?"

Hanna chewed on her straw. Aria's boobs had always been there—she and Alison had been the only two of the friends who needed a bra in seventh grade. Ali always flaunted hers, but the only time Aria seemed to notice she even *had* boobs was when she knit everyone bras as Christmas gifts and had to make herself a larger size. "She just doesn't seem the type," Hanna answered. Talking to Mona about her old friends was awkward territory. Hanna still felt bad about how she and Ali and the others used to tease Mona back in seventh grade, but it always seemed too weird to bring up now.

Mona stared at her. "Are you all right? You look different today."

Hanna flinched. "I do? How?"

Mona gave her a tiny smirk. "Whoa! Somebody's jumpy!"

"I'm not jumpy," Hanna said quickly. But she was: Ever since the police station and that e-mail she had gotten last night, she'd been freaking. This morning, her eyes even seemed more dull brown than green, and her arms looked disturbingly puffy. She had this horrible sense that she really was going to spontaneously morph back into her seventh-grade self.

A blond, giraffelike waitress interrupted them. "Have you decided?"

Mona looked at the menu. "I'll have the Asian chicken salad, no dressing."

Hanna cleared her throat. "I want a garden salad with sprouts, no dressing, and an extra-large order of sweet potato fries. In a carry-out box, please."

As the waitress took their menus, Mona pushed her sunglasses down her nose. "Sweet potato fries?"

"For my mom," Hanna answered quickly. "She lives on them."

Down on the golf course, a group of older guys teed up, along with one young good-looking guy in fatigue shorts. He looked a little out of place with his messy brown hair, cargos, and . . . was that a . . . *Rosewood Police* polo? Oh no. It was.

Wilden scanned the terrace and coolly nodded when he saw Hanna. She ducked.

"Who is *that*?" Mona purred.

"Um . . . ," Hanna mumbled, half under the table. Darren Wilden was a *golfer*? Come *on*. Back in high school, he was the type to flick lit matches at the guys on Rosewood's golf team. Was the whole world out to get her? Mona squinted. "Wait. Didn't he go to our school?" She grinned. "Oh my God. It's the girls' diving team guy. Hanna, you little bitch! How does he know *you*?"

"He's . . . " Hanna paused. She ran her hand along the waistband of her jeans. "I met him on the Marwyn trail a couple of days ago when I was running. We stopped at the water fountain at the same time."

"Nice," Mona said. "Does he work around here?"

Hanna paused again. She really wanted to avoid this. "Um . . . I think he said he was a cop," she said nonchalantly.

"You're kidding." Mona took out her Shu Uemura lip moisturizer from her blue leather hobo bag and lightly dabbed her bottom lip. "That guy's hot enough to be in a policeman's calendar. I could just see it: Mr. April. Let's ask if we can see his nightstick!"

"Shhh," Hanna hissed.

Their salads came. Hanna pushed the Styrofoam container of sweet potato fries to the side and took a bite of an undressed grape tomato.

Mona leaned closer. "I bet you could hook up with him."

"Who?"

"Mr. April! Who else?"

Hanna snorted. "Right."

"Totally. You should bring him to the Kahn party. I heard some cops came to the party last year. That's how they never get busted."

Hanna sat back. The Kahn party was a legendary Rosewood tradition. The Kahns lived on twenty-some acres of land, and the Kahn boys—Noel was the youngest—held a back-to-school party every year. The kids raided their parents' extremely well-stocked liquor supply in the basement, and there was *always* a scandal. Last year, Noel shot his best friend James in the bare ass with his BB gun because James had tried to make out with Noel's then-girlfriend, Alyssa Pennypacker. They were both so drunk they laughed the whole way to the ER and couldn't remember how or why it happened. The year before that, a bunch of stoners smoked too much and tried to get Mr. Kahn's Appaloosas to take hits from a bong.

"Nah." Hanna bit into another tomato. "I think I'm going with Sean."

Mona scrunched up her face. "Why waste a perfectly good party night on Sean? He took a virginity pledge! He probably won't even go."

"Just because you sign a virginity pledge doesn't mean you stop partying, too." Hanna took a big bite of her salad, crunching the dry, unappetizing vegetables in her mouth.

"Well, if you're not gonna ask Mr. April to Noel's, I will." Mona stood up.

Hanna grabbed her arm. "No!"

"Why not? C'mon. It'd be fun."

Hanna dug her fingernails into Mona's arm. "I said no."

Mona sat back down and stuck out her lip. "Why not?"

Hanna's heart galloped. "All right. You can't tell *anyone*, though." She took a deep breath. "I met him at the police station, not the trail. I was called in for questioning for the Tiffany's thing. But it's not a big deal. I'm not busted."

"Oh my *God*!" Mona yelled. Wilden looked up at them again.

"Shhh!" Hanna hissed.

"Are you all right? What happened? Tell me everything," Mona whispered back.

"There isn't much to tell." Hanna threw her napkin over her plate. "They brought me to the station, my mom came with me, and we sat for a while. They let me off with a warning. Whatever. The whole thing took like twenty minutes."

"Yikes." Mona gave Hanna an indeterminate look; Hanna wondered for a second if it was a look of pity.

"It wasn't, like, dramatic or anything," Hanna said defensively, her throat dry. "Not much happened. Most of the cops were on the phone. I text-messaged the whole time." She paused, considering whether she should tell Mona about that "not it" text message she'd received from A, whoever A was. But why waste her breath? It couldn't have actually meant anything, right?

Mona took a sip of her Perrier. "I thought you'd never get caught."

Hanna swallowed hard. "Yeah, well . . . "

"Did your mom totally kill you?"

Hanna looked away. On the drive home, her mom had asked Hanna if she'd meant to steal the bracelet and earrings. When Hanna said no, Ms. Marin answered, "Good. It's settled then." Then she flipped open her cell to make a call.

Hanna shrugged and stood up. "I just remembered—I gotta go walk Dot."

"Are you sure you're okay?" Mona asked. "Your face looks kind of splotchy."

"No biggie." She smacked her lips glamorously at Mona and turned for the door.

Hanna sauntered coolly out of the restaurant, but once she got to the parking lot, she broke into a run. She climbed inside her Toyota Prius—a car her mom had bought for herself last year but had recently handed off to Hanna because she'd grown tired of it—and checked her face in the rearview mirror. There were hideous bright red patches on her cheeks and forehead.

After her transformation, Hanna had been neurotically

careful about not only looking cool and perfect at all times, but *being* cool and perfect, too. Terrified that the tiniest mistake would send her spiraling back to dorkdom, she labored over every last detail, from little things like the perfect IM screen name and the right mix for her car's built-in iPod, to bigger stuff like the right combo of people to invite over before someone's party and choosing the perfect *it* boy to date—who, luckily, was the same boy she'd loved since seventh grade. Had getting caught for shoplifting just tarnished the perfect, controlled, über-cool Hanna everyone had come to know? She hadn't been able to read that look on Mona's face when she said "yikes." Had the look meant, *Yikes, but no big deal?* Or, *Yikes, what a loser?*

She wondered if maybe she shouldn't have told Mona at all. But then . . . someone else already knew. A.

Know what Sean's going to say? Not it!

Hanna's field of vision went blurry. She squeezed the steering wheel for a few seconds, then jammed the key into the ignition and rolled out of the country club parking lot to a gravelly, dead-end turn-off a few yards down the road. She could hear her heart pounding at her temples as she turned off the engine and took deep breaths. The wind smelled like hay and just-mown grass.

Hanna shut her eyes tight. When she opened them, she stared at the container of sweet potato fries. *Don't,* she thought. A car swished by on the main road.

Hanna wiped her hands on her jeans. She snuck another peek at the container. The fries smelled delicious. *Don't, don't, don't.*

She reached over for them and opened the lid. Their sweet, warm smell wafted into her face. Before she could stop herself, Hanna shoved handful after handful of fries into her mouth. The fries were still so hot that they burned her tongue, but she didn't care. It was such a relief; this was the only thing that made her feel better. She didn't stop until she'd eaten them all and even licked the sides of the container for the salt that had gathered at the bottom.

At first she felt much, much calmer. But by the time she pulled into her driveway, the old, familiar feelings of panic and shame had welled up inside her. Hanna was amazed how, even though it had been years since she'd done this, everything felt exactly the same. Her stomach ached, her pants felt tight, and all she wanted was to be rid of what was inside of her.

Ignoring Dot's excited cries from her bedroom, Hanna bolted to the upstairs bathroom, slammed the door, and collapsed onto the tiled floor. Thank God her mom wasn't home from work yet. At least she wouldn't hear what Hanna was about to do.

12

MMM, LOVE THAT
NEW-TEST-SCORE SMELL

Okay. Spencer had to calm down.

Wednesday night, she pulled her black Mercedes C-Class hatchback—her sister's castoff car, since she got the new, "practical" Mercedes SUV—into the circular driveway of her house. Her student council meeting had gone extra late and she'd been on edge driving through Rosewood's dark streets. All day, she'd felt like someone was watching her, like whoever had written that "covet" e-mail could jump out at her at any second.

Spencer kept thinking uneasily about that familiar ponytail in Alison's bedroom window. Her mind kept going back to Ali—all the things she knew about Spencer. But no, that was crazy. Alison had been gone—and most likely dead—for three years. Plus, a new family lived in her house now, right?

Spencer ran to the mailbox and pulled out a pile, tossing everything back that wasn't hers. Suddenly, she saw it. It was a long envelope, not too thick, not too thin, with Spencer's name typed neatly in the windowpane. The return address said, *The College Board*. It was here.

Spencer ripped open the envelope and scanned the page. She read the PSAT results six times before it sunk in.

She'd gotten a 2350 out of 2400.

"Yessssss!" she screamed, clutching the papers so tightly they wrinkled.

"Whoa! Someone's happy!" called a voice from the road.

Spencer looked up. Hanging out the driver's-side window of a black Mini Cooper was Andrew Campbell, the tall, freckly, long-haired boy that beat out Spencer for class president. They were number-one and number-two in the class in practically every subject. But before Spencer could brag about her score—telling Andrew about her PSATs would feel *so* good—he peeled away. *Freak.* Spencer turned back to her house.

As she excitedly scampered inside, something stopped her: she remembered her sister's near-perfect score and quickly converted it from the 1600-scale they used to use into the 2400-scale the College Board used nowadays. It was a full 100 points lower than Spencer's. And weren't they supposed to be harder these days, too?

Well, *now* who's the genius?

An hour later, Spencer sat at the kitchen table reading *Middlemarch*—a book on the English AP "suggested reading" list—when she began to sneeze.

"Melissa and Wren are here," Mrs. Hastings said to Spencer as she bustled into the kitchen, carrying in the mail Spencer had left in the box. "They've brought all of their luggage to move in!" She opened the oven a crack, checking on the rotisserie chicken and seven-grain rolls, and then bustled into the living room.

Spencer sneezed again. A cloud of Chanel No. 5 always preceded her mom—even though she spent the whole day working around horses—and Spencer was certain she was allergic. She considered announcing her PSAT news, but a twinkly voice from the foyer stopped her.

"Mom?" Melissa called. She and Wren strolled into the kitchen. Spencer pretended to study *Middlemarch*'s boring back cover.

"Hey," Wren said above her.

"Hey," she answered coolly.

"Whatcha reading?"

Spencer hesitated. It was better to steer clear of Wren, especially now that he was moving in.

Melissa brushed by without saying hello and began to unpack purple pillows from a Pottery Barn bag. "These are for the couch in the barn," she practically yelled.

Spencer cringed. Two could play at this game. "Oh,

Melissa!" Spencer cried. "I forgot to tell you! Guess who I ran into!"

Melissa continued to unpack the pillows. "Who?"

"Ian Thomas! He's coaching my field hockey team now!"

Melissa froze. "He . . . what? He is? He's *here*? Did he ask about me?"

Spencer shrugged and pretended to think. "No, I don't think so."

"Who's Ian Thomas?" Wren asked, leaning against the marble island counter.

"No one," Melissa snapped, turning back to the pillows. Spencer slapped her book shut and skipped off to the dining room. There. That felt better.

She sat down at the long, mission-style farmhouse table, running her finger around the stemless wineglass Candace, the family's housekeeper, had just filled with red wine. Her parents didn't care if their kids drank while they were at home as long as no one was driving, so she grabbed the glass with both hands and greedily took a large gulp. When she looked up, Wren was smirking at her from across the table, his spine very straight in his dining chair.

"Hey," he said. She raised her eyebrows in answer.

Melissa and Mrs. Hastings sat down, and Spencer's father adjusted the chandelier lights and took a seat as well. For a moment everyone was quiet. Spencer felt for the PSAT score papers in her pocket. "So guess what happened to me," she began.

"Wren and I are so happy you're letting us stay here!" Melissa said at the same time, grabbing Wren's hand.

Mrs. Hastings smiled at Melissa. "I'm always happy when the family's all here."

Spencer bit her lip, her stomach nervously gurgling. "So, Dad. I got my—"

"Uh-oh," Melissa interrupted, staring down at the plates Candace had just brought in from the kitchen. "Do we have anything other than chicken? Wren's trying not to eat meat."

"It's all right," Wren said hastily. "Chicken is perfect."

"Oh!" Mrs. Hastings stood up halfway. "You don't eat meat? I didn't know! I think we may have some pasta salad in the fridge, although it might have ham in it. . . ."

"Really, it's okay." Wren rubbed his head uncomfortably, making his messy black hair stand up in peaks.

"Oh, I feel terrible," Mrs. Hastings said. Spencer rolled her eyes. When the whole family was together, her mom wanted all meals—even sloppy cereal breakfasts—to be perfect.

Mr. Hastings eyed Wren suspiciously. "I'm a steak man, myself."

"Absolutely." Wren lifted his glass so forcefully that a little wine spilled on the tablecloth.

Spencer was considering a good segue into her big announcement when her father laid down his fork.

"I've got a brilliant idea. Since we're all here, why don't we play Star Power?"

"Oh, Daddy." Melissa grinned. "No."

Her father smiled. "Oh yes. I had a terrific day at work. I'm going to kick your butt."

"What's Star Power?" Wren asked, his eyebrows arched.

A nervous glow grew in Spencer's stomach. Star Power was a game her parents had made up when Spencer and Melissa were little kids that she'd always suspected they'd pilfered from some company power-retreat. It was simple: Everyone shared their biggest achievement of the day, and the family would select one Star. It was supposed to make people feel proud and accomplished, but in the Hastings family, people just got ruthlessly competitive.

But if there was one perfect way for Spencer to announce her PSAT results, Star Power was it.

"You'll catch on, Wren," Mr. Hastings said. "I'll start. Today, I prepared a defense so compelling for my client, he actually offered to pay me *more* money."

"Impressive," her mother said, taking a tiny bite of a golden beet. "Now me. This morning, I beat Eloise at tennis in straight sets."

"Eloise is tough!" her father cried before taking another sip of wine. Spencer peeked at Wren across the table. He was carefully peeling the skin off his chicken thigh, so she couldn't catch his eye.

Her mother dabbed her mouth with her napkin. "Melissa?"

Melissa laced her stubby-nailed fingers together.

"Well, hmm. I helped the builders tile the entire bathroom—the only way it'd be perfect is if I did it myself."

"Good for you, dear!" her father said.

Spencer jiggled her legs nervously.

Mr. Hastings finished sipping his wine. "Wren?"

Wren looked up, startled. "Yes?"

"It's your turn."

Wren fiddled with his wineglass. "I don't know what I should say. . . . "

"We're playing Star Power," Mrs. Hastings chirped, as if Star Power were as common a game as Scrabble. "What wonderful thing did you, Mr. Doctor, achieve today?"

"Oh." Wren blinked. "Well. Um, nothing, really. It was my day off from school and the hospital, so I went down to the pub with some hospital friends and watched the Phillies game."

Silence. Melissa shot Wren a disappointed look.

"I think that's awesome," Spencer offered. "The way they've been playing, it's a feat to watch the Phillies all day."

"I know, they're kind of crap, aren't they?" Wren smiled at her gratefully.

"Well, anyway," her mother interrupted. "Melissa, when do you start class?"

"Wait a minute," Spencer piped up. They were *not* about to forget her! "I have something for Star Power."

Her mother's salad fork hung in the air. "I'm sorry."

"Oops!" her father agreed jocularly. "Go ahead, Spence."

"I got my PSAT results," she said. "And, well . . . here."
She pulled out the scores and shoved them at her father.

As soon as he took them, she knew what would happen. They wouldn't care. What did PSATs matter, anyway? They'd go back to their Beaujolais and to Melissa and Wharton and that would be that. Her cheeks felt hot. Why did she even bother?

Then her dad put down his wineglass and studied the paper. "Wow." He motioned Mrs. Hastings over. When she saw the paper, she gasped.

"You can't get much higher than this, can you?" Mrs. Hastings said.

Melissa craned her neck to look too. Spencer could hardly breathe. Melissa glared at her over the lilac and peony centerpiece. It was a look that made Spencer think that maybe Melissa *had* written that creepy e-mail yesterday. But when Spencer met her eye, Melissa broke into a smile. "You really studied, didn't you?"

"It's a good score, yeah?" Wren asked, glancing at the page.

"It's a fantastic score!" Mr. Hastings bellowed.

"This is wonderful!" cried Mrs. Hastings. "How would you like to celebrate, Spencer? Dinner in the city? Is there something you've had your eye on?"

"When I got my SAT scores, you got me a Fitzgerald first edition at that estate auction, remember?" Melissa beamed.

"That's right!" Mrs. Hastings trilled.

Melissa turned to Wren. "You would've loved it. It was so amazing to bid."

"Well, why don't you give it some thought." Mrs. Hastings said to Spencer. "Try to think of something memorable, like what we got for Melissa."

Spencer slowly sat up. "Actually, there is something that I have in mind."

"What's that?" Her father leaned forward in his chair.

Here goes, Spencer thought. "Well, what I'd really, really, *really* love, right now, not a few months from now, would be to move into the barn."

"But—," Melissa started, before stopping herself.

Wren cleared his throat. Her father furrowed his brow. Spencer's stomach made a loud, hungry growl. She covered it with her hand.

"Is that what you *really* want?" her mother asked.

"Uh-huh," Spencer answered.

"Okay," Mrs. Hastings said, looking at her husband. "Well . . ."

Melissa loudly laid down her fork. "But, um, what about Wren and me?"

"Well, you said yourself the renovations wouldn't take too long." Mrs. Hastings put her hand to her chin. "You guys could stay in your old bedroom, I suppose."

"But it has a twin bed," Melissa said in an uncharacteristically childish voice.

"I don't mind," Wren said quickly. Melissa scowled sharply at him.

"We could move the queen bed from the barn to Melissa's room and put Spencer's bed out there," Mr. Hastings suggested.

Spencer couldn't believe her ears. "You would do that?"

Mrs. Hastings raised her eyebrows. "Melissa, you can survive, can't you?"

Melissa pushed her hair back from her face. "I guess," she said. "I mean, I personally got much more out of the auction and the first edition, but that's just me."

Wren discreetly took a sip of his wine. When Spencer caught his eye, he winked. Mr. Hastings turned to Spencer. "Done, then."

Spencer jumped up and hugged her parents. "Thank you, thank you, thank you!"

Her mother beamed. "You should move in tomorrow."

"Spencer, you're certainly the Star." Her father held up her scores, now slightly stained with red wine. "We should frame this as a memento!"

Spencer grinned. She didn't need to frame anything. She'd remember this day for as long as she lived.

13

ACT ONE: GIRL MAKES
BOY WANT HER

"Want to come with me to an artist reception at the
Chester Springs studio next Monday night?" Aria's
mother, Ella, asked.

It was Thursday morning, and Ella was sitting across
from Aria at the breakfast table, doing the *New York Times*
crossword puzzle with a leaky black pen and eating a bowl
of Cheerios. She had just returned to her part-time job at
the Davis contemporary art gallery on Rosewood's main
drag, and she was on the mailing list for all the benefits.

"Isn't Dad going to go with you?" Aria asked.

Her mom pursed her lips together. "He has a lot of
work to do for his classes."

"Oh." Aria picked at a loose strand of wool on the
fingerless gloves she'd knitted during a long train ride to
Greece. Was that suspicion she detected in her mom's

voice? Aria always worried Ella would find out about Meredith and never forgive her for keeping the secret.

Aria squeezed her eyes closed. *You're not thinking about it*, she thought. She poured some grapefruit juice into a glass. "Ella?" she asked. "I need some love advice."

"Love advice?" her mother teased, securing her jet-black bun with a take-out chopstick that had been lying on the table.

"Yeah," Aria said. "I like this guy, but he's kind of . . . unattainable. I'm out of ideas on how to convince him he should like me."

"Be yourself!" Ella said.

Aria groaned. "I've tried that."

"Go out with an attainable boy, then!"

Aria rolled her eyes. "Are you going to help or not?"

"Ooh, someone's sensitive!" Ella smiled, then snapped her fingers. "I just read this study in the paper." She held up the *Times*. "It was a survey about what men find most attractive in women. You know what was the number-one thing? Intelligence. Here, let me find it for you. . . . " She rifled through the paper and handed the page to Aria.

"Aria likes a guy?" Mike swept into the kitchen and grabbed a glazed donut from the box on the island.

"No!" Aria quickly responded.

"Well, someone likes *you*," Mike said. "Gross as that is." He made a barfing sound.

"Who?" Ella asked in an excited voice.

"Noel Kahn," Mike answered, talking with a huge,

chewed-up bite of donut in his mouth. "He asked about you at lacrosse practice."

"Noel Kahn?" Ella echoed, looking back and forth from Mike to Aria. "Which one is he? Was he here three years ago? Do I know him?"

Aria groaned and rolled her eyes. "He's nobody."

"Nobody?" Mike sounded disgusted. "He's, like, the coolest guy in your grade."

"Whatever," Aria said, kissing her mother on the top of her head. She headed to the hallway, staring at the newspaper clipping in her hands. So men liked brains? Well, Icelandic Aria could certainly be brainy.

"Why don't you like Noel Kahn?" Mike's voice made Aria jump. He stood a few feet away from Aria with a carton of orange juice in his hand. "He's the man."

Aria groaned. "If you like him so much, why don't *you* go out with him?"

Mike drank straight from the carton, wiped his mouth, and stared at her. "You've been acting freaky. Are you high? Can I have some if you are?"

Aria snorted. In Iceland, Mike had been constantly trying to score drugs and freaked when some guys at the harbor sold him a dime bag of pot. The stuff turned out to be skunky, but Mike proudly smoked it anyway.

Mike started stroking his chin. "I think I know why you're acting freaky."

Aria turned back to the closet. "You're full of crap."

"You think so?" Mike answered. "I don't. And you

know what? I'm going to find out if my suspicions are true."

"Good luck, Sherlock." Aria pulled at her jacket. Even though she knew Mike was probably full of shit, she hoped he hadn't noticed the quiver in her voice.

As the other kids filed into English—most of the boys sporting a few days' growth of stubble and most of the girls in copycat Mona-and-Hanna platform sandals and charm bracelets—Aria reviewed her just-scrawled stack of note cards. Today, they had to give an oral report about a play called *Waiting for Godot*. Aria adored oral reports—she had the perfect, sexy, gravelly voice for them—and she happened to know the play really well. Once, she'd spent a whole Sunday in a Reykjavík bar, vehemently arguing with an Adrien Brody look-alike about its theme . . . between swilling delicious apple vodka martinis and playing footsie with him under the table, that is. So not only was this an excellent day to become über student, it was also a great opportunity to show everyone how cool Icelandic Aria was.

Ezra strolled in, looking rumpled, bookish, and completely edible, and clapped his hands. "Okay, class," he said. "We have a lot of stuff to get through today. Quiet down."

Hanna Marin turned around and smirked at Aria. "What kind of underwear do you think he's wearing?"

Aria smiled blandly—striped cotton boxers, of course—but snapped her attention back to Ezra.

"All right." Ezra walked to the chalkboard. "Everyone did the reading, right? Everyone has a report? Who wants to go first?"

Aria's hand shot up. Ezra nodded at her. She walked to the podium at the front of the room, arranged her black hair around her shoulders so that it looked extra gorgeous, and made sure that her chunky coral necklace wasn't caught in the collar of her shirt. Quickly, she reread the first few scene-setting sentences on her index cards.

"Last year, I attended a performance of *Waiting for Godot* in Paris," she began.

She noticed Ezra raise his eyebrow just the tiniest bit.

"It was a small theater off the Seine, and the air smelled like the cheese brioche baking next door." She paused. "Picture the scene: a huge line of people waiting to go in, a woman toting her two little white poodles, the Eiffel Tower in the distance."

She briefly looked up. Everyone seemed so transfixed! "I could feel the energy, the excitement, the *passion* in the air. And it wasn't just the beer they were selling to *everyone*—even my little brother," she added.

"Nice!" Noel Kahn interjected.

Aria smiled. "The seats were very velvety and purple, and smelled like this type of butter in France that's sweeter than American butter. It's what makes the pastries so delicious."

"Aria," Ezra said.

"It's the kind of butter that even makes *escargot* taste good!"

"Aria!"

Aria stopped. Ezra leaned against the chalkboard with his arms crossed over his Rosewood blazer. "Yes?" She smiled.

"I have to stop you."

"But . . . I'm not even halfway done!"

"Well, I need less about velvet seats and pastries and more about the play itself."

The class snickered. Aria shuffled back to her seat and sat down. Didn't he know she was creating *ambiance*?

Noel Kahn raised his hand.

"Noel?" Ezra asked. "You want to go next?"

"No," Noel said. The class laughed. "I just wanted to say I thought Aria's report was good. I liked it."

"Thanks," Aria said quietly.

Noel swiveled around. "Is there really no drinking age?"

"Not really."

"I might go with my family to Italy this winter."

"Italy's amazing. You're going to love it."

"Are you two through?" Ezra asked. He shot Noel an exasperated look. Aria dug her hot-pink nails into the wood grain of her desk.

Noel turned back to her again. "Did they have absinthe?" he whispered.

She nodded, amazed Noel had even heard of absinthe.

"Mr. Kahn," Ezra interrupted sternly. A little too sternly. "That's enough."

Was this *jealousy* she detected?

"Damn," Hanna twisted around. "What crawled up his ass?"

Aria stifled a giggle. It seemed to her like a certain über student was making a certain teacher a little twitchy.

Ezra called on Devon Arliss next and she started her speech. As Ezra turned to the side and put his finger on his chin, listening, Aria throbbed. She wanted him so badly it made her whole body buzz.

No, wait. That was just her cell phone, which was nestled in her oversize lime-green tote next to her foot.

The thing kept buzzing. Aria slowly reached down and pulled it out. One new text message:

Aria,

Maybe he fools around with students all the time. A lot of teachers do. . . . Just ask your dad! —A

Aria quickly snapped her cell phone shut. But then she opened it and read the message again. And again. As she did, the little hairs on her arms stood straight up.

No one in the room had their phones out—not Hanna, not Noel, nobody. And no one was looking at her, either. She even looked up on the ceiling and out the classroom door, but nothing seemed out of place.

Everything was quiet and still.

"This can't be happening," Aria whispered.

The only person who knew about Aria's dad was . . . Alison. And she'd sworn *on her grave* she wouldn't tell a soul. Was she *back*?

14

THAT'LL TEACH YOU TO GOOGLE-STALK WHEN YOU'RE SUPPOSED TO BE STUDYING

During her free period Thursday afternoon, Spencer strode into the Rosewood Day reading room. With its ceiling-high stacks of reference books, giant pedestal globe in the corner, and stained-glass window on the far wall, it was her favorite place on campus. She stood in the middle of the empty room, closed her eyes, and inhaled the old, leather-bound book smell.

Everything had gone her way today: The unusual cold snap had allowed her to wear her brand-new Marc Jacobs pale blue wool coat, the Rosewood Day café barista had made her a perfect double skim latte, she'd just aced a French oral exam, and tonight she would be moving into the barn, while Melissa had to sleep in her old, cramped bedroom.

Despite all that, an uneasy haze hung over her. It was a cross between a bothersome feeling she sometimes had

when she'd forgotten to do something and the sense that
someone was . . . well, watching her. It was obvious why
she was feeling so off: that creepy "covet" e-mail. The flash
of blond hair in Ali's old window. The fact that only Ali
knew about Ian . . .

Trying to shake it off, she sat down at the computer,
adjusted the waistband of her navy blue Wolford
patterned stockings, and logged on to the Internet. She
began research for her upcoming AP bio project, but after
scrolling through a list of Google results, she typed, *Wren
Kim,* into the search engine.

Trolling through the results, she stifled a giggle. On a
site called *Mill Hill School, London,* there was a photo of a
longer-haired Wren standing next to a Bunsen burner
and a bunch of test tubes. Another link was to Oxford
University's Corpus Christi College student portal; there
was a photo of Wren looking gorgeous in Shakespearean
garb, holding a skull. She hadn't known Wren was into
drama. As she tried to magnify the photo to check out
the fit of his tights, someone tapped her on the shoulder.

"That your boyfriend?"

Spencer jumped, knocking her crystal-studded Sidekick
cell phone to the floor. Andrew Campbell grinned awkwardly behind her.

She quickly closed the window. "Of course not!"

Andrew bent down to pick up her Sidekick, pushing a
lock of straight, shoulder-length hair out of his eyes.
Spencer noticed that he might actually have a chance at

being cute if he cut off that lion's mane.

"Oops," he said, handing the Sidekick back to her. "I think a jewel thing fell off."

Spencer grabbed it from him. "You scared me."

"Sorry about that." Andrew smiled. "So your boyfriend's an actor?"

"I said he wasn't my boyfriend!"

Andrew stepped back. "Sorry. Just making conversation."

Spencer eyed him suspiciously.

"Anyway," Andrew went on, hefting his North Face backpack higher on his shoulder. "I was wondering. You going to Noel's tomorrow? I could give you a ride."

Spencer looked at him blankly and then remembered: Noel Kahn's field party. She'd gone to last year's. Kids did beer funnels, and practically every girl cheated on her boyfriend. This year would be more of the same. And what—Andrew seriously thought she'd ride with him in his Mini? Would they both even *fit*? "Doubt it," she said.

Andrew's face fell. "Yeah, I guess you're probably kind of busy."

Spencer furrowed her brow. "What's that supposed to mean?"

Andrew shrugged. "You seem to have a lot going on. Your sister's home, right?"

Spencer leaned back in her chair and drew her bottom lip into her mouth. "Yeah, she just got home last night. How'd you know tha—"

She stopped. Wait a *second*. Andrew drove his Mini up

and down her street all the time. She'd seen him just yesterday, when she was at the mailbox getting her test scores. . . .

She swallowed hard. Now that she thought about it, she might have seen his black Mini drive by the day she and Wren were in the hot tub together. He must've been driving it up and down her street a lot to notice Melissa was home. What if . . . what if *Andrew* was the one skulking around spying on her? What if Andrew wrote that creepy "covet" e-mail? Andrew was so competitive it seemed possible. Wouldn't sending threatening messages be a good way to throw someone off her game and make it easier to be reelected as next year's class president . . . or, *even better,* beat out his competition for valedictorian? And the long hair! Maybe she'd seen *him* in Ali's old window?

Unbelievable! Spencer stared at Andrew incredulously.

"Is something wrong?" Andrew asked, looking concerned.

"I have to go." She gathered up her books and walked out of the reading room.

"Wait," Andrew called.

Spencer kept going. But as she pushed through the library doors, she realized that she didn't feel enraged. Sure, it was bizarre that Andrew was spying on her, but if Andrew was A, Spencer was safe. Whatever Andrew *thought* he had on her, it was nothing . . . *nothing* . . . compared to what Alison knew.

She reached the door to the commons—coming in at the same time was Emily Fields.

"Hey," Emily said. A nervous look crossed her face.

"Hey," Spencer answered.

Emily readjusted her Nike backpack. Spencer pushed her bangs off her face. When was the last time she'd spoken to Emily?

"It got cold out, huh?" Emily asked.

Spencer nodded. "Yeah."

Emily smiled in that I-don't-know-what-to-say-to-you way. Then Tracey Reid, another swimmer, grabbed Emily's arm. "When is our swimsuit money due?" she asked.

As Emily answered, Spencer wiped some nonexistent dirt off her blazer and wondered if she could just walk away or if she had to say a formal good-bye. Then something on Emily's wrist caught her eye. Emily was still wearing her blue string bracelet from sixth grade. Alison had made them for everyone right after the accident—The Jenna Thing—happened.

Initially, they'd just wanted to get Jenna's brother, Toby; it was supposed to be a prank. After the five of them planned it, Ali went across the street to watch through Toby's tree house window, and then when it happened, it did something . . . *horrible* . . . to Jenna.

After the ambulance pulled away from Jenna's house, Spencer discovered something about the accident none of the other girls ever found out: Toby saw Ali, but Ali saw Toby doing something *just as bad*. He couldn't tell on her, because then she'd tell on *him*.

Not long after, Ali made everyone the bracelets to remind them they were best friends *forever* and now that they shared a secret like this, they had to protect one another *forever*. Spencer waited for Ali to tell the others that someone saw her, but she never did.

When the cops questioned Spencer after Ali went missing, they asked if Ali had any enemies, anyone who hated her so much they might want to hurt her. Spencer said that Ali was a popular girl, and like any popular girl, there were some girls who didn't like her, but it was just jealousy.

That, of course, was a bold-faced lie. There *were* people who hated Ali, and Spencer knew she should tell the police what Ali told her about The Jenna Thing . . . that maybe Toby wanted to hurt Ali . . . but how could she tell them that without telling them *why*? Spencer couldn't get through a day without passing Toby and Jenna's house on her street. But they'd been sent away to boarding school and hardly ever came home, so she thought their secret was safe. They were safe from Toby. And Spencer was safe from ever having to tell her best friends what she alone knew.

As Tracey Reid said good-bye, Emily turned around. She seemed surprised Spencer was still standing there. "I've got to get to class," she said. "Good to see you, though."

"'Bye," Spencer answered, and she and Emily exchanged one last awkward smile.

15

INSULTING HIS MASCULINITY
IS SUCH A DEAL BREAKER

"You guys are looking lazy. I want to see better form!"
Coach Lauren yelled at them from the deck.

On Thursday afternoon, Emily bobbed with the other
swimmers in the crystal blue water of Rosewood's
Anderson Memorial Natatorium, listening to their
youngish, former-Olympian coach, Lauren Kinkaid,
scream at them. The pool was twenty-five yards wide, fifty
yards long, with a small diving well. Huge skylights mir-
rored the length of the pool, so when you did backstrokes
in the evening, you could look up and see the stars.

Emily held on to the wall and pulled her cap over her
ears. Okay, better form. She needed to really concentrate
today.

Last night, after getting back from the creek with
Maya, she'd lain on her bed for a long time, flip-flopping
from feeling warm and happy about the fun she and

Maya had had . . . to feeling uneasy and antsy about Maya's confession. *I'm not sure I like guys. I think I'd like someone more like me.* Did Maya mean what Emily thought she meant?

Thinking about how giddy Maya had been at the waterfall—not to mention how much they'd tickled and touched each other—Emily felt nervous. After getting home last night, she'd rifled through her swimming bag for that note from A from the day before. She read it over and over again, picking apart every word until her eyes blurred.

By dinnertime, Emily decided she needed to throw herself back into swimming. No more skipped practices. No more slacking. From now on, she'd be the model swimmer girl.

Ben paddled over to her and put his hands on the wall. "I missed you yesterday."

"Mmmm." She should make a new start with Ben, too. With his freckles, piercing blue eyes, slightly stubbly jaw, and beautifully chiseled swimmer's body, he was hot, right? She tried to imagine Ben jumping off the Marwyn trail bridge. Would he laugh or think it was immature?

"So where were you?" Ben asked, blowing on his goggles to defog them.

"Tutoring for Spanish."

"Wanna come over to my house after practice? My parents won't be home till eight."

"I . . . I'm not sure if I can." Emily pushed away from

the wall and started to tread water. She stared down at her blurrily pumping legs and feet.

"Why not?" Ben pushed off the wall to join her.

"Because . . . " She couldn't come up with an excuse.

"You know you want to," Ben whispered. He took some water into his hands and began splashing her. Maya had done the same thing yesterday, but this time Emily jerked away.

Ben stopped splashing. "What?"

"Don't."

Ben put his hands around her waist. "No? You don't like to get splashed?" he asked in a baby voice.

She took his hands off her. *"Don't."*

He backed away. "Fine."

Sighing, Emily floated over to the other side of the lane. She liked Ben, she really did. Maybe she *should* just go over to Ben's after swimming. They'd watch TiVo'ed episodes of *American Chopper,* eat pizza delivered from DiSilvio's, and he'd feel underneath her unsexy sports bra. Suddenly tears sprang to her eyes. She really didn't want to sit on Ben's itchy blue basement couch, picking oregano spices out of her teeth and rolling her tongue around the inside of his mouth. She just *didn't.*

She wasn't the kind of girl who could fake things. But did that mean she wanted to break up? It was hard to make up your mind about a boy when he was right in your swimming lane, four feet away.

Her sister Carolyn, who was practicing in the lane

next to her, tapped Emily on the shoulder. "Everything all right?"

"Yeah," Emily mumbled, grabbing a blue kickboard.

"Okay." Carolyn looked as if she wanted to say more. After her trip with Maya to the creek yesterday, Emily had skidded the Volvo into the parking lot just in time to see Carolyn exiting the natatorium's double doors. When Carolyn asked where Emily had been, Emily had told her she had to tutor for Spanish. It seemed like Carolyn believed her, despite Emily's damp hair and the funny ticky noise the car was making—something it did only when it was cooling down from a drive.

Even though the sisters looked alike—both had broad freckles over their noses, chlorine-bleached reddish brown hair, and had to wear a lot of Maybelline Great Lash to lengthen their stubby lashes—and even though they shared a room, they weren't close. Carolyn was a quiet, demure, and obedient girl, and although Emily was all those things too, Carolyn seemed really satisfied to be that way.

Coach Lauren blew the whistle. "Kicking time! Line up!"

The swimmers lined up from fastest to slowest, kickboards in front of them. Ben was in front of Emily. He looked at her and raised an eyebrow.

"I can't come over tonight," she said quietly, so the other boy swimmers—who were crowded around behind her and laughing at Gemma Curran's fake tan gone wrong—couldn't hear. "Sorry."

Ben's mouth flattened into a straight line. "Yeah. As if

that's a surprise." Then, as Lauren blew the whistle, he pushed off the wall and began dolphin-kicking. Uneasy, Emily waited until Lauren blew the whistle again, and pushed off behind him.

As she swam, Emily stared at Ben's pumping legs. It was so dorky how he wore a cap over his already-short hair. He got so OCD before races, too, shaving off every hair on his body, including the ones on his arms and legs. Now, his feet made exaggeratedly huge splashes, which sprayed right into Emily's face. She glared at his head bobbing in front of her and pumped her legs harder.

Even though she'd left five seconds behind him, Emily reached the opposite wall at almost the same time Ben did. He turned to her, pissed. Swim team etiquette dictated that no matter how big a swimming star you were, if someone caught your feet on a set, you let them go ahead of you. But Ben just pushed back off the wall.

"Ben!" Emily called, the irritation in her voice showing.

He stood up in the shallow end and turned around. "What?"

"Let me go in front of you."

Ben rolled his eyes and ducked back underwater.

Emily shoved off the wall and kicked crazily until she caught up to him. He reached the wall and turned to face her.

"Would you stay off my ass?" he practically yelled.

Emily burst out laughing. "You're supposed to let me go!"

"Maybe if you didn't leave right on top of me you wouldn't *be* on top of me."

She snorted. "I can't help it if I'm faster than you."

Ben's mouth fell open. Oops.

Emily licked her lips. "Ben . . . "

"No." He held up his hand. "Just go swim really fast, okay?" He tossed his goggles onto the deck. They bounced awkwardly and landed back in the water, narrowly missing Gemma's fake-tanned shoulder.

"Ben . . . "

He glared at her, then turned and got out of the pool. "Whatever."

Emily watched him angrily push open the boys' locker room door.

She shook her head, watching the door slowly swing back and forth. Then she remembered the thing Maya said yesterday.

"Fuck a moose," she tried out quietly, and smiled.

16

NEVER TRUST AN INVITE
WITHOUT A RETURN ADDRESS

"So are you coming over tonight?" Hanna switched her BlackBerry to her other ear and waited for Sean's answer.

It was Thursday after school. She and Mona had just met for a quick cappuccino on campus, but Mona had to leave early to practice her drive for the mother/daughter golf tournament she was competing in this weekend. Now, Hanna sat on her front porch, talking to Sean and watching the six-year-old twins next door draw surprisingly anatomically correct naked boys in chalk all over their driveway.

"I can't," Sean answered. "I'm really sorry."

"But Thursday is *Nerve* night; you know that!"

Hanna and Sean were hooked on this reality show *Nerve*, which documented the lives of four couples who'd met online. Tonight's episode was extremely important, because their favorite two characters, Nate and Fiona, were about to do it. Hanna thought it might at least start a conversation.

"I . . . I have a meeting tonight."

"A meeting for what?"

"Um . . . V Club."

Hanna's mouth fell open. *V Club?* As in *Virginity Club?* "Can you skip it?"

He was quiet for a minute. "I can't."

"Well, are you at least coming to Noel's tomorrow?"

Another pause. "I don't know."

"Sean! You have to!" Her voice squeaked.

"All right," he answered. "I guess Noel would be kinda pissed if I didn't."

"*I* would be pissed too," Hanna added.

"I know. See you tomorrow."

"Sean, wait—" Hanna started. But he'd already hung up.

Hanna unlocked her house. Sean *had* to come to the party tomorrow. She'd hatched a foolproof, romantic plan: She'd take him to Noel's woods, they'd confess their love for each other, and then they'd have sex. V Club couldn't argue with having sex if you were in love, could it? Besides, the Kahn woods were legendary. They were known as the Manhood Woods, because so many guys at so many Kahn parties had lost their virginity there. It was rumored that the trees whispered sex secrets to new recruits.

She stopped at the mirror in the hallway and pulled

up her shirt to examine her taut stomach muscles. She swiveled sideways to investigate her small, round butt. Then she bent forward to look at her skin. Yesterday's blotchiness was gone. She bared her teeth. One bottom front tooth crossed over a canine. Had they always been that way?

She threw her thick-strapped, gold leather handbag onto the kitchen table and opened the freezer. Her mom didn't buy Ben & Jerry's, so Tofutti Cutie 50-percent-less sugar faux ice-cream sandwiches would have to do. She took out three and began to greedily unwrap the first one. As she took a bite, she felt that familiar tug to eat more.

"Here, Hanna, have another profiterole," Ali had whispered to her that day they visited her dad in Annapolis. Then Ali turned to Kate, her dad's girlfriend's daughter, and said, "Hanna's so lucky—she can eat anything and not gain an ounce!"

It wasn't true, of course. That's what made it so mean. Hanna was already chubby and seemed to be getting more so. Kate giggled, and Ali—who was supposed to be on Hanna's side—laughed too.

"I got you something."

Hanna jumped. Her mom sat at the little telephone table in a hot pink Champion sports bra and black flared-leg yoga pants. "Oh," Hanna said quietly.

Ms. Marin appraised Hanna, her eyes settling on the ice-cream sandwiches in her hands. "Do you really need *three*?"

Hanna looked down. She'd chomped through one sandwich in less than ten seconds, hardly even tasting it, and had already unwrapped the next.

She smiled faintly at her mom and quickly stuffed the remaining Cuties back into the freezer. When she turned back around, her mother set a little blue Tiffany bag on the table. Hanna looked at it questioningly. *"This?"*

"Open it."

Inside was a little blue Tiffany box, and inside that was the complete Tiffany toggle set—the charm bracelet, round silver earrings, plus the necklace. The very same kind she'd had to hand over to the Tiffany's woman at the police station. Hanna held them up, letting them sparkle in the overhead light. "Wow."

Ms. Marin shrugged. "You're welcome." Then, to signify that the conversation was finished, she retreated to the den, unrolled her purple yoga mat, and turned on her Power Yoga DVD.

Hanna slowly slid the earrings back in the bag, confused. Her mom was so *weird.* That was when she noticed a creamy, square card envelope sitting on the little telephone table. Hanna's name and address were typewritten in all caps. She smiled. An invite to a sweet party was just the thing she needed to cheer up.

Breathe in through your nose, out through your mouth, the soothing yogi instructed from the TV in the den. Ms. Marin stood with her arms placidly by her sides. She didn't even move when her BlackBerry started singing

Flight of the Bumblebee, which meant she had an e-mail. This was her Me time.

Hanna grabbed the envelope and climbed upstairs to her room. She sat down on her four-poster bed, felt the edges of her billion-thread-count sheets, and smiled at Dot, sleeping peacefully on his doggie bed.

"Come here, Dot," she whispered. He stretched and sleepily climbed into her arms. Hanna sighed. Maybe she just had PMS, and these jittery, uneasy, the-world-is-caving-in feelings would go away in a few days.

She sliced the envelope open with her fingernail and frowned. It wasn't an invitation, and the note didn't really make sense.

Hanna,

Even Daddy doesn't love you best! —A

What was that supposed to mean? But when she unfolded the accompanying page stuffed inside the envelope, she yelped.

It was a color printout from a private school's online newsletter. Hanna looked at the familiar people in the photo. The caption said, *Kate Randall was Barnbury School's student speaker at the benefit. Pictured here with her mother, Isabel Randall, and Ms. Randall's fiancé, Tom Marin.*

Hanna blinked quickly. Her father looked the same as when she'd last seen him. And although her heart stopped when she read the word *fiancé*—when had *that* happened?—it was the image of Kate that made her skin itch. Kate looked more perfect than ever. Her skin was glowing and her hair was perfect. She had her arms gleefully wrapped around her mom and Mr. Marin.

Hanna would never forget the moment she first saw Kate. Ali and Hanna had just gotten off Amtrak in Annapolis, and at first Hanna saw only her dad leaning up against the hood of his car. But then the car door opened, and Kate stepped out. Her long chestnut hair was straight and shiny, and she held herself like the kind of girl who'd taken ballet since she was two. Hanna's first instinct was to crouch behind a pole. She looked at her snug jeans and stretched-out cashmere sweater and tried not to hyperventilate. *This was why Dad left,* she thought. *He wanted a daughter who wouldn't embarrass him.*

"Oh my God," Hanna whispered, searching the envelope for a return address. Nothing. Something occurred to her. The only person who really knew about Kate was Alison. Her eyes moved to the *A* on the note.

The Tofutti Cutie burbled in her stomach. She ran for the bathroom and grabbed the extra toothbrush in the ceramic cup next to the sink. Then she knelt down over the toilet and waited. Tears dotted the corners of her eyes. *Don't start this again,* she told herself, gripping the toothbrush hard by her side. *You're better than this.*

Hanna stood up and stared in the mirror. Her face was flushed, her hair was strewn around her face, and her eyes were red and puffy. Slowly, she put the toothbrush back in the cup.

"I'm Hanna and I'm fabulous," she said to her reflection.

But it didn't sound convincing. Not at all.

17

DUCK, DUCK, GOOSE!

"Okay." Aria blew her long bangs out of her eyes. "In this scene, you have to wear this colander on your head and talk a lot about a baby we don't have."

Noel frowned and brought his thumb to his pink, bow-shaped lips. "Why do I have to wear a colander on my head, Finland?"

"Because," Aria answered. "It's an absurdist play. It's supposed to be, like, absurd."

"Gotcha." Noel grinned. It was Friday morning, and they were sitting on desks in English class. After yesterday's *Waiting for Godot* disaster, Ezra's next assignment had been for them to break up into groups and write their own existentialist plays. *Existentialist* was another way of saying, "silly and out there." And if anyone could do silly and out there, it was Aria.

"I know something really absurd we could do," Noel said. "We could have this character drive a Navigator and, like, after a couple of beers, crash it into his duck pond. But he's, like, fallen asleep at the wheel, so he doesn't notice he's in the duck pond until the next day. There could be ducks in the Navigator."

Aria frowned. "How could we stage all that? It sounds impossible."

"I don't know." Noel shrugged. "But that happened to me last year. And it was really absurd. And awesome."

Aria sighed. She hadn't exactly chosen Noel to be her partner because she thought he'd be a good cowriter. She looked around for Ezra, but he unfortunately wasn't watching them in fitful jealousy. "How about if we make one of the characters *think* he's a duck?" she suggested. "He could randomly quack."

"Um, sure." Noel wrote that down on a piece of lined paper with a gnawed-up Montblanc pen. "Hey, maybe we could shoot this with my dad's Canon DV camera? And have this as a movie instead of a boring play?"

Aria paused. "Actually, that would be kind of cool."

Noel smiled. "Then we could keep the Navigator scene!"

"I guess." Aria wondered if the Kahns really had a spare Navigator to crash. Probably.

Noel nudged Mason Byers, who was paired up with James Freed. "Dude. We're going to have a Navigator in our play! And pyrotechnics!"

"Wait. Pyrotechnics?" Aria asked.

"Nice!" Mason said.

Aria clamped her lips shut. Honestly, she didn't have the energy for this. Last night, she hardly slept. Plagued by yesterday's cryptic text message, she'd spent half the night thinking and furiously knitting a purple hat with earflaps.

It was awful to think that someone knew not only about her and Ezra, but also about that stuff with her dad. What if this A person sent her mom messages next? What if A already had? Aria didn't want her mom to find out—not now, and not that way.

Aria also couldn't shake the idea that the A message might actually be from *Alison*. There just weren't that many people who knew. A few faculty members maybe, and Meredith knew, obviously. But they didn't know Aria.

If the text was from Alison, that meant she was alive. Or . . . *not*. What if the texts were from Ali's ghost? A ghost could have easily slid between the cracks of the women's bathroom at Snooker's. And spirits from the dead sometimes contacted the living to make amends, right? It was like their final homework assignment before graduating to heaven.

If Ali needed to make amends, though, Aria could think of a more deserving candidate than her. Try Jenna. Aria put her hands over her eyes, blocking out the memory. Screw therapy that said you should face your demons: She tried to block out The Jenna Thing as much as she tried to block out her dad and Meredith.

Aria sighed. At times like this, she wished she hadn't drifted from her old friends. Like Hanna, a few desks over—if only Aria could walk up to Hanna and talk to her about this, ask her questions about Ali. But time really changed people. She wondered if it would be easier to talk to Spencer or Emily instead.

"Hey there."

Aria straightened up. Ezra was standing in front of her desk. "Hi," she squeaked.

She met his blue eyes and her heart ached.

Ezra tilted his hips awkwardly. "How are you?"

"Um, I'm . . . great. Really awesome." She sat up straight. On the plane back from Iceland, Aria had read in a *Seventeen* she found in her seat pocket that boys liked enthusiastic, positive girls. And since brilliant hadn't worked yesterday, why not try out peppy?

Ezra clicked and unclicked his Bic pen. "Listen, sorry to cut you off yesterday in the middle of your speech. Do you want to give me your index cards so I can take a look at them and grade you?"

"Okay." Huh. Would Ezra do that for the other students? "So . . . how are you?"

"Good." Ezra smiled. His lips twitched as if he wanted to say more. "What're you working on, there?" He placed his hands on her desk and leaned over to look at her notebook. Aria stared at his hands for a moment, then slid her pinkie finger up against his. She tried to make it look like an accident, but he didn't pull away. It felt like electricity was surging between their two pinkies.

"Mr. Fitz!" Devon Arliss's hand shot up in the back row. "I have a question."

"Be right there," Ezra said, straightening up.

Aria put the pinkie finger that had touched Ezra's into her mouth. She watched him for a few seconds, thinking he might come back to her, but he didn't.

Well then. Back to plan J, for *Jealous*. She turned to Noel. "I think our movie should have a sex scene in it."

She said it really loud, but Ezra was still bent over Devon's desk.

"Awesome," Noel said. "Does the guy who thinks he's a duck get some?"

"Yep. With a woman who kisses like a goose."

Noel laughed. "How does a goose kiss?"

Aria turned toward Devon's desk. Ezra was facing them now. Good.

"Like this." She leaned over and smacked Noel on the cheek with her lips. Surprisingly, Noel smelled pretty good. Like Kiehl's Blue Eagle shaving cream.

"Nice," Noel whispered.

The rest of the class burbled with activity, unaware of any goose kissing, but Ezra, still next to Devon's desk, stood absolutely still.

"So did you know I'm having a party tonight?" Noel put his hand on Aria's knee.

"Yeah, I heard something about that."

"You should totally come. We're going to have a lot of beer. And other things . . . like Scotch. Do you like Scotch? My dad has a collection, so . . . "

"I love Scotch." Aria felt Ezra's eyes burning into her back. Then she leaned over to Noel, and said: "I'll totally come to your party tonight."

By the way his pen fell out of his hand and clattered to the ground, it wasn't hard to guess whether or not Ezra had heard them.

18

WHERE'S OUR OLD EMILY AND WHAT HAVE YOU DONE WITH HER?

"Are you going to the Kahn party later?" Carolyn asked, steering the car into the Fieldses' driveway.

Emily ran a comb through her still-wet hair. "I don't know." Today at practice, she and Ben hadn't said two words to each other, so she wasn't exactly sure about going with him. "Are you?"

"I don't know. Topher and I might just go to Applebee's instead."

Of course Carolyn would have a hard time deciding between a Friday night field party and Applebee's.

They slammed the doors of the Volvo and walked up the stone path to the Fieldses' thirty-year-old colonial-style house. It wasn't nearly as big or flashy as most of the houses in Rosewood. The blue-painted shingles were chipping a little and some of the stones in the front path had disappeared. The deck furniture looked kind of outdated.

Their mother greeted them at the front door, holding the cordless phone. "Emily, I need to speak with you."

Emily glanced at Carolyn, who ducked her head and ran upstairs. Uh-oh. "What's up?"

Her mom smoothed her hands over her gray pleated slacks. "I was on the phone with Coach Lauren. She said your head seems to be somewhere else, not focused on swimming. And . . . you missed practice on Wednesday."

Emily swallowed hard. "I was tutoring some kids in Spanish."

"That's what Carolyn told me. So I called Ms. Hernandez."

Emily stared down at her green Vans. Ms. Hernandez was the Spanish teacher in charge of tutoring.

"Don't lie to me, Emily." Mrs. Fields frowned. "Where were you?"

Emily walked into the kitchen and slumped into a chair. Her mom was a rational person. They could discuss this.

She fiddled with the silver loop at the top of her ear. Years ago, Ali had asked Emily to come to the Piercing Palace with her when she got her belly button pierced, and they'd ended up getting matching piercings at the top of their ears, too. Emily still wore the same little silver hoop. Afterward, Ali bought Emily a pair of leopard-print earmuffs to hide the evidence. Emily still wore those earmuffs on the coldest days in the winter.

"Look," she finally said. "I was just hanging out with that new girl, Maya. She's really nice. We're friends."

Her mother looked confused. "Why didn't you just do something after practice, or on Saturday?"

"I don't see why it's such a big deal," Emily said. "I missed one day. I'll swim a double this weekend—I promise."

Her mother pursed her thin lips in a straight line and sat down. "But Emily . . . I just don't understand. When you signed up for swimming this year, you made a commitment. You can't go running off with friends if you're supposed to be swimming."

Emily stopped her. "*Signed up* for swimming? Like I had a choice?"

"What's going on with you? You're using a strange tone of voice; you're lying about where you've been." Her mother shook her head. "What's with this lying? You've never lied before."

"*Mom* . . . " Emily paused, feeling very tired. She wanted to point out that yes, she *had* lied, plenty. Even though she'd been the good girl of her seventh-grade friends, she'd done all kinds of stuff her mom never knew about.

Right after Ali went missing, Emily worried that Ali's disappearance was somehow . . . cosmically . . . her fault— as punishment, maybe, for how Emily had secretly disobeyed her parents. For getting that piercing. For The Jenna Thing. Since then, she'd tried to be perfect, to do everything her parents asked. She'd made herself into this model daughter, inside and out.

"I just like to know what's going on with you," her mother said.

Emily laid her hands on the place mat, remembering how she'd become this version of herself that wasn't *really* her. Ali wasn't gone because Emily had disobeyed her parents—she realized that now. And the same way she couldn't imagine sitting on Ben's itchy couch, feeling his slimy tongue on her neck, she also couldn't see herself spending the next two years of high school—and then the next four years of college—in a pool for hours every day. Why couldn't Emily just be . . . Emily? Couldn't her time be better served studying or—God forbid—having some fun?

"If you want to know what's going on with me," Emily started, pushing her hair out of her face. She took a deep breath. "I don't think I want to swim anymore."

Mrs. Fields's right eye twitched. Her lips parted slightly. Then she spun around to face the fridge, staring at all the chicken magnets on the freezer. She didn't speak, but her shoulders shook. Finally, she turned. Her eyes were slightly red, and her face looked saggy, as if she'd aged ten years in just a few moments. "I'm calling your father. He'll talk some sense into you."

"I've already made up my mind." As she said it, she realized she had.

"No you haven't. You don't know what's best for you."

"Mom!" Emily suddenly felt tears fill her eyes. It was scary and sad to have her mother angry with her. But now that she'd made the decision, she felt like she'd finally been allowed to take off a big goose down jacket in the middle of a heat wave.

Her mom's mouth trembled. "Is it because of that new friend of yours?"

Emily cringed and wiped her nose. "What? Who?"

Mrs. Fields sighed. "That girl who moved into the DiLaurentis house. She was the one you skipped practice to spend time with, right? What were you two doing?"

"We . . . we just went to the trail," Emily whispered. "And talked."

Her mother looked down. "I don't have a good feeling about girls . . . like that."

Wait. What? Emily stared at her mother. She . . . *knew?* But how? Her mom hadn't even met Maya. Unless you could look at her and just *know?*

"But Maya's really nice," Emily managed. "I forgot to tell you, but she said the brownies were great. She said thank you."

Her mother pinched her lips together. "I went over there. I was trying to be neighborly. But this . . . this is too much. She's not a good influence for you."

"I don't—"

"Please, Emily," her mom interrupted.

Emily's words stuck in her throat.

Her mom sighed. "There are just so many cultural differences with . . . her . . . and I just don't understand what you and Maya have in common, anyway. And who knows about her family? Who knows what they could be into?"

"Wait, *what*?" Emily stared at her mother. Maya's *family*? As far as Emily knew, Maya's father was a civic engineer and her mom worked as a nurse practitioner. Her brother was a senior at Rosewood and a tennis prodigy; they were building a tennis court for him in the backyard. What did her family have to do with anything?

"I just don't trust those people," her mother said. "I know that sounds really narrow-minded, but I don't."

Emily's mind screeched to a halt. *Her family. Cultural differences. Those people?* She went over everything her mother just said. Oh. My. God.

Mrs. Fields wasn't upset because she thought Maya was gay. She was upset because Maya—and the rest of her family—were *black*.

19

SPICY HOT

Friday evening, Spencer lay on her maple four-poster bed in the middle of her brand-new converted barn bedroom with Icy Hot slathered on her lower back, staring at the gorgeous beamed ceiling. You'd never guess that fifty years ago, cows slept in this barn. The room was huge, with four gigantic windows and a little patio. After dinner last night, she'd moved all of her boxes and furniture there. She'd organized all of her books and CDs according to author and artist, set up her surround-sound, and even reset TiVo to her preferences, including her brand-new favorite programs on BBC America. It was perfect.

Except, of course, for her throbbing back. Her body ached as if she'd gone bungee jumping without a ripcord. Ian had made them run three miles—at a sprint—followed by practice drills. All the girls had been talking about what they were wearing to Noel's party tonight, but after the hellish practice, Spencer was just as happy to stay home with some calc homework. Especially since home was now her very own little barn utopia.

Spencer reached for the jar of Icy Hot and realized it was empty. She sat up slowly, and put her hand on her back like an old woman. She'd just have to get some more from the main house. Spencer just *loved* that she could now call it *the main house*. It felt terribly grown up.

As she crossed her long, hilly lawn, she let her mind return to one of her favorite topics *du jour,* Andrew Campbell. Yes, it was a relief that A was Andrew and not Ali, and yes, she felt a billion times better and a zillion times less paranoid since yesterday, but still—what a horrible, meddling spy! How dare he ask such intrusive, gossipy questions in the reading room and write her a creepy e-mail! And everyone thought he was so sweet and innocent, with his perfectly knotted tie and his luminous skin—he was probably the type who brought Cetaphil to school and washed up after gym class. Weirdo.

Shutting the door of the upstairs bathroom, she found the jar of Icy Hot in the closet, pulled down her Nuala Puma warm-up pants, twisted around to see herself in the mirror, and started rubbing the balm all over her back and hamstrings. The Icy Hot's stinky menthol smell instantly wafted around the room, and she closed her eyes.

The door burst open. Spencer tried to pull her pants up as quickly as she could.

"Oh my God," Wren said, his eyes wide. "I . . . shit. I'm sorry."

"It's all right," Spencer said, scrambling to tie her waistband.

"I'm still confused about this house. . . . " Wren was wearing his blue hospital scrubs, which consisted of a V-neck draped top and tie-waist wide-leg pants. He looked all ready for bed. "I thought this was our bedroom."

"Happens all the time," Spencer said, even though it obviously didn't.

Wren paused in the doorway. Spencer felt him looking at her and quickly looked down to make sure her boob wasn't hanging out and there wasn't a glob of Icy Hot on her neck.

"So, um, how's the barn?" Wren asked.

Spencer grinned, then self-consciously covered her mouth. Last year, she'd had her teeth whitened at the dentist and they'd come out looking a little *too* white. She'd had to purposely dull them with tons of coffee. "Awesome. How's my sister's old bedroom?"

Wren smiled wryly. "Um. It's rather . . . pink."

"Yeah. All those frilly curtains," Spencer added.

"I found a disturbing CD, too."

"Oh yeah? What?"

"*Phantom of the Opera.*" He grimaced.

"But aren't you into plays?" Spencer blurted out.

"Well, Shakespeare and stuff." Wren raised an eyebrow. "How'd you know that?"

Spencer paled. It might sound sort of weird if she told

Wren she'd Googled him. She shrugged and leaned back on the counter. A shooting pain exploded through her lower back, and she winced.

Wren hesitated. "What's the matter?"

"Um, you know." Spencer leaned against the sink. "Field hockey again."

"What'd you do this time?"

"Pulled something. See the Icy Hot?" Holding her towel in one hand, she reached for the jar, scooped some into her palm, and slid her hand down her pants to rub it into her hamstring. She groaned slightly, and hoped it was a sexy-sounding groan. Fine, so sue her for being a *teensy* bit dramatic.

"Do you need some help?"

Spencer hesitated. But Wren looked so concerned. And it *was* excruciating—well, painful, anyway—to twist her back that way, even if she was doing it on purpose.

"If you don't mind," she said softly. "Thanks."

Spencer nudged the door a little more closed with her foot. She smeared the Icy Hot goop from her hand onto his. Wren's large hands felt sexy all slimed up with balm. She caught sight of their figures in the mirror and shivered. They looked awesome together.

"So where's the damage?" Wren asked.

Spencer pointed. The muscle was right below her butt. "Hang on," she murmured. She grabbed a towel from the rack, wrapped it around herself, and then slid off her pants under the towel. She motioned to where it hurt, indicating that Wren reach below the towel. "But, um, try not to get too much on the towel," she said. "I begged my mom to order these special from France a couple years ago, and Icy Hot ruins them. You can't get the smell out in the wash."

She heard Wren stifle a laugh and stiffened. Had that come out way too uptight and Melissa-ish?

Wren slicked back his floppy hair with his goop-free hand and knelt down, slathering the Icy Hot on her skin. He reached his hands under her towel and began to rub slow, gentle circles across her muscles. Spencer relaxed and then leaned into him slightly. He stood but didn't back away from her. She felt his breath on her shoulder, and then on her ear. Her skin felt radiant and fiery.

"Feel better?" Wren murmured.

"Feels amazing." She might have said it in her head, she wasn't sure.

I should do it, Spencer thought. *I should kiss him.* He pressed his hands more firmly on her back, his nails digging in a little. Her chest fluttered.

In the hall, the phone rang.

"Wren, dear?" Spencer's mother called from downstairs. "Are you upstairs? Melissa's on the phone for you."

He sprang backward. Spencer jolted forward and pulled the towel around her. He quickly wiped the Icy Hot off his hands onto another towel. Spencer was too panicked to tell him not to. "Um," he murmured.

She looked away. "You should . . . "

"Yeah."

He pushed the door back open. "I hope that worked."

"Yeah, thanks," she murmured back, closing the door behind him. Then she draped herself over the sink and stared at her reflection.

Something flickered in the mirror, and for a second, she thought someone was by the shower. But it was only the flapping shower curtain, lifted by a breeze from the open window. Spencer turned back to the sink.

They'd spilled a few globs of Icy Hot on the counter. It was white and gooey, sort of like frosting. With her pointer finger, Spencer spelled out Wren's name. Then she drew a heart around it.

Spencer considered leaving it there. But when she heard Wren stomp down the hall and say, "Hey, love. Missed you," she frowned and rubbed it out with the heel of her hand.

20

ALL EMILY NEEDS IS A LIGHT SABER AND A BLACK HELMET

It was just getting dark as Emily slid into Ben's green Jeep Cherokee. "Thanks for convincing my parents that my punishment starts tomorrow."

"No prob," Ben answered. He didn't give her a hello kiss. And he was blasting Fall Out Boy, who he knew Emily hated.

"They're kinda pissed at me."

"I heard." He kept his eyes on the road.

Interesting that Ben didn't ask why. Maybe he already knew. Bizarrely, Emily's father had come into her room earlier and said, "Ben's going to pick you up in twenty minutes. Be ready." *Okay.* Emily had thought she was grounded for life for denouncing the Swimming Gods, but she had the feeling they actually *wanted* her to go out with Ben. Maybe he'd talk some sense into her.

Emily heaved a sigh. "Sorry about practice yesterday. I'm just under some stress."

Ben finally turned down the volume. "It's all right. You're just confused."

Emily licked her just-ChapSticked lips. *Confused? About what?*

"I'll forgive you this time," Ben added. He reached over and squeezed her hand.

Emily bristled. *This time?* And shouldn't he say he was sorry too? He had, after all, stormed off into the locker room like a baby.

They pulled through the Kahns' open wrought-iron gates. The property was set back from the road, so the driveway was half a mile long and surrounded by tall, thick pines. Even the air smelled cleaner. The redbrick house sat behind massive Doric columns. It had a portico with a little horse statue on top and a gorgeous all-glass sun room off to the side. Emily counted fourteen windows on the second floor, from one end to the other.

But the house didn't matter tonight. They were going to the field. It was set way off from the property by high, British-racing-green hedges and a stone wall and went on for acres. Half of it housed the Kahn horse farm; on the other side were a huge lawn and a duck pond. Surrounding the whole yard were thick woods.

As Ben parked the car in a makeshift grass parking lot, Emily climbed out, hearing The Killers blaring from the backyard. Familiar faces from Rosewood climbed out of their Jeeps, Escalades, and Saabs. A group of immaculately made-up girls took cigarette packs out of their little chain-link quilted bags and lit up, talking on their tiny cell phones. Emily looked down at her worn blue Converse All-Stars and touched her messy ponytail.

Ben caught up with her and they cut through the hedges and across a secluded stretch of woods and entered the party zone. There were a lot of kids Emily didn't know, but that was because the Kahns invited all the *it* kids from the area's other private schools, in addition to Rosewood. There were a keg and a drinks table by the bushes, and they'd set up a wooden dance floor, tiki lights, and tents in the middle of the field. On the other side of the field, near the woods, there was an old-school photo booth lit up with Christmas lights. The Kahns dragged it out of their basement for this party every year.

Noel greeted them. He wore a gray T-shirt that said WILL FLEX FOR FOOD, ripped-up faded blue jeans, and no shoes or socks. "What up." He handed them both a beer.

"Thanks, man." Ben took his cup and started drinking. The amber beer messily dribbled down his chin. "Nice party."

Someone tapped Emily on the shoulder.

Emily turned. It was Aria Montgomery, wearing a tight, faded red University of Iceland T-shirt, a frayed denim mini, and red John Fluevog cowboy boots. Her black hair was pulled back into a high ponytail.

"Wow, hi," Emily said. She'd heard Aria was back but she hadn't seen her yet. "How was Europe?"

"Awesome." Aria smiled. The girls looked at each other for a few seconds. Emily paused, wanting to tell Aria she was glad she'd ditched her fake nose ring and pink hair stripes but wondered if it would be weird to make a reference to their old friendship. She took a sip of her beer and pretended to be fascinated with the ridges on the cup.

Aria fidgeted. "Listen, I'm glad you're here. I've been wanting to talk to you."

"You have?" Emily met her eyes and then looked back down.

"Well . . . either you or Spencer."

"Really?" Emily felt her chest tighten. *Spencer?*

"So, promise me you won't think I'm crazy. I've been away for such a long time, and . . . " Aria made a puckered face that Emily remembered well. It meant she was considering her words carefully.

"And what?" Emily raised her eyebrows, waiting. Maybe Aria wanted all her old friends to have a reunion—of course, being away, she wouldn't know how far apart they'd grown. How uncomfortable would *that* be?

"Well . . ." Aria looked around warily. "Was there any more news about Ali's disappearance while I was away?"

Emily jerked back, hearing Ali's name come out of her old friend's mouth. "Her disappearance? What do you mean?"

"Like, did they ever find out who took her? Did she ever come back?"

"Um . . . no . . . " Emily chewed on her thumbnail uncomfortably.

Aria leaned into Emily. "Do you think she's dead?"

Emily's eyes widened. "I . . . I don't know. *Why?*"

Aria set her jaw. She looked deep in thought.

"What's this about?" Emily asked, her heart pounding.

"Nothing."

Then Aria's eyes focused on someone behind her. She clamped her mouth shut.

"Hey," said a gravelly voice behind Emily.

Emily turned. Maya. "Hey," she answered, nearly dropping her cup. "I . . . I didn't know you were coming."

"I didn't either," Maya said. "But my brother wanted to. He's here somewhere."

Emily turned to introduce Aria, but she was gone.

"So is this Maya?" Ben reappeared next to them. "The girl that's turned Emily to the dark side?"

"Dark side?" Emily squeaked. "What dark side?"

"Quitting swimming," Ben answered. He turned to Maya. "You know she's quitting, right?"

"*You are?*" Maya turned to Emily and grinned excitedly.

Emily shot Ben a look. "Maya didn't have anything to do with that. And we don't have to talk about it now."

Ben took another big sip of beer. "Why not? Isn't it your big news?"

"I don't know. . . . "

"Whatever." He clapped his heavy hand on her shoulder a little roughly. "I'm going to get another beer. You want another?"

Emily nodded, even though she only ever drank one beer at parties, max. Ben didn't ask Maya if she wanted a drink. As he walked away, she noticed his saggy jeans. Yuck.

Maya took Emily's hand and squeezed. "How's it feel?"

Emily stared at their entwined hands, blushed, but kept holding on. "Good." Or scary. Or, at some moments, like a bad movie. "Confusing, but good."

"I have just the thing to celebrate with," Maya whispered. She reached into her Manhattan Portage knapsack and showed Emily the top of a Jack Daniel's bottle. "Stole it from the liquor table. Wanna help kill it with me?"

Emily gazed at Maya. Her hair was pulled off her face, and she wore a simple black sleeveless shirt and an army green cargo skirt. She looked effervescent and fun—way more fun than Ben in his saggy-butt jeans.

"Why not?" she answered, and followed Maya toward the woods.

21

HOT GIRLS—THEY'RE
JUST LIKE US!

Hanna took a sip of her vodka lemonade and lit another cigarette. She hadn't seen Sean since they parked his car on the Kahns' lawn two hours ago, and even Mona had vanished. Now she was stuck talking to Noel's best friend, James Freed, Zelda Millings—a beautiful blond girl who only wore clothes and shoes made out of hemp—and a bunch of squeally, cliquey girls from Doringbell Friends, the ultra-hip Quaker school in the next town over. The girls had come to Noel's party last year and even though Hanna had hung out with them then, she couldn't remember any of their names.

James stubbed out his Marlboro on the heel of his Adidas shell-tops and took a swig of beer. "I heard Noel's brother has a ton of pot."

"Eric?" asked Zelda. "Where's he at?"

"Photo booth," James answered.

Suddenly, Sean darted through the pines. Hanna

stood up, adjusted her hopefully slimming BCBG slip dress, and tied the straps of her brand-new pale blue Christian Louboutin sandals back around her ankles. As she ran to catch up with him, her heel sunk into the dewy grass. She flailed her arms, dropped her drink, and suddenly she was on her butt.

"And she's down!" James called out drunkenly. The Doringbell girls all laughed.

Hanna quickly scrambled up, pinching her palm to keep herself from crying. This was the biggest party of the year, but she felt way off her game: Her dress felt snug around her hips, she hadn't been able to get Sean to crack a smile during the car ride over here—despite the fact that he'd scored his dad's BMW 760i for the night—and she was on her third calorie-laden vodka lemonade and it was only nine-thirty.

Sean held out his hand to help her up. "Are you okay?"

Hanna hesitated. Sean was dressed in a plain white T-shirt that accentuated his strong-from-soccer chest and flat-from-good-genes stomach, dark blue Paper Denim jeans that made his butt look awesome, and ragged black Pumas. His blondish brown hair was messily styled, his brown eyes looked extra soulful, and his pink lips extra kissable. For the past hour, she'd watched Sean bond with every guy there and carefully avoid her.

"I'm fine," she said, sticking her lip out in a Hanna-patented pout.

"What's the matter?"

She tried to balance in her shoes. "Can we . . . go somewhere private for a while? Maybe the woods? To talk?"

Sean shrugged. "Okay."

Yes.

Hanna led Sean down a path to the Manhood Woods, the trees casting long, dark shadows across their bodies. The only other time Hanna had ever been here was in seventh grade, when her friends had a secret rendezvous with Noel Kahn and James Freed. Ali made out with Noel, Spencer made out with James, and she, Emily, and Aria sat on logs, shared cigarettes, and miserably waited for them to finish. Tonight, she vowed, would be different.

She sat down on a thick patch of grass and pulled Sean down with her. "You having fun?" She passed her drink to Sean.

"Yeah, it's cool." Sean took a small sip. "You?"

Hanna hesitated. Sean's skin shone in the moonlight. His shirt had a tiny smear of dirt on it near the collar. "I guess."

All right, chatting time was over. Hanna took the drink out of Sean's hand and grabbed his sweet, square jaw and started to kiss him. *There.* It sort of sucked that the world was kind of spinning, and that instead of tasting the inside of Sean's mouth, she tasted Mike's Hard Lemonade, but whatever.

After a minute of kissing, she felt Sean pulling away. Maybe this called for upping the ante a little. She hiked up her navy dress, exposing her legs and tiny lavender Cosabella lace thong. The woodsy air was cold. A mosquito landed on her upper thigh.

"Hanna," Sean said gently, reaching to pull her dress back down. "This isn't . . . "

He wasn't fast enough, though; Hanna had already torn the dress over her head. Sean's eyes canvassed her whole body. Amazingly, this was only the second time he'd seen her in her underwear—unless you counted the week they spent at his parents' place in Avalon on the Jersey Shore, when she was in her bikini. But that was different.

"You don't *really* want to stop, do you?" She reached toward him, hoping she looked smoldering yet wholesome.

"Yeah." Sean caught her hand. "I do."

Hanna wrapped herself up in her dress as best she could. She probably had a hundred mosquito bites already. Her lip trembled. "But . . . I don't get it. Don't you love me?" The words felt very small and frail coming out of her mouth.

Sean took a long time to respond. Hanna heard another couple from the party giggling nearby. "I don't know," he answered.

"Jesus," Hanna said, rolling away from him. The vodka lemonades sloshed in her stomach. "Are you *gay*?" It came out a little meaner than she meant it to.

"No!" Sean sounded hurt.

"Well then what? Am I not hot enough?"

"Of course not!" Sean said, sounding shocked. He thought for a moment. "You're one of the prettiest girls I know, Hanna. Why don't *you* know that?"

"What are you talking about?" Hanna asked, disgusted.

"I just . . . ," Sean started. "I just think that maybe if you could have a little more respect for yourself—"

"I have plenty of self-respect!" Hanna shouted at him. She shifted onto her butt, rolling onto a pine cone.

Sean stood up. He looked deflated and sad. "Look at you." His eyes traveled from her shoes to the top of her head. "I'm just trying to help you, Hanna—I *care* about you."

Hanna felt tears gathering at the corners of her eyes and tried to choke them back down. She would not cry right now. "I respect myself," she repeated. "I just wanted to . . . to . . . show you how I feel."

"I'm just trying to be choosy about sex." He sounded not kind, but not mean, either. Just . . . detached. "I want it to be at the right time with the right person. And it doesn't look like that's going to be you." Sean sighed and took a step away from her. "I'm sorry." Then he pushed through the trees and was gone.

Hanna was so embarrassed and angry, she couldn't speak. She tried to stand up to follow Sean, but her heel caught again and she fell over. She splayed her arms out and stared up at the stars, holding her thumbs over her eyes, so tears wouldn't pour out of them.

"She looks like she might puke."

Hanna opened one eye and saw two freshman boys—most likely crashers—hovering over her as if she were a girl they'd created on their computers.

"Fuck off, pervs," she said to the ogling freshmen as she stood up. Across the lawn, she could see Sean running after Mason Byers, wielding a yellow croquet mallet. Hanna sniffed as she brushed herself off and headed back toward the party. Didn't *anyone* care about her? She thought of the letter she'd gotten yesterday. *Even Daddy doesn't love you best!*

Hanna wished, suddenly, that she had her dad's number, her mind flashing back to that day she'd met her dad and Isabel and Kate with Ali.

Although it had been February, the weather in Annapolis had been freakishly warm, and Hanna, Ali, and Kate had been sitting outside on the porch, trying to get tan. Ali and Kate were bonding over their favorite shades of MAC nail polish, but Hanna couldn't get into it. She felt heavy and awkward. She'd seen Kate's relieved expression when she and Ali first emerged from the train—surprise at how gorgeous Ali was, and then relief when she laid eyes on Hanna. It was as if Kate was thinking, *Well, I don't need to worry about her!*

Without realizing it, Hanna had eaten the entire bowl of cheese popcorn that was on the table. And six of the profiteroles. And some of the Brie wedge that was meant for Isabel and her dad. She clutched her bloated stomach, gazed at Ali's and Kate's flat six-packs, and groaned out loud, without meaning to.

"Little piggy doesn't feel good?" Hanna's dad asked, squeezing her small toe.

Hanna shuddered at the memory and touched her now-slim stomach. A—whoever A was—was totally right. Her dad *didn't* love her best.

"Everyone in the pond!" Noel shouted, snapping Hanna out of her thoughts.

Across the field, Hanna watched Sean pull off his T-shirt and run toward the water. Noel, James, Mason, and some other boys threw off their shirts, but Hanna didn't even care. Of all the nights to see Rosewood's hottest boys without their shirts on . . .

"They're all so gorgeous," murmured Felicity McDowell, who was mixing tequila with Fanta Grape, next to her. "Aren't they?"

"Mmm," she muttered.

Hanna ground her teeth together. Fuck her happy father and his perfect soon-to-be stepdaughter, and fuck Sean and his choosiness! She grabbed a bottle of Ketel One from the table and drank straight from it. She put the bottle back down but at the last second decided to bring it to the pond with her. Sean wasn't going to get away with dumping her, insulting her, and then straight-up ignoring her. No way.

She stopped at a pile of clothes that were no doubt
Sean's—the jeans were neatly folded, and he'd anally
stuffed his little white socks into his Pumas. Making sure
no one was looking, she balled up the jeans in her hands
and started backing away from the pond. What would the
V Club say if they caught him driving home in his boxers?

As she walked toward the trees with Sean's jeans,
something fell and bounced off her foot. Hanna picked
it up and stared at it for a moment, waiting for her vision
to un-double.

The key to the BMW.

"Sweet," she whispered, stroking the alarm button
with her finger. Then she dropped the jeans back on the
ground and shoved the keys into her blue quilted
Moschino bag.

It was a gorgeous night for a drive.

22

BEER BATHS ARE GOOD
FOR THE PORES

"Check it out," Maya whispered excitedly. "There used to be one of these in my favorite café back in Cali!"

Emily and Maya stared at the old-school photo booth at the perimeter of Noel's yard and the woods. A long, orange extension cord wound its way to the booth from Noel's house across the lawn. As they admired it, Noel's older brother, Eric, and a very-giddy Mona Vanderwaal fell out of the booth, grabbed their photos, and skipped away.

Maya glanced at Emily. "Wanna try it?"

Emily nodded. Before they ducked inside, she quickly glanced around the party. Some kids were gathered around the keg and a lot of other people held their red plastic cups in the air as they danced. Noel and a bunch of boys were swimming in the duck pond in their boxers. Ben was nowhere to be seen.

Emily sat beside Maya on the photo booth's little orange seat and closed the curtain. They were so squeezed together, their shoulders and thighs touched.

"Here." Maya handed her the Jack Daniel's bottle and hit the green start button. Emily did a shot, then held it up triumphantly as the camera snapped the first picture. Then they squished their faces together and donned huge grins. Emily rolled her eyes back into her head, and Maya puffed her cheeks out like a monkey for the third picture. Then the camera caught them looking seminormal, if maybe a bit nervous.

"Let's go see how they look," Emily said.

But as she stood up, Maya grabbed her sleeve. "Can we stay in here a sec? This is such a great hiding spot."

"Um, sure." Emily sat back down. She swallowed loudly, without meaning to.

"So, how have you been?" Maya asked, pushing hair out of Emily's eyes.

Emily sighed, trying to get comfy on the cramped seat. *Confused. Upset at my possibly racist parents. Afraid I made the wrong decision about swimming. Kinda freaked that I'm sitting so close to you.*

"I'm all right," she said finally.

Maya snorted and took a swig of whiskey. "I don't believe that for one second."

Emily paused. Maya seemed like the only person who actually understood her. "Yeah, I guess not," she said.

"Well, what's going on?"

But suddenly, Emily didn't want to talk about swimming or Ben or her parents. She wanted to talk about . . . something else completely. Something that had been slowly dawning on her. Maybe seeing Aria had triggered it. Or maybe finally having a real friend again had brought the feeling back. Emily thought Maya would understand.

She took a deep breath. "So, you know that girl Alison, the one who used to live in your house?"

"Yeah."

"We were really close and I, like, really loved her. Like, everything about her."

She heard Maya breathe out and nervously took another sip of Jack Daniel's from the bottle.

"We were best friends," Emily said, rubbing her fingers between the ratty blue fabric of the photo booth curtain. "I cared about her so much. So this one day, sort of out of the blue, I did it."

"Did what?"

"Well, Ali and I were in this tree house in her backyard—we went there a lot to talk. We were sitting up there, talking about this guy that she liked, some older boy whose name she wouldn't say, and I just felt like I couldn't hold any of it in anymore. So I leaned over . . . and kissed her."

Maya made a small sniffing noise.

"She wasn't into it, though. She was even kind of distant and said, like, 'Well, now I know why you get so quiet when we're changing for gym!'"

"God," Maya said.

Emily took another sip of whiskey and felt dizzy. She'd never had this much to drink. And here was one of her biggest secrets, hanging out like granny underwear on a clothesline. "Ali said she didn't think best friends should kiss," she went on. "So I tried to play it off as a joke. But when I went home, I realized how I really felt. So I wrote her this letter, telling her that I loved her. I don't think she ever got it, though. If she did, she never said anything."

A tear plopped on Emily's bare knee. Maya noticed it, and smeared it with her finger.

"I still think about her a lot." Emily sighed. "I'd sort of pushed that memory back, told myself it was just about her being my very best friend but not anything, you know . . . *else* . . . but now I don't know."

They sat there for a few minutes. The party sounds filtered in. Every few seconds, Emily heard the rough flicker of someone's Zippo lighting a cigarette. She wasn't that surprised about what she'd just said about Ali. It was scary, of course—but it was also the truth. In a way, it felt good to have finally figured it out.

"Since we're sharing," Maya said quietly, "I have something to tell you, too."

She turned her forearm over to show Emily the white, raised scar on her wrist. "You might have seen this."

"Yeah," Emily whispered, squinting at it in the pale, semidarkness of the booth.

"It's from one of the times I cut myself with a razor blade. I didn't know it was going to go so deep. There was so much blood. My parents took me to the emergency room."

"You cut yourself on purpose?" Emily whispered.

"Um . . . yeah. I mean, I don't really do it anymore. I try not to."

"Why do you do that?"

"I don't know," Maya said. "Sometimes I just . . . feel like I need to. You can touch it, if you want."

Emily did. It was puckered and smooth, not like real skin at all. Touching it felt like the most intimate thing Emily had ever done. She reached over to hug Maya.

Maya's body shook. She buried her head in Emily's neck. Like before, she smelled like artificial bananas. Emily pressed herself to Maya's slight chest. What was it like to cut yourself, to watch yourself bleed like that? Emily had her fair share of baggage, but even in the wake of her absolute worst memories—like of when Ali rejected her, or of The Jenna Thing—she'd felt guilty and horrible and strange, but she'd *never* wanted to hurt herself.

Maya raised her head and met Emily's eyes. Then smiling a little sadly, she kissed Emily's lips. Emily blinked at her, surprised.

"Sometimes best friends *do* kiss," Maya said. "See?"

They hung apart, nose practically touching nose. Outside, the crickets sawed away furiously.

Then Maya reached for her. Emily melted into her lips. Their mouths were open and she felt Maya's soft tongue. Emily's chest clenched up excitedly as she raked her hands through Maya's rough hair, then down to her shoulders, then her back. Maya stuck her hands under Emily's polo shirt and pressed her fingers flat against her belly. Emily self-consciously flinched but then relaxed. This felt a zillion times different than kissing Ben.

Maya's hands traveled up her body and felt over her bra. Emily shut her eyes. Maya's mouth tasted delicious, like Jack Daniel's and licorice. Next, Maya kissed Emily's chest and shoulders. Emily threw her head back. Someone had painted a moon and a bunch of stars on the photo booth's ceiling.

Suddenly, the curtain started to open. Emily jumped, but it was too late—someone had torn the curtain back completely. Then Emily saw who it was. "Oh my God," she sputtered.

"Shit," Maya echoed. The Jack Daniel's bottle swished onto the floor.

Ben held two cups of beer, one in each hand. "Well. This explains things."

"Ben . . . I . . . " Emily scrambled out of the booth, bumping her head on the door.

"Don't get up for me," Ben said in a horrible, mocking, angry-yet-hurt voice Emily had never heard before.

"No . . . ," Emily squeaked. "You don't understand."

She climbed out of the booth completely. So did Maya. Out of the corner of her eye, Emily noticed Maya pick up their strip of photos and stuff it into her pocket.

"Don't even talk," Ben spat. Then he turned and threw one of the cups of beer at her. It splashed warmly all over Emily's legs, her shoes, and her shorts. The cup bounced crazily into the bushes.

"Ben!" Emily cried.

Ben hesitated, then threw the other one more directly at Maya. It splashed her face and hair. Maya screamed.

"Stop it!" Emily gasped.

"You fucking dykes," Ben said. She heard the crackly tears in his voice. Then he turned and ran crookedly into the darkness.

23

ICELANDIC ARIA GETS
WHAT SHE WANTS

"Finland! I've been looking everywhere for you!"

It was an hour later, and Aria was just stepping out of the photo booth. Noel Kahn stood in front of her, naked except for his Calvin Klein boxers, which were wet and clingy. He was holding a yellow plastic cup of beer and her just-developed strip of pictures. Noel shook his hair around a little, and water from his hair sprayed onto her APC miniskirt.

"Why are you all wet?" Aria asked.

"We were playing water polo."

Aria glanced at the pond. The boys were batting one another in the heads with pink fun-noodles. On the banks, girls in nearly identical Alberta Ferrari minidresses huddled together, gossiping. Over by the hedges, not that far from them, she spied her brother, Mike. He was with a petite girl in a plaid micromini and platform heels.

Noel followed her gaze. "That's one of those Quaker school girls," he murmured. "Those chicks are nuts."

Mike glanced up and saw Aria and Noel together. He gave Aria an approving nod.

Noel tapped Aria's photo strip with his thumb. "These are gorgeous."

Aria looked at them. Bored out of her skull, she'd been taking pictures of herself in the booth for twenty minutes. This round, she'd made sultry, sex-kitten expressions.

Très sigh. She'd come here thinking that Ezra, jealous and lustful, would come and whisk her away. But, duh, he was a teacher, and a teacher wouldn't go to a students' party.

"Noel!" James Freed called from across the lawn. "Keg's tapped!"

"Shit," Noel said. He gave Aria a wet kiss on her cheek. "This beer's for you. Don't leave."

"Uh-huh," Aria said drolly, watching him scamper away, his boxers slowly sliding down to reveal his pale, defined-from-running butt.

"He really likes you, you know."

Aria turned. Mona Vanderwaal sat on the ground a few feet away. Her blond hair was in coils around her face and her gold-rimmed bug-eye sunglasses had slid down her nose. Noel's older brother, Eric, had his head in her lap.

Mona blinked slowly. "Noel's awesome. He'd make such a good friendboy."

Eric burst out laughing. "What?" Mona bent down to him. "What's so funny?"

"She's so stoned," Eric said to Aria.

As Aria scoured her brain for something to say, her Treo beeped. She wrenched it out of her purse and looked at the number. Ezra. *Oh my God, oh my God!*

"Um, hello?" she answered quietly.

"Hey. Um, Aria?"

"Oh. Hey! What's up?" She tried to sound as controlled and cool as possible.

"I'm at home, having a Scotch, thinking about you."

Aria paused, closed her eyes, and a glow passed through her. "Really?"

"Yep. You at that big party?"

"Uh-huh."

"You bored?"

She laughed. "A little."

"Wanna come by?"

"Okay." Ezra started to give her directions, but Aria already knew where it was. She'd looked up his address on MapQuest and Google Earth, but she couldn't exactly tell *him* that.

"Cool," she said. "See you soon."

Aria shoved the phone back into her purse as calmly as she could, and then banged the rubbery soles of her boots together. *Yessss!!!*

"Hey, I know where I know you from."

Aria looked over. Noel's brother, Eric, was squinting

at her while Mona kissed his neck. "You're the friend of that chick who disappeared, right?"

Aria looked at him and pushed her hair out of her eyes. "I don't know who you're talking about," she said, and walked away.

A lot of Rosewood was gated estates and renovated fifty-acre horse farms, but near the college there was a series of rambling, cobblestone streets lined with falling-to-pieces Victorian houses. The houses in Old Hollis were painted crazy colors like purple, pink, and teal and were usually split into apartments and leased to students. Aria's family had lived in an Old Hollis house until Aria was five, which was when her dad got his first teaching job at the college.

As Aria drove slowly down Ezra's street, she noticed one house with Greek letters mounted onto its siding. Toilet paper wound through its trees. Another house had a half-finished painting on an easel in the front yard.

She pulled up to Ezra's house. After parking, she climbed up the stone front steps and rang the bell. The door flung open, and there he was.

"Wow," he said. "Hey." His mouth spread into a wiggly smile.

"Hi," Aria answered, smiling back at him in the same way.

Ezra laughed. "I . . . um, you're here. Wow."

"You already said wow," Aria teased.

They entered into a hallway. Ahead of her, a creaky staircase with a different swatch of carpet on each step wound its way upstairs. On the right, a door was ajar. "This apartment's mine."

Aria walked in and noticed a claw-foot bathtub in the middle of Ezra's living room. She pointed at it.

"It's too heavy to move," Ezra said sheepishly. "So I store books in there."

"Cool." Aria looked around, taking in Ezra's gigantic bay window, dusty built-in bookshelves, and yellow crushed velvet sofa. It smelled faintly of macaroni and cheese but there was a crystal chandelier hanging from the ceiling, a funky mosaic tile around the mantel, and real logs in the fireplace. This was so much more Aria's style than the Kahns' million-dollar duck pond and twenty-seven-room estate.

"I totally want to live here," Aria said.

"I can't stop thinking about you," Ezra said at the same time.

Aria looked over her shoulder. "Really?"

Ezra came up behind her and put his hands on her waist. Aria leaned slightly into him. They stood there for a moment, and then Aria turned. She stared at his clean-shaven face, at the bump at the edge of his nose, the green flecks in his eyes. She touched a mole on his ear-lobe and felt him shudder.

"I just . . . couldn't ignore you in class," he whispered. "It was torture. When you were giving that report . . ."

"You touched my hand today," Aria teased. "You were looking at my notebook."

"You kissed Noel," Ezra said back. "I was so jealous."

"Then it worked," Aria whispered.

Ezra sighed and wrapped his arms around her. She met his mouth with hers and they kissed feverishly, their hands crawling up each other's backs. They backed up for a second, breathlessly staring into each other's eyes.

"No more talk about class," Ezra said.

"Deal."

He guided her into a tiny back bedroom that had clothes all over the floor and an open bag of Lay's on the nightstand. They sat down on his bed. The mattress was barely bigger than a twin, and even though the comforter was made of stiff denim and the mattress probably had potato chip crumbs in the cracks, Aria had never felt anything so perfect in her life.

Aria was still on the bed, staring up at a crack in the ceiling. The streetlight outside the window cast long shadows across everything, turning Aria's bare skin a weird shade of pink. A stiff, chilly breeze from the open window blew out the sandalwood candle next to the bed. She heard Ezra turn on the faucet in the bathroom.

Wow. Wow wow *wow*!

She felt alive. She and Ezra had nearly had sex . . . but then, at exactly the same time, they'd agreed that they should wait. So then they'd snuggled up to each other, naked, and started to talk. Ezra told her about the time he was six and sculpted a red squirrel out of clay, only to have his brother squash it. How he used to smoke a lot of pot after his parents got divorced. About the time he had to take the family's fox terrier to the vet to have her put to sleep. Aria told him about how when she was little, she kept a can of split pea soup named Pee as a pet and cried when her mom tried to cook Pee for dinner. She told him about her furious knitting habit and promised to knit him a sweater.

It was easy to talk to Ezra—so easy she could imagine doing it forever. They could travel together to faraway places. Brazil would be amazing. . . . They could sleep in a tree and eat nothing but plantains and write plays for the rest of their lives. . . .

Her Treo beeped. *Ugh.* It was probably Noel, wondering what happened to her. She hugged one of Ezra's pillows close to her—mmm, it smelled just like him—and waited for him to come out of the bathroom and kiss her some more.

Then it beeped again. And again and again.

"Jesus," Aria groaned, leaning her naked body off the bed to pull it out of her bag. Seven new text messages. More kept beeping in.

Opening her inbox, Aria frowned. The messages all had the same title: STUDENT-TEACHER CONFERENCE! Her stomach turned as she opened the first one.

Aria,

That's some kind of extra credit!

Love ya, A

P.S. Wonder what your mom would think if she found out about your dad's little, uh, study buddy . . . and that you knew!

Aria read the next text message and the next and the next. *All the messages said the same thing.* She dropped the Treo on the floor. She had to sit down.

No. She had to get out of here.

"Ezra?" She frantically peered out Ezra's windows. Was she watching, right this second? What did she want? Was it really *her*? "Ezra, I have to go. It's an emergency."

"What?" Ezra called from behind the bathroom door. "You're leaving?"

Aria couldn't quite believe it, either. She yanked her shirt over her head. "I'll call you, okay? I just have to go do something."

"Wait. What?" he asked, opening the bathroom door.

Aria grabbed her bag and tore out the door and across the yard. She needed to get away. Now.

24

THERE'S MORE THAN JUST SHOES AND JEANS IN SPENCER'S CLOSET

"The limit of x is . . . ," Spencer murmured to herself. She propped herself up on one elbow on her bed and stared at her brand-new, just-covered-with-a-brown-bag calculus book. Her lower back still burned with Icy Hot.

She checked her watch: It was after midnight. Was she crazy to stress over her calc homework on the school year's first Friday night? The Spencer of last year would've whizzed over to the Kahns' in her Mercedes, drunk bad keg beer, and maybe made out with Mason Byers or some other cute lax boy. But not the Spencer of now. She was the Star, and the Star had homework to do. Tomorrow, the Star was visiting home design stores with her mom to properly accessorize the barn. She might even hit Main Line Bikes with her dad in the afternoon—he'd pored over some bicycling catalogues with her during dinner, asking her which Orbea frame she liked better. He'd never asked her opinion about bikes before.

She cocked her head. Was that a tiny, tentative knock at the door? Putting down her mechanical pencil, Spencer gazed out the barn's large front window. The moon was silvery and full, and the windows of the main house blazed a warm yellow. There was the knock again. She padded over to the heavy wooden door and opened it a crack.

"Hey," Wren whispered. "Am I interrupting?"

"Of course not." Spencer opened the door wider. Wren was barefoot, in a slim-fitting white T-shirt that said, UNIVERSITY OF PENNSYLVANIA MEDICAL, and baggy khaki shorts. She looked down at her black French Connection baby tee, short track-star gray sweat shorts from Villanova, and bare legs. Her hair was pulled back in a low, messy ponytail; wisps hanging around her face. It was a completely different look from her everyday Thomas Pink striped button-down and Citizens jeans. That look said, *I'm sophisticated and sexy*, this look said, *I'm studying . . . but still sexy*.

Okay, so maybe she'd planned for the off chance this would happen. But it goes to show you shouldn't just throw on your high-waisted underwear and old, ratty I HEART PERSIAN CATS T-shirt.

"How's it going?" she asked. A warm breeze lifted the wispy ends of her hair. A pine cone fell out of a nearby tree with a thump.

Wren hovered in the doorway. "Shouldn't you be out partying? I heard there was a huge field party somewhere."

Spencer shrugged. "Not into it."

Wren met her eyes. "No?"

Spencer's mouth felt cottony. "Um . . . where's Melissa?"

"She's sleeping. Too much renovating, I guess. So I thought maybe you could give me a tour of this fabulous barn I don't get to live in. I never even got to see it!"

Spencer frowned. "Do you have a housewarming gift?"

Wren paled. "Oh. I . . . "

"I'm kidding." She opened the door. "Enter the Spencer Hastings barn."

She'd spent some of the night daydreaming about all the potential scenarios of being alone with Wren, but nothing compared to actually having him right here, next to her.

Wren strolled over to her Thom Yorke poster and stretched his hands behind his head. "You like Radiohead?"

"Love."

Wren's face lit up. "I've seen them like twenty times in London. Every show gets better."

She smoothed down the duvet on her bed. "Lucky. I've never seen them live."

"We have to remedy that," he said, leaning against her couch. "If they come to Philly, we're going."

Spencer paused. "But I don't think . . . " Then she stopped. She was about to say *I don't think Melissa likes them*, but . . . maybe Melissa wasn't invited.

She led him to the walk-in closet. "This is my, um, closet," she said, accidentally bumping into the doorjamb. "It used to be a milking station."

"Oh yeah?"

"Yep. This is where the farmers squeezed the cow's nipples or whatever."

He laughed. "Don't you mean *udders?*"

"Uh, yeah." Spencer blushed. Oops. "You don't have to look in there to be polite. I mean, I know closets aren't that interesting to guys."

"Oh no." Wren grinned. "I've come all this way; I absolutely want to see what Spencer Hastings has in her closet."

"As you wish." Spencer flicked on the closet light. The closet smelled like leather, mothballs, and Clinique Happy. She'd stashed all her undies, bras, nightgowns, and grubby hockey clothes in wicker pull-out baskets, and her shirts hung in neat rows, arranged according to color.

Wren chuckled. "It's like being in a shop!"

"Yeah," Spencer said bashfully, running her hands against her shirts.

"I've never heard of a window in a closet." Wren pointed to the open window on the far wall. "Seems funny."

"It was part of the original barn," Spencer explained.

"You like people watching you naked?"

"There are *blinds*," Spencer said.

"Too bad," Wren said softly. "You looked so beautiful in the bathroom. . . . I hoped I'd get to see you . . . like that . . . again."

When Spencer whirled around—*what* did he just say?—Wren was staring at her. He rubbed his fingers over the cuff of a hung-up pair of Joseph trousers. She slid her Tiffany Elsa Peretti heart ring up and down her finger, afraid to speak. Wren took a step forward, then another, until he was right next to her. Spencer could see the light smattering of freckles over his nose. The well-behaved Spencer of a parallel universe would have ducked around him and shown him the rest of the barn. But Wren kept staring at her with his huge, gorgeous brown eyes. The Spencer who was here now rubbed her lips together, afraid to speak, yet dying to do . . . something.

So then she did. She closed her eyes, reached up, and kissed him right on the lips.

Wren didn't hesitate. He kissed her back, then held on to the back of her neck and kissed her harder. His mouth was soft, and he tasted a tiny bit like cigarettes.

Spencer sank back into her wall of shirts. Wren followed. A few slipped off the hangers, but Spencer didn't care.

They sank down onto the soft carpeted floor. Spencer kicked her field hockey cleats out of the way. Wren rolled on top of her, groaning slightly. Spencer grabbed fistfuls of his worn T-shirt in her hands and pulled it over his head. He took hers off next and ran his feet up and down her legs. They rolled over and now Spencer was on top of him. A huge, overwhelming surge of—well, she didn't know what—overcame her. Whatever it was, it was so intense it didn't occur to her to feel guilty. She paused over him, breathing hard.

He reached up and kissed her again, then kissed her nose and her neck. Then he pushed himself up. "I'll be right back."

"Why?"

He motioned his eyes to his left, the direction of her bathroom.

As soon as she heard Wren shut the door, Spencer threw her head back onto the floor and stared dizzily up at her clothes. Then she scrambled up and examined herself in the three-way mirror. Her hair had come out of its ponytail and cascaded over her shoulders. Her bare skin looked luminous, and her face was slightly flushed. She grinned at the three Spencers in the mirror. This. Was. *Unbelievable*.

That was when the reflection of her computer screen, directly opposite her closet, caught her eye.

It was flashing. She turned around and squinted. It looked like she had hundreds of instant messages, piled one on top of the other. Another IM popped on the screen, this time written in 72-point font. Spencer blinked.

A A A A A: I already told you: Kissing your sister's boyfriend is WRONG.

Spencer ran up to her computer screen and read the IM again. She turned and glanced toward the bathroom; a tiny strip of light shone from underneath the door.

A was definitely not Andrew Campbell.

When she kissed Ian back in seventh grade, she told Alison about it, hoping for some advice. Ali examined her French-manicured toenails for a long moment before she finally said, "You know, I've been in your corner when it comes to Melissa. But this is different. I think you should tell her."

"*Tell her?*" Spencer shot back. "No way. She'd kill me."

"What, do you think Ian's going to go out with you?" Ali said nastily.

"I don't know," Spencer said. "Why not?"

Ali snorted. "If you don't tell her, maybe I will."

"No you won't!"

"Oh yeah?"

"If you tell Melissa," Spencer said after a moment, her heart pounding wildly, "I'll tell everyone about The Jenna Thing."

Ali barked out a laugh. "You're just as guilty as I am."

Spencer stared at Ali long and hard. "But no one saw *me*."

She turned to Spencer and gave her a fierce, angry look—scarier than any look she'd ever given any of the girls before. "You know I took care of that."

Then there was that sleepover in the barn on the last day of seventh grade. When Ali said how cute Ian and Melissa were together, Spencer realized Ali really might tell on her. Then, strangely, a light, free feeling swept over her. *Let her,* Spencer thought. She suddenly didn't care anymore. And even though it sounded horrible to say now, the truth was, Spencer wanted to be free of Ali, right then and there.

Now Spencer felt nauseous. She heard the toilet flush. Wren strode out and stood in the closet's doorway. "Now, where were we?" he cooed.

But Spencer still had her eyes on her computer screen. Something on it—a flicker of red—just moved. It looked like . . . a reflection.

"What's the matter?" Wren asked.

"Shh," Spencer said. Her eyes focused. It *was* a reflection. She spun around. There was someone outside her window.

"Holy shit," Spencer said. She held her T-shirt up against her naked chest.

"What is it?" Wren asked.

Spencer stepped back. Her throat was dry. "Oh," she croaked.

"Oh," Wren echoed.

Melissa stood outside the window, her hair messy and Medusa-like, her face absolutely expressionless. A cigarette shook in her tiny, usually steady fingers.

"I didn't know you smoked," Spencer finally said.

Melissa didn't answer. Instead, she took one more drag, threw the butt in the dewy grass, and turned back toward the main house.

"You coming, Wren?" Melissa called frostily over her shoulder.

25

STUDENT DRIVERS THESE DAYS!

Mona's mouth dropped open when she came around the corner to Noel's front lawn. "Holy shit."

Hanna leaned out the window of Sean's father's BMW and grinned at Mona. "You love it?"

Mona's eyes lit up. "I'm speechless."

Hanna smiled gratefully and took a swig from the Ketel One bottle she'd swiped from the booze table. Two minutes ago, she'd texted Mona a picture of the BMW with the message, *I'm all lubed up and out front. Come ride me.*

Mona opened the heavy passenger door and slid into the seat. She leaned over and stared intensely at the BMW insignia on the steering wheel. "It's so beautiful. . . . " She traced the little blue and white triangles with her pinkie.

Hanna flicked her hand off. "Get stoned much?"

Mona raised her chin and appraised Hanna's dirty hair, crooked dress, and tear-stained face. "Things didn't go well with Sean?"

Hanna looked down and jammed the key into the ignition.

Mona moved to hug her. "Oh Han, I'm sorry. . . . What happened?"

"Nothing. Whatever." Hanna jerked away and put on her sunglasses—which made it a little hard to see, but who cared?—and started the car. It burst into action, all of the BMW's dashboard lights switching on.

"Pretty!" Mona cried. "It's like the lights at Club Shampoo!"

Hanna slammed the gear into reverse and the tires rolled through the thick grass. Then she jerked it into drive, cut the wheel, and off they went. Hanna was too keyed up to worry about the fact that the double lines on the road were quadrupling in her vision.

"*Yee haw*," Mona whooped. She rolled down the window to let her long, blond hair flutter behind her. Hanna lit a Parliament and swiveled the Sirius radio dial until she found a retro rap station playing "Baby Got Back." She turned the volume up and the cabin throbbed—of *course* the car had the best bass money could buy.

"That's more like it," Mona said.

"Hells yeah," Hanna answered.

As she navigated a sharp turn a little too quickly, something in the back of her mind made a *ping*.

It's not gonna be you.

Ouch.

Even Daddy doesn't love you best!

Double ouch.

Well, fuck it. Hanna pressed down on the gas and nearly took out someone's dog-shaped mailbox.

"We've got to go somewhere and show this bitch off." Mona put her Miu Miu heels up on the dashboard, smearing bits of grass and dirt on it. "How 'bout Wawa? I'm jonesing for some Tastykake."

Hanna giggled and took another swig of Ketel One. "You must be super-baked."

"I'm not just baked, I'm broiled!"

They parked crookedly in the Wawa lot and sang, *"I like big BUTTS and I cannot lie!"* as they stumbled into the store. A couple of grubby delivery guys, holding 64-ounce cups of coffee and leaning against their trucks, stared with their mouths open.

"Can I have your hat?" Mona asked the skinnier of the two, pointing to his mesh ball cap that said WAWA FARMS. Without a word, the guy gave it to her.

"Ew," Hanna whispered. "That thing is germy!" But Mona had already put it on her head.

In the store, Mona bought sixteen Tastykake Butterscotch Krimpets, a copy of *Us Weekly*, and a huge bottle of Tahitian Treat; Hanna bought a Tootsie Pop for ten cents. When Mona wasn't looking, she shoved a Snickers and a pack of M&M's into her purse.

"I can hear the car," Mona said dreamily as they paid. "It's screaming."

It was true. In her drunken haze, Hanna had activated the alarm on the keychain. "Oops." She giggled.

Hooting with laughter, they ran back to the car and slid inside. They stopped at a red light, heads bobbing. The supermarket strip mall to their left was empty except for some loose shopping carts. The store's neon signs glowed vacantly; even the Outback Steakhouse bar was dead.

"People in Rosewood are such losers." Hanna gestured to the darkness.

The highway was barren too, so Hanna let out a startled, "Eep!" when a car stealthily rolled up in the lane next to her. It was a silver, pointy-nosed Porsche with tinted windows and those creepy blue headlights.

"Check that out," Mona said, Krimpet crumbs falling out of her mouth.

As they stared, the car revved its engine.

"It wants to race," Mona whispered.

"Bull," Hanna answered. She couldn't make out who was inside the car—only the red, glowing tip of a lit cigarette. An uneasy feeling washed over her.

The car revved its engine again—impatiently, this time—and she could finally see a vague outline of the driver. He revved his engine again.

Hanna raised an eyebrow at Mona, feeling drunk, hyped, and completely invincible.

"Do it," Mona whispered, pulling down the brim of the Wawa milk hat.

Hanna swallowed hard. The light turned green. As

Hanna hit the gas, the car launched forward. The Porsche growled ahead of her.

"You pussy, don't let him beat you!" Mona cried.

Hanna stepped down on the gas pedal and the engine roared. She pulled alongside the Porsche. They were doing 80, then 90, then 100. Driving this fast felt better than stealing.

"Kick his ass!" Mona screamed.

Heart pounding, Hanna pressed the pedal to the floor. She could hardly hear what Mona was saying over the engine noise. As they rounded a turn, a deer stepped into their lane. It came out of nowhere.

"Shit!" Hanna screamed. The deer stood dumbly still. She gripped the wheel tightly, hit the brakes, and swerved right, and the deer jumped out of the way. Quickly, she wrenched the wheel to straighten it out, but the car began to skid. The tires caught on a patch of gravel on the side of the road, and suddenly, they were spinning.

The car spun around and around, and then they hit something. All at once, there was a crunch, splintering glass and . . . darkness.

A split second later, the only sound in the car was a vigorous hissing noise from under the hood.

Slowly, Hanna felt her face. It was okay; nothing had hit it. And her legs could move. She pushed herself up through a bunch of folded, puffy fabric—the airbag. She checked on Mona. Her long legs kicked wildly from behind her airbag.

Hanna wiped tears from the corners of her eyes. "You okay?"

"Get this thing off me!"

Hanna got out of the car and then pulled Mona out. They stood on the side of the highway, breathing hard. Across the street were the SEPTA tracks and the dark Rosewood station. They could see far up the highway: There was no sign of the Porsche—or the deer that they'd missed. Ahead of them, the stoplights swung, turning from yellow to red.

"That was something," Mona said, her voice quivering.

Hanna nodded. "You sure you're all right?" She looked at the car.

The whole front end had crumpled into a telephone pole. The bumper hung off the car, touching the ground. One of the headlights had twisted around to a crooked angle; the other flashed crazily. Stinky steam poured out of the hood.

"You don't think it's gonna blow up, do you?" Mona asked.

Hanna giggled. This shouldn't have been funny, but it was. "What should we do?"

"We should bolt," Mona said. "We can walk home from here."

Hanna swallowed more giggles. "Oh my God. Sean's gonna shit!"

Then both girls started to laugh. Hiccupping, Hanna turned around on the empty road and spread her arms out. There was something empowering about standing in the middle of an empty four-lane highway. She felt like she owned Rosewood. She also felt like she was spinning, but maybe that was because she was still wasted. She tossed the key ring next to the car. It hit the pavement hard, and the alarm started wailing again.

Hanna quickly bent down and hit the deactivate button. The alarm stopped. "Does it have to be so *loud*?" she complained.

"Totally." Mona put her sunglasses back on. "Sean's dad should really get that fixed."

26

DO U LOVE ME? Y OR N?

The grandfather clock in the hall rang at 9 A.M. on Saturday morning as Emily padded quietly down the stairs to the kitchen. She never got up this early on the weekends, but this morning, she couldn't sleep.

Someone had made coffee, and there were sticky buns sitting out on a chicken-print plate on the table. It looked as if her parents had gone out for their never-fail, rain-or-shine Saturday crack-of-dawn walk. If they did their two loops around the neighborhood, Emily could get out of here without anybody noticing.

Last night, after Ben caught her and Maya in the photo booth, Emily had bolted from the party—without saying good-bye to Maya. Emily had called Carolyn—who *was* at Applebee's—and asked for a ride, pronto. Carolyn and Topher, her boyfriend, came, no questions asked, although her sister gave Emily—who stank of whiskey—a stern, parental look when she climbed in the backseat. At home, she'd hidden under her covers so she wouldn't have to talk to Carolyn and dropped off into a deep sleep. But this morning, she felt worse than ever.

She didn't know what to think about what happened at the party. It was all a blur. She wanted to believe that kissing Maya had been a mistake, and that she could explain everything to Ben and it would be okay. But Emily kept returning to how everything felt. It was like . . . before last night, she'd never been kissed before.

But there was nothing, *nothing* about Emily that said lesbian. She bought girly hot-oil treatments for her chlorine-damaged hair. She had a poster of the hot Australian swimmer Ian Thorpe on her wall. She giggled with the other swimmer girls about the boys in their Speedos. She'd only kissed one other girl, years ago, and that didn't count. Even if it did, it didn't mean anything, right?

She broke a Danish in half and stuffed a piece in her mouth. Her head throbbed. She wanted things to go back to the way they were. To throw a fresh towel in her duffel and head to practice, to happily make goofy pig faces into someone's digital camera on the away-meet bus. To be content with herself and her life and to not be an emotional yo-yo.

So that was it. Maya was awesome and all, but they were just confused—and sad, for their own reasons. But not gay. Right?

She needed some air.

It was desolate outside. The birds were chirping

noisily, and someone's dog kept barking, but everything was still. Freshly delivered papers were still waiting on front lawns, wrapped in blue plastic.

Her old, red Trek mountain bike was propped up against the side of the toolshed. Emily jerked it upright, hoping she'd be coordinated enough to handle a bike after last night's whiskey. She pushed off to the street, but her bike's front wheel made a flapping noise.

Emily bent down. There was something caught in the wheel. A piece of notebook paper was woven through the spokes. She pulled it out and read a few lines. Wait. This was her own handwriting.

. . . I love staring at the back of your head in class, I love how you chew gum whenever we're talking on the phone together, and I love that when you jiggle your Skechers during class when Mrs. Hat starts talking about famous American court cases, I know you're totally bored.

Emily's eyes darted around her empty front yard. Was this what she thought it was? She nervously skimmed down to the bottom, her mouth dry.

. . . and I've done a lot of thinking about why I kissed you the other day. I realized: It wasn't a joke, Ali. I think I love you. I can understand if you never want to speak to me again, but I just had to tell you. —Em

There was something else written on the other side of the paper. She flipped it over.

Thought you might want this back.

Love, A

Emily let her bike clatter to the ground.

This was *the* letter to Ali, the very one Emily had sent right after the kiss. The one she'd wondered if Ali had ever gotten.

Calm down, Emily told herself, realizing her hands were trembling. *There's a logical explanation for this.*

It had to be Maya. She lived in Ali's old room. Emily had told Maya about Alison and the letter last night. Maybe she was just giving it back?

But then . . . *Love, A*. Maya wouldn't write that.

Emily didn't know what to do or who to talk to. Suddenly, she thought of Aria. So much had happened last night after Emily ran into her, she'd forgotten their conversation. What had all Aria's bizarre Alison questions been about? And there was something about her expression last night. Aria seemed . . . nervous.

Emily sat on the ground and looked at the "Thought you might want this back" message again. If Emily recalled correctly, Aria had spiky handwriting that looked a lot like this.

In the last days before Ali had gone missing, she'd held the kiss over Emily's head, forcing Emily to go along with whatever she wanted to do. It hadn't occurred to Emily that maybe Ali had told the rest of their friends. But maybe . . .

"Honey?"

Emily jumped. Her parents stood above her, dressed in sensible white sneakers, high-waisted shorts, and preppy pastel golf shirts. Her father had a red fanny pack, and her mom swung turquoise arm weights back and forth.

"Hey," Emily croaked.

"Going for a bike ride?" her mother asked.

"Uh-huh."

"You're supposed to be grounded." Her father put on his glasses, as if he needed to see Emily to scold her. "We only let you out last night because you were going with Ben. We hoped he'd get through to you. But bike rides are off limits."

"Well," Emily groaned, standing up. If only she didn't have to explain things to her parents. But then . . . whatever. She wouldn't. Not now. She threw her leg over the bar and sat on her seat.

"I have somewhere to go," she mumbled, pedaling down the driveway.

"Emily, come back here," her father yelled gruffly.

But Emily, for the first time in her life, just kept pedaling.

27

DON'T MIND ME, I'M JUST DEAD!

Aria awoke to her doorbell ringing. Except it wasn't her family's normal doorbell chime, it was "American Idiot," by Green Day. Huh—when had her parents changed that?

She threw back her duvet, slid on the blue-flowered, fur-lined clogs she'd bought in Amsterdam, and clomped down the spiral staircase to see who it was.

When she opened the door, she gasped. It was Alison. She was taller and her blond hair was cut in long shaggy layers. Her face looked more glamorous and angular than it had in seventh grade.

"Ta-*daa!*" Ali grinned and spread out her arms. "I'm back!"

"Holy . . . " Aria choked on her words, blinking furiously a couple of times. "*Wh*-where have you been?"

Ali rolled her eyes. "My stupid parents," she said. "Remember my aunt Camille, the really cool one who was born in France and married my uncle Jeff when we

were in seventh? I went to visit her in Miami that summer. Then, I liked it so much that I just stayed. I totally
told my parents about all of it, but I guess they forgot to
tell everyone else."

Aria rubbed her eyes. "So, wait. You've been in . . .
Miami? You're *okay*?"

Ali twirled around a little. "I look more than okay,
don't I? Hey, did you like my texts?"

Aria's smile faded. "Um . . . no, actually."

Ali looked hurt. "Why not? That one about your
mom was *so* funny."

Aria stared at her.

"God, you're sensitive." Ali narrowed her eyes. "Are
you going to blow me off again?"

"Wait, what?" Aria stammered.

Alison gave Aria a long look, and a black, gelatinous
substance began dripping out her nostrils. "I told the others, you know. About your dad. I told them everything."

"Your . . . nose . . . " Aria pointed. Suddenly it started
seeping out of Ali's eyeballs. Like she was crying oil. It
was dripping from her fingernails, too.

"Oh, I'm just rotting." Ali smiled.

Aria jerked up in bed. Sweat drenched the back of her
neck. The sun streamed in through her window, and she
heard "American Idiot" on her brother's stereo next door.
She checked her hands for black goo, but they were
squeaky clean.

Whoa.

"Morning, honey."

Aria staggered down her spiral staircase to see her father, dressed only in thin, tartan plaid boxer shorts and a sleeveless T-shirt, reading the *Philadelphia Inquirer.* "Hey," she murmured back.

Shuffling to the espresso machine, she stared for a long time at her father's pale, randomly hairy shoulders. He jiggled his feet and made *hmmm* noises at the paper.

"Dad?" Her voice cracked slightly.

"Mmm?"

Aria leaned against the stone-topped island. "Can ghosts send text messages?"

Her father looked up, surprised and confused. "What's a text message?"

She stuck her hand into an open box of Frosted Mini Wheats and pulled out a handful. "Never mind."

"You sure?" Byron asked.

She chewed nervously. What did she want to ask? *Is a ghost sending me texts?* But c'mon, she knew better. Anyway, she didn't know why Ali's ghost would come back and do this to her. It was as if she wanted revenge, but was that possible?

Ali had been great the day they caught her dad in the car. Aria had fled around the corner and ran until she had to start walking. She kept walking all the way home, not sure what else to do with herself. Ali hugged her for a long time. "I won't tell," she whispered.

But the next day, the questions started. *Do you know that girl? Is she a student? Is your dad going to tell your mom? Do you think he's doing it with lots of students?* Usually, Aria could take Ali's inquisitiveness and even her teasing—she was okay with being the "weird kid" of the group. But this was different. This *hurt.*

So the last few days of school, before she disappeared, Aria avoided Alison. She didn't send her "I'm bored" texts during health class or help her clean out her locker. And she certainly didn't talk about what happened. She was mad that Ali was prying—as if it was some celebrity gossip in *Star* and not her life. She was mad that Ali knew. Period.

Now, three years later, Aria wondered who she'd really been mad at. It wasn't really Ali. It was her dad.

"Really, never mind," Aria answered her father, who'd been waiting patiently, sipping his coffee. "I'm just sleepy."

"Okay," Byron answered incredulously.

The doorbell rang. It wasn't the Green Day song but their normal *bong, bong* chime. Her father looked up. "I wonder if that's for Mike," he said. "Did you know that some girl from the Quaker school came by here at eight-thirty, looking for him?"

"I'll get it," Aria said.

She tentatively pulled open the front door, but it was only Emily Fields on the other side, her reddish-blond hair messy and her eyes swollen.

"Hey," Emily croaked.

"Hey," Aria answered.

Emily puffed up her cheeks with air—her old nervous habit. She stood there for a moment. Then she said, "I should go." She started to turn.

"Wait." Aria caught her arm. "What? What's going on?"

Emily paused. "Um. Okay. But . . . this is going to sound weird."

"That's okay." Aria's heart started to pound.

"I was thinking about what you were saying yesterday at the party. About Ali. I was wondering . . . did Ali ever tell you guys something about me?"

Emily said it very quietly. Aria pushed her hair out of her eyes.

"What?" Aria whispered. "Recently?"

Emily's eyes widened. "What do you mean, *recently*?"

"I—"

"In seventh grade," Emily interrupted. "Did she tell you . . . like . . . something about me in seventh grade? Was she telling everybody?"

Aria blinked. At the party yesterday, when she'd seen Emily, she'd wanted more than anything to tell her about the texts. "No," Aria answered slowly. "She never talked behind your back."

"Oh." Emily stared at the ground. "But I—" she started.

"I've been getting these—" Aria said at the same time. Then Emily looked past her and her eyes grew still.

"Miss Emily Fields! Hello!"

Aria turned. In the living room stood Byron. At least he'd thrown on a striped bathrobe. "I haven't seen you in ages!" Byron boomed.

"Yeah." Emily puffed out her cheeks again. "How are you, Mr. Montgomery?"

He frowned. "Please. You're old enough to call me Byron." He scratched his chin with the top edge of his coffee cup. "How's your life? Good?"

"Absolutely." Emily looked like she was about to cry.

"Do you need something to eat?" Byron asked. "You look hungry."

"Oh. No. Thanks. I, um, I guess I didn't really sleep well."

"You girls." He shook his head. "You never sleep! I always tell Aria she needs eleven hours—she needs to bank sleep for when she gets to college and parties all night!" He began climbing the stairs to the second floor.

As soon as he was out of sight, Aria whirled back around. "He's so—" she started. But then she realized Emily was halfway across her lawn, on the way to her bike. "Hey!" she called. "Where are you going?"

Emily picked her bike up off the ground. "I shouldn't have come."

"Wait! Come back! I . . . I need to talk to you!" Aria
called out.

Emily paused and looked up. Aria felt all of her words
swarming like bees in her mouth. Emily seemed terrified.

But suddenly Aria was too afraid to ask. How would
she talk about the texts from A without mentioning her
secret? She still didn't want anyone to know. Especially
with her mom just upstairs.

Then she thought of Byron in his bathrobe and how
uncomfortable Emily seemed around him just now. Emily
had asked, *Did Alison tell you something about me in seventh
grade?* Why would she ask that?

Unless . . .

Aria bit her pinkie nail. What if Emily already *knew*
Aria's secret? Aria clamped her mouth shut, paralyzed.

Emily shook her head. "I'll see you later," she mumbled, and before Aria could compose herself, Emily was
biking furiously away.

28

BRAD AND ANGELINA ACTUALLY MET AT THE ROSEWOOD POLICE STATION

"Ladies, discover yourselves!"

As Oprah's audience clapped wildly, Hanna sank into her coffee-colored leather couch cushions, balancing the TiVo remote on her bare stomach. She could use a little self-discovery on this crisp Saturday morning.

Last night was pretty blurry—like she'd gone through the night without her contacts in—and her head was throbbing. Had it involved some sort of animal? She'd found some empty candy wrappers in her purse. Had she eaten them? *All* of them? Her stomach hurt, after all, and it looked a little puffy. And why did she have a distinct memory of a Wawa dairy truck? It felt like piecing together a puzzle, except Hanna was too impatient for puzzles—she always jammed pieces together that didn't actually fit.

The doorbell rang. Hanna groaned, then rolled off the couch, not bothering to fix her army-green ribbed tank top, which was turned around and practically exposing her boob. She cracked the oak door and then slammed it shut again.

Whoa. It was that cop, Mr. April. Er, Darren Wilden.

"Open up, Hanna."

She checked him out through the peephole. He stood with his arms crossed, seeming all business, but then his hair was a mess and she didn't see his gun anywhere. And what kind of cop worked at 10 A.M. on a cloudless Saturday morning like this?

Hanna glanced at her reflection in the round mirror across the room. Jesus. Sleep marks from the pillow? Yes. Puffy eyes, lips in need of gloss? Absolutely. She quickly ran her hands over her face, pushed her hair into a ponytail, and put on her round Chanel sunglasses. Then she flung open the door.

"Hey!" she said brightly. "How are you?"

"Is your mom home?" he asked.

"Nope," Hanna said flirtatiously. "She's out all morning."

Wilden pursed his lips together, looking stressed. Hanna noticed Wilden had a little clear Band-Aid right above his eyebrow. "What, did your girlfriend deck you?" she asked, pointing at it.

"No . . . " Wilden touched the Band-Aid. "I banged it on my medicine cabinet when I was washing my face."

He rolled his eyes. "I'm not the most graceful person in the morning."

Hanna smiled. "Join the club. I fell on my ass last night. It was so random."

Wilden's kind expression was suddenly grim. "Was that before or after you stole the car?"

Hanna stood back. "What?"

Why was Wilden looking at her as if she were the love child of space aliens? "There was an anonymous tip that you stole a car," he enunciated slowly.

Hanna's mouth fell open. "I . . . *what*?"

"A black BMW? Belonging to a Mr. Edwin Ackard? You crashed it into a phone pole? After you drank a bottle of Ketel One? Any of this sound familiar?"

Hanna shoved her sunglasses up her nose. Wait, *that* was what happened? "I wasn't drunk last night," she lied.

"We found a vodka bottle on the driver's-side floor in the car," Wilden said. "So, *someone* was drunk."

"But—" Hanna started.

"I have to bring you into the station," Wilden interrupted, sounding a little disappointed.

"I didn't steal it," Hanna squeaked. "Sean—his son—said I could take it!"

Wilden raised an eyebrow. "So you admit you were driving it?"

"I—" Hanna started. *Shit.* She took a step back into the house. "But my mom's not even here. She won't know what happened to me." Embarrassingly, tears rushed to her eyes. She turned away, trying to get her shit together.

Wilden shifted his weight uncomfortably. It seemed like he didn't know what to do with his hands—first he put them in his pockets, then they hovered near Hanna, then he wrung them together. "Listen, we can call your mom at the station, all right?" he said. "And I won't cuff you. And you can ride up front with me." He walked back to his car and opened the passenger door for her.

An hour later, she sat on the police station's same yellow plastic bucket seats, staring at the same *Chester County's Most Wanted* poster, fighting back the urge to start crying again. She'd just been given a blood test to see if she was still drunk from last night. Hanna wasn't sure if she was—did alcohol stay in your body for that long? Now Wilden was hunching over his same desk, which held the same Bic pens and a metallic Slinky. She pinched her palm with her fingernails and swallowed.

Unfortunately, the events of last night had coalesced in her head. The Porsche, the deer, the airbag. *Had* Sean said she could take the car? She doubted it; the last thing she could remember was his little self-esteem speech before he'd ditched her in the woods.

"Hey, were you at the Swarthmore battle of the bands last night?"

A college-age guy with a buzz cut and a uni-brow sat next to her. He wore a ripped flannel surfer's shirt, paint-spattered jeans, and no shoes. His hands were cuffed. "Um, no," Hanna muttered.

He leaned close to her, and Hanna could smell his beery breath. "Oh. I thought I saw you there. I was and I drank too much and started terrorizing someone's cows. That's why I'm here! I was trespassing!"

"Good for you," she answered frostily.

"What's your name?" He jingled his cuffs.

"Um, Angelina." Like hell she was giving him her real name.

"Hey, Angelina," he said. "I'm Brad!"

Hanna cracked a smile at how lame that line was.

Just then, the station's front door opened. Hanna jerked back in her seat and pushed her sunglasses up her nose. Great. It was her mom.

"I came as soon as I heard," Ms. Marin said to Wilden.

This morning, Ms. Marin wore a simple white boat-neck tee, low-waisted James jeans, Gucci slingbacks, and the exact same Chanel shades that Hanna was wearing. Her skin radiated—she'd been at the spa all morning—and her red-gold hair was pulled back into a simple ponytail. Hanna squinted. Had her mom stuffed her bra? Her boobs looked like they belonged to someone else.

"I'll talk to her," Ms. Marin said to Wilden in a low voice. Then she walked over to Hanna. She smelled of seaweed body wrap. Hanna, certain that she smelled of Ketel One and Eggo waffles, tried to shrink in her seat.

"I'm sorry," Hanna squeaked.

"Did they make you take a blood test?" she hissed.

She nodded miserably.

"What else did you tell them?"

"N-n-nothing," she stuttered.

Ms. Marin laced her French-manicured hands together. "Okay. I'll handle this. Just be quiet."

"What are you going to do?" she whispered back. "Are you going to call Sean's dad?"

"I said I'll *handle* it, Hanna."

Her mother rose up from the plastic bucket seats and leaned over Wilden's desk. Hanna tore through her purse for her emergency pack of Twizzlers Pull-n-Peel. She'd just have a couple, not the whole pack. It had to be in here somewhere.

As she pulled out the Twizzlers, she felt her BlackBerry buzzing. Hanna hesitated. What if it was Sean, chewing her out via voice mail? What if it was Mona? Where the hell *was* Mona? Had they actually let her go to the golf tourney? She hadn't stolen the car, but she'd come along for the ride. That had to count for something.

Her BlackBerry had a few missed calls. Sean . . . six times. Mona, twice, at 8 A.M. and 8:03. There were also some new text messages: a bunch from kids at the party, unrelated, and then one from a cell number she didn't know. Hanna's stomach knotted.

Hanna: Remember the KATE toothbrush? Thought so! —A

Hanna blinked. A cold, clammy sweat gathered on the back of her neck. She felt dizzy. *The Kate toothbrush?* "Come on," she said shakily, trying to laugh. She glanced up at her mother, but she was still bent over Wilden's desk, talking.

When she was in Annapolis, after her father told Hanna that she was, essentially, a pig, Hanna shot up from the table and ran inside. She ducked into the powder room, shut the door, and sat down on the toilet.

She took deep breaths, trying to calm down. Why couldn't she be beautiful and graceful and perfect like Ali or Kate? Why did she have to be who she was, dumpy and clumsy and a wreck? And she wasn't sure who she was angriest at—her dad, Kate, herself, or . . . Alison.

As Hanna choked on hot, angry tears, she noticed the three framed pictures on the wall across from the toilet. All three were close-ups of someone's eyes. She recognized her father's squinty, expressive eyes right away. And there were Isabel's small, almond-shaped ones. The third pair of eyes were large, intoxicating. They looked like they were straight out of a Chanel mascara ad. They were obviously Kate's.

They were all watching her.

Hanna stared at herself in the mirror. A peal of laughter floated in from outside. Her stomach felt like it was bursting from all the popcorn everyone had watched her eat. She felt so sick, she just wanted it *out* of there, but when she leaned over the toilet, nothing happened. Tears spilled down her cheeks. As she reached for a Kleenex, she noticed a green toothbrush sitting in a little porcelain cup. It gave her an idea.

It took her ten minutes to work up the nerve to put it into her throat, but when she did, she felt worse—but also better. She started crying even harder, but she also wanted to do it again. As she eased the toothbrush back in her mouth, the bathroom door burst open.

It was Alison. Her eyes swept over Hanna kneeling on the floor, the toothbrush in her hand. "Whoa," she said.

"Please go away," Hanna whispered.

Alison took a step into the bathroom. "Do you want to talk about it?"

Hanna looked at her desperately. "At least close the door!"

Ali shut the door and sat on the side of the tub. "How long have you been doing this for?"

Hanna's lip quivered. "Doing what?"

Ali paused, looking at the toothbrush. Her eyes widened. Hanna looked at it too. She hadn't noticed before, but KATE was printed on the side in white letters.

A phone rang loudly in the police station and Hanna flinched. *Remember the Kate toothbrush?* Someone else might have known about Hanna's eating problem, or might have seen her going into the police station, or might even know about Kate. But the *green toothbrush*? There was only one person who knew about that.

Hanna liked to believe that if Ali were alive, she'd be rooting for her, now that her life was so perfect. That was the scene she replayed in her mind constantly—Ali impressed by her size 2 jeans. Ali oohing over her Chanel lip gloss. Ali congratulating Hanna on how she'd planned the perfect pool party.

With shaking hands, Hanna typed, *Is this Alison?*

"Wilden," a cop shouted. "We need you in the back."

Hanna looked up. Darren Wilden rose from his desk, excusing himself from Hanna's mom. Within seconds, the whole precinct burst into action. A cop car flew out of the parking lot; three more followed. Phones rang maniacally; four cops sprinted through the room.

"It looks like something big," said Brad, the drunk trespasser sitting next to her. Hanna flinched—she'd forgotten he was there.

"A donut shortage?" she asked, trying to laugh.

"Bigger." He jiggled his handcuffed hands excitedly. "Looks like something *very* big."

29

GOOD MORNING, WE HATE YOU

The sun streamed in through the barn's window, and for the first time in Spencer's life, she was awakened by the chirping of high-on-life sparrows instead of the frightening '90s techno mix her dad blasted from the main house's exercise room. But could she enjoy it? Nope.

Although she hadn't drunk a drop last night, her body felt achy, chilled, and hungover. There was zero sleep in her fuel tank. After Wren left, she'd tried to sleep, but her mind spun. The way Wren held her felt so . . . different. Spencer had never felt anything remotely like that before.

But then that IM. And Melissa's calm, spooky expression. And . . .

As the night wore on, the barn creaked and groaned, and Spencer pulled the covers up to her nose, shaking. She chided herself for feeling paranoid and immature, but she couldn't help it. She kept thinking of the possibilities.

Eventually, she'd gotten up and rebooted her computer. For a few hours, she searched the Internet. First she looked at technical websites, searching for answers on how to trace IMs. No luck. Then she tried to find where that first e-mail—the one titled "covet"—had come from. She wanted, desperately, for the trail to end at Andrew Campbell.

She found that Andrew had a blog, but after scouring the whole thing, she found nothing. The entries were all about the books Andrew liked to read, dorky boy philoso-phizing, a couple of melancholy passages about an unre-quited crush on some girl he never named. She thought he might slip up and give himself away, but he didn't.

Finally, she plugged in the key words *missing persons* and *Alison DiLaurentis.*

She found the same stuff from three years ago—the reports on CNN and in the *Philadelphia Inquirer,* search groups, and kooky sites, like one showing what Ali might look like with different hairstyles. Spencer stared at the school picture they'd used; she hadn't seen a photo of Ali in a long time. Would she recognize Ali if she had, for instance, a short, black bob? She certainly looked different in this picture they'd created.

The main house's screen door squeaked as she nervously pushed through it. Inside, she smelled freshly brewed coffee, which was odd, because usually her mom was already at the stables by now and her dad was riding or at the golf course. She wondered what had happened between Melissa and Wren after last night, praying she wouldn't have to face them.

"We've been waiting for you."

Spencer jumped. At the kitchen table were her parents and Melissa. Her mother's face was pale and drained and her dad's cheeks were beet red. Melissa's eyes were red-rimmed and puffy. Even the two dogs didn't jump up to greet her as they normally did.

Spencer swallowed hard. So much for praying.

"Sit down, please," her father said quietly.

Spencer scraped back a wooden chair and sat next to her mother. The room was so still and silent, she could hear her stomach, nervously on spin cycle.

"I don't even know what to say," her mother croaked. "How *could* you?"

Spencer's stomach dropped. She opened her mouth, but her mother held up her hand. "You have no right to talk right now."

Spencer clamped her mouth shut and lowered her eyes.

"Honestly," her father said, "I am so mortified you're my daughter right now. I thought we raised you better."

Spencer picked at a rough cuticle on her thumb and tried to stop her chin from wobbling.

"What were you thinking?" her mother asked. "That was her *boyfriend*. They were planning to move *in* together. Do you realize what you've done?"

"I–" Spencer started.

"I mean . . . ," her mother interrupted, then wrung her hands and looked down.

"You're under eighteen, which means we're legally responsible for you," her father said. "But if it were up to me, I'd lock you out of this house right now."

"I wish I never had to see you again," Melissa spat.

Spencer felt faint. She half-expected them to set down their coffee cups and tell her they were just kidding, that everything was all right. But they couldn't even *look* at her. Her dad's words stung in her ears: *I am so mortified you're my daughter.* No one had ever said anything like that to her before.

"One thing's for certain; Melissa will be moving into the barn," her mother continued. "I want all of your stuff out and back into your old bedroom. And once her town house is ready, I'm turning the barn into a pottery studio."

Spencer balled up her fists under the table, willing herself not to cry. She didn't care about the barn, not really. It was what came with the barn that mattered. It was that her dad was going to build shelves for her. Her mom was going to help her pick out new curtains. They'd said she could get a kitten and they'd all spent a few minutes thinking up funny names for it. They were excited for her. They *cared*.

She reached out for her mother's arm. "I'm sorry–"

Her mother slid her body away. "Spencer, don't."

Spencer couldn't manage to swallow her sob. Tears started running down her cheeks.

"It's not me you need to apologize to, anyway," her mother said in a low voice.

Spencer looked at Melissa, sniveling across the table. She wiped her nose. As much as she hated Melissa, she'd never seen her sister this miserable—not since Ian broke up with her back in high school. It was wrong to flirt with Wren, but Spencer hadn't thought it would go as far as it did. She tried to put herself in Melissa's place—if she'd met Wren first, and Melissa had kissed him, she'd be shattered too. Her heart softened. "I'm sorry," she whispered.

Melissa shuddered. "Rot in hell," she spat.

Spencer bit the inside of her mouth so hard she tasted blood.

"Just get your things out of the barn." Her mother sighed. "Then get out of our sight."

Spencer's eyes widened. "But—" she squeaked.

Her father gave her a withering look.

"It's just so despicable," her mother murmured.

"You're such a bitch," Melissa threw in.

Spencer nodded—perhaps if she agreed with them, they would stop. She wanted to shrivel up into a tiny ball and evaporate. Instead, she mumbled, "I'll go do it now."

"Good." Her father took another sip of coffee and left the table.

Melissa made a small squeak and pushed back her chair. She sobbed the whole way up the stairs and slammed her bedroom door.

"Wren left last night," Mr. Hastings said as he paused in the doorway. "We won't be hearing from him, ever again. And if you know what's best for you, *you* won't talk about him ever again."

"Of course," Spencer mumbled, and set her head down on the cool oak table.

"Good."

Spencer kept her head firmly on the table, breathing yoga fire breaths and waiting for someone to come back and tell her that everything would be okay. Nobody did. Outside, she heard an ambulance siren screaming in the distance. It sounded like it was coming toward the house.

Spencer sat up. *Oh God.* What if Melissa had . . . hurt herself? She wouldn't, would she? The sirens howled, coming closer. Spencer shoved back her chair.

Holy shit. What had she done?

"Melissa!" she yelled, running to the stairs.

"You're a whore!" came a voice. "You're a fucking whore!"

Spencer slumped back against the railing. Well, then. It seemed Melissa was just fine, after all.

30

THE CIRCUS IS BACK IN TOWN

Emily biked furiously away from Aria's house, narrowly missing a jogger on the side of the road. "Watch it!" he yelled.

As she passed a neighbor walking two huge Great Danes, Emily made a decision. She had to go to Maya's. It was the only answer. Maybe Maya had meant it in a nice way, like she was just returning the note after Emily told her about Alison last night. Maybe Maya wanted to mention the letter last night but, for whatever reason, she didn't. Maybe the *A* was really an *M*?

Besides, she and Maya had tons of other stuff to talk about—besides the note. Try everything that happened at the party. Emily closed her eyes, remembering. She could practically smell Maya's banana gum and feel the soft contours of her mouth. Opening her eyes, she swerved away from the curb.

Okay, they definitely needed to work that out. But what did Emily want to say?

I loved it.

No. Of course she wouldn't say that. She would say, *We should just be friends.* She was going back to Ben, after all. If he'd have her. She wanted to rewind time, to go back to being the Emily who was happy with her life, who her parents were happy with. The Emily who only worried about her breaststroke reach and her algebra homework.

Emily pedaled past Myer Park, where she and Ali used to swing for hours. They tried to pump together in unison, and when they were completely even, Ali always called out, "We're married!" Then they'd squeal and jump off at the same time.

But what if Maya hadn't put that note on her bike? When Emily asked Aria if Ali had told her Emily's secret, Aria had replied, "What, recently?" Why would Aria say that? Unless . . . unless Aria knew something. Unless Ali was back.

Was that possible?

Emily skidded through the gravel. No, that was crazy. Her mother still exchanged holiday cards with Mrs. DiLaurentis; she would've heard if Ali had returned. Back when Ali vanished, it was on the news 24/7. These days, her parents usually had on CNN while they ate breakfast. It would surely be a top story again.

Still, it was thrilling to consider. Every night for almost a year after Ali's disappearance, Emily had asked her Magic 8 Ball if Alison would come back. Although it sometimes said, *Wait and see*, it never, ever said, *No*. She made bets with herself, too: *If two kids get on the school bus today wearing red shirts*, she would whisper to herself, *Ali is okay*. *If they're serving pizza at lunch, Ali's not dead*. *If Coach makes us practice starts and turns, Ali will come back*. Nine times out of ten, according to Emily's little superstitions, Ali was on her way back to them.

Maybe she'd been right all along.

She pumped uphill and around a sharp turn, narrowly avoiding a stone Revolutionary War battle memorial sign. If Ali was back, what would that mean for Emily's friendship with Maya? She sort of doubted she could have two best friends . . . two best friends she felt so similarly about. She wondered what Ali would even think of Maya. What if they hated each other?

I loved it.

We should just be friends.

She swept past the beautiful farmhouses, crumbling stone inns, and gardeners' pickups parked on the road's shoulder. She used to bike this exact route to Ali's house; the last time, in fact, had been before the kiss. Emily hadn't planned to kiss Ali before she came; something had come over her in the heat of the moment. She would never forget how soft Ali's lips were or the stunned look on Ali's face when she pulled back. "What did you do that for?" she'd asked.

Suddenly, a siren wailed behind her. Emily barely had time to move to the edge of the road again before a Rosewood ambulance screamed past. A gust of wind kicked up, blowing dust into her face. She wiped her eyes and stared as the ambulance got to the top of the hill and paused at Alison's street.

Now it was turning onto Alison's street. Fear seized Emily. Ali's street was . . . Maya's street. She gripped the rubber handles of her bike.

With all the craziness, she'd forgotten the secret Maya had told her last night. The cutting. The hospital. That huge, jagged scar. *Sometimes I just feel like I need to,* Maya had said.

"Oh my God," Emily whispered.

She pedaled furiously and skidded around the corner. *If the ambulance sirens stop by the time I get around the corner,* she thought, *Maya will be okay.*

But then the ambulance pulled to a stop in front of Maya's house. The sirens were still roaring. Police cars were everywhere.

"No," Emily whispered. White-coated medics got out of the vehicle and ran for the house. A ton of people littered Maya's yard, some with cameras. Emily threw her bike at the curb and ran crookedly toward the house.

"Emily!"

Maya burst through the crowd. Emily gasped, then ran into Maya's arms, tears messily running down her face.

"You're okay." Emily sobbed. "I was afraid—"

"I'm fine," Maya said.

But there was something in her voice that was clearly *not* fine. Emily stood back. Maya's eyes were red and watery. Her mouth was drawn down nervously.

"What is it?" Emily asked. "What's going on?"

Maya swallowed. "They found your friend."

"What?" Emily stared at her, then at the scene on Maya's lawn. It was all so eerily familiar: the ambulance, the cop cars, the crowds of people, the long-lensed cameras. A news helicopter hovered overhead. This was exactly the same scene as three years ago, when Ali went missing.

Emily stepped back out of Maya's arms, grinning in disbelief. She *had* been right!

Alison was back at her house, like nothing had ever happened. "I knew it!" she whispered.

Maya took Emily's hand. "They were digging for our tennis court. My mom was there. She . . . saw her. I heard her scream from my bedroom."

Emily dropped her hand. "Wait. What?"

"I tried to call you," Maya added.

Emily wrinkled her brow and stared back at Maya. Then she looked at the twenty-strong team of cops.

At Mrs. St. Germain sobbing by the tire swing. At the POLICE LINE, DO NOT CROSS tape loops around the back-yard. And then at the van parked in the driveway. It said, ROSEWOOD PD MORGUE. She had to read it six times for it to make sense. Her heart sped up and suddenly she couldn't breathe.

"I don't . . . understand," Emily sputtered, taking another step back. "Who did they find?"

Maya looked at her sympathetically, her eyes shiny with tears. "Your friend Alison," she whispered. "They just found her body."

31

HELL *IS* OTHER PEOPLE

Byron Montgomery took a big sip of coffee and shakily lit his pipe. "They found her when they were excavating the concrete slab in the DiLaurentises' old backyard to put in a tennis court."

"She was under the concrete," Ella jumped in. "They knew it was her from the ring she was wearing. But they're doing DNA tests to make sure."

It felt like a fist was pummeling Aria's stomach. She remembered Ali's white-gold initialed ring. Ali's parents had gotten it for her at Tiffany's when she was ten after she got her tonsils out. Ali liked to wear it on her pinkie.

"Why did they have to do DNA tests?" Mike asked. "Was she all decomposed?"

"Michelangelo!" Byron frowned. "That's not a very sensitive thing to say in front of your sister."

Mike shrugged and jammed a piece of sour green-apple Bubble Tape into his mouth. Aria sat opposite him, tears quietly running down her cheeks, absentmindedly unraveling the edge of a rattan place mat. It was 2 P.M., and they were sitting around the kitchen table.

"I can handle it." Aria's throat constricted. "*Was* she decomposed?"

Her parents looked at each other. "Well, yes," her father said, scratching his chest through a little hole in his shirt. "Bodies break down pretty fast."

"Sick," Mike whispered.

Aria shut her eyes. Alison was dead. Her body was rotted. Someone had probably killed her.

"Sweetheart?" Ella asked quietly, cupping her hand over Aria's. "Honey, are you all right?"

"I don't know," Aria murmured, trying not to start bawling all over again.

"Would you like a Xanax?" Byron asked.

Aria shook her head.

"*I'll* take a Xanax," Mike said quickly.

Aria nervously picked at the side of her thumb. Her body felt hot and then cold. She didn't know what to do or think. The only person who she thought might make her feel better was Ezra; she thought she could explain all of her feelings to him. At the very least, he would let her curl up on his denim futon and cry.

Scraping back her chair, she started for her room. Byron and Ella exchanged glances and followed her to the spiral staircase.

"Sweetie?" Ella asked. "What can we do?"

But Aria ignored them and pushed through her bedroom door. Her room was a disaster. Aria hadn't cleaned
since she'd moved back from Iceland, and she wasn't the
neatest girl in the world to start with. Her clothes were all
over the floor in unorganized piles. On her bed were
CDs, sequins she was using to make a beaded hat, poster
paints, playing cards, Pigtunia, line drawings of Ezra's
profile, several skeins of yarn. The carpet had a big, red
candle wax stain on it. She searched in the covers of her
bed and on the surface of her desk for her Treo—she
needed it to call Ezra. But it wasn't there. She checked
the green bag she'd taken to the party last night, but her
phone wasn't in that, either.

Then she remembered. After she received that text,
she'd dropped the phone like it was poisonous. She must
have left it behind.

She stormed down the stairs. Her parents were still on
the landing.

"I'm taking the car," she mumbled, grabbing the keys
off the ring by the foyer table.

"Okay," her father said.

"Take your time," her mother added.

Someone had propped the front door to Ezra's house
open with a large metal sculpture of a terrier. Aria
stepped around it and walked inside the hallway. She
knocked on Ezra's door. She had the same feeling she
did when she had to pee really badly—it might be

torture, but you knew that very soon, you were going to feel a whole hell of a lot better.

Ezra flung open the door. As soon as he saw her, he tried to shut it again.

"Wait," Aria squeaked, her voice still filled with tears. Ezra retreated into his kitchen, his back to her. She followed him in.

Ezra whirled around to face her. He was unshaven and looked exhausted. "What are you doing here?"

Aria chewed on her lip. "I'm here to see you. I got some news. . . . " Her Treo sat on his sideboard. She picked it up. "Thanks. You found it."

Ezra glared at the Treo. "Okay, you got it. Can you leave now?"

"What's going on?" She walked toward him. "I got this news. I had to see—"

"Yeah, I got some news too," he interrupted. Ezra moved away from her. "Seriously, Aria. I can't . . . I can't even look at you."

Tears sprang to her eyes. *"What?"* Aria stared at him, confused.

Ezra lowered his eyes. "I found what you said about me on your cell phone."

Aria wrinkled her eyebrows. "My cell phone?"

Ezra raised his head. His eyes flashed with anger. "Do you think I'm stupid? Was this all just a game? A *dare?*"

"What are you . . . ?"

Ezra sighed angrily. "Well, you know what? You got

me. Okay? I'm the brunt of your big joke. You happy? Now get out."

"I don't understand," Aria said loudly.

Ezra slapped his palm against the wall. The force of it made Aria jump. "Don't play dumb! I'm not some boy, Aria!"

Aria's whole body started to tremble. "I swear to God, I don't know what you're talking about. Can you explain, please? I'm kind of falling apart here!"

Ezra took his hand off the wall and started to pace around the tiny room. "Fine. After you left, I tried to sleep. There was this . . . this *beeping*. You know what it was?" He pointed to the Treo. "Your cell phone thing. The only way to shut it up was to open your *text messages*."

Aria wiped her eyes.

Ezra crossed his arms over his chest. "Shall I *quote* them for you?"

Then Aria realized. The text messages. "Wait! No! You don't understand!"

Ezra trembled. "*Student-teacher conference? Extra credit? This sound familiar?*"

"No, Ezra," Aria stammered. "You don't understand." The world was spinning. Aria gripped the edge of Ezra's kitchen table.

"I'm waiting," Ezra said.

"This friend of mine was killed," she began. "They just found her body." Aria opened her mouth to say more, but couldn't find the words. Ezra stood at the farthest point in the room from her, behind the bathtub.

"It's all so silly," Aria said. "Can you please come over here? Can you at least hug me?"

Ezra crossed his arms over his chest and looked down. He stood that way for what felt like a long time. "I *really* liked you," he finally said, his voice thick.

Aria choked back a sob. "I really like you, too. . . . " She walked over to him.

But Ezra stepped away. "No. You have to get out of here."

"But . . . "

Ezra clapped his hand over her mouth. "Please," he said a little desperately. "*Please* leave."

Aria widened her eyes and her heart started to pound. Alarms went off in her head. This felt . . . *wrong*. On impulse, she bit down into Ezra's hand.

"What the *fuck*?" he shrieked, pulling away.

Aria stood back, dazed. Blood dripped out of Ezra's hand onto the floor.

"You're insane!" Ezra cried.

Aria breathed heavily. She couldn't speak even if she wanted to. So she turned and ran for the door. As her hand turned the doorknob, something screamed past her, bounced off the wall, and landed next to her foot. It was a copy of *Being and Nothingness*, by Jean-Paul Sartre. Aria turned back to Ezra, her mouth open in shock.

"Get *out*!" Ezra boomed.

Aria slammed the door behind her. She tore down across the lawn as fast as her legs would carry her.

32

A FALLEN STAR

The next day, Spencer stood at her old bedroom window, smoking a Marlboro and looking across her lawn into Alison's old bedroom. It was dark and empty. Then, her eyes moved to the DiLaurentises' yard. The flashing lights hadn't stopped since they found her.

The police had put up DO NOT CROSS tape all around the concrete area of Alison's old backyard, even though they had already removed her body from the ground. They'd put huge tents around the area while doing that, too, so Spencer hadn't seen anything. Not that she'd have wanted to. It was beyond awful to think that Ali's body had been next door to her, rotting in the ground for three years. Spencer remembered the construction before Ali disappeared. They dug the hole right around the night she went missing. She knew, too, that they'd filled it after Ali disappeared but wasn't sure when. Someone had just *dumped* her there.

She stubbed out her Marlboro in the brick siding of her house and turned back to *Lucky* magazine. She'd hardly exchanged a word with her family since yesterday's confrontation and she'd been trying to calm herself down by going methodically through it and marking everything she wanted to buy with the magazine's little YES stickers. As she looked at a page on tweed blazers, though, her eyes glazed over.

She couldn't even talk to her parents about this. Yesterday, after they confronted her at breakfast, Spencer had wandered outside to see what the sirens were all about—ambulances still made her nervous, from both The Jenna Thing and Ali's disappearance. As she walked across her lawn to the DiLaurentis house, she sensed something and turned back. Her parents had come out to see what was going on too. When they saw her turn, they quickly looked away. The police told her to stand back, that this area was off limits. Then Spencer saw the morgue van. One of the policeman's walkie-talkies crackled, "Alison."

Her body had grown very cold. The world spun. Spencer slumped down on the grass. Someone spoke to her, but she couldn't understand him. "You're in shock," she finally heard. "Just try to calm down." Spencer's field of vision was so narrow, she wasn't sure who it was—only that it wasn't her mom or dad. The guy came back with a blanket and told her to sit there for a while and keep warm.

Once Spencer felt well enough to get up, whoever had

helped her was gone. Her parents had left too. They hadn't even bothered to see if she was okay.

She'd spent the rest of Saturday and most of Sunday in her room, only going out into the hall to the bathroom when she knew no one else was around. She hoped someone would come up and check on her, but when she heard a small, tentative knock on her door earlier this afternoon, Spencer didn't answer. She wasn't sure why. She listened to whoever it was sigh and pad back down the hall.

And then, only a half hour ago, Spencer had watched her dad's Jaguar back out of the driveway and turn toward the main road. Her mom was in the passenger seat; Melissa was in the back. She had no idea where they were going.

She slumped down in her computer chair and pulled up that first e-mail from A, the one talking about coveting things she couldn't have. After reading it a few times, she clicked REPLY. Slowly she typed, *Are you Alison?*

She hesitated before hitting SEND. Were all the police lights making her trippy? Dead girls didn't have Hotmail accounts. Nor did they have Instant Messenger screen names. Spencer had to get a grip—someone was pretending to be Ali. But who?

She stared up at the Mondrian mobile she'd bought last year at the Philadelphia Art Museum. Then she heard a *plink* sound. There it was again.

Plink.

It sounded really close, actually. Like at her window. Spencer sat up just as a pebble hit her window again. Someone was throwing rocks.

A?

As another rock hit, she went to the window—and gasped. On the lawn was Wren. The blue and red lights from the police cars kept making streaky shadows across his cheeks. When he saw her, he broke into a huge smile. Immediately, she bolted downstairs, not caring how horrible her hair looked or that she was wearing marinara-stained Kate Spade pajama pants. Wren ran for her as she came out the door. He threw his arms around her and kissed her scruffy head.

"You're not supposed to be here," she murmured.

"I know." He stood back. "But I noticed your parents' car was gone, so . . . "

She pushed her hand through his soft hair. Wren looked exhausted. What if he had to sleep in his little Toyota last night?

"How did you know I'd be back in my old room?"

He shrugged. "A hunch. I also thought I saw your face at the window. I wanted to come earlier, but there was . . . all that." He gestured to the police cars and random news vans next door. "You okay?"

"Yeah," Spencer answered. She tilted her head up to Wren's mouth and bit her chapped lip to keep from crying. "Are *you* okay?"

"Me? Sure."

"Do you have somewhere to live?"

"I can stay on a friend's couch until I find something. Not a big deal."

If only Spencer could stay on a friend's couch too. Then something occurred to her. "Are you and Melissa over?"

Wren cupped her face in his hand and sighed. "Of course," he said softly. "It was kind of obvious. With Melissa, it wasn't like . . . "

He trailed off, but Spencer thought she knew what he was going to say. *It wasn't like being with you.* She smiled shakily and laid her head against his chest. His heart thumped in her ear.

She looked over at the DiLaurentis house. Someone had started a little shrine to Alison on the curb, complete with pictures and Virgin Mary candles. In the center were little alphabet magnet letters that spelled *Ali.* Spencer herself had propped up a smiling picture of Alison in a tight blue Von Dutch T-shirt and spanking new Sevens. She remembered when she'd taken that picture: They were in sixth grade, and it was the night of the Rosewood Winter Formal. The five of them had spied on Melissa as Ian picked her up. Spencer had gotten hiccups from laughing when Melissa, trying to make a grand entrance, tripped down the Hastingses' front walk on the way to the tacky rented Hummer limo. It was probably their last really fun, carefree memory. The Jenna Thing happened not too long after. Spencer glanced at Toby and Jenna's house. No one was home, as usual, but it still made her shiver.

As she blotted her eyes with the back of her pale, thin hand, one of the news vans drove by slowly, and a guy in a red Phillies cap stared at her. She ducked. Now would not be the time to capture some emotional-girl-breaks-down-at-the-tragedy footage.

"You'd better go." She sniffed and turned back to Wren. "It's so crazy here. And I don't know when my parents will be back."

"All right." He tilted her head up. "But can we see each other again?"

Spencer swallowed, and tried to smile. As she did, Wren bent down and kissed her, wrapping one hand around the back of her neck and the other around the very spot on her lower back that, just Friday, hurt like hell.

Spencer broke away from him. "I don't even have your number."

"Don't worry," Wren whispered. "I'll call you."

Spencer stood out on the edge of her vast yard for a moment, watching Wren walk to his car. As he drove away, her eyes stung with tears again. If only she had someone to talk to—someone who wasn't banned from her house. She glanced back at the Ali shrine and wondered how her old friends were dealing with this.

As Wren pulled to the end of her street, Spencer noticed another car's headlights turn in. She froze. Was that her parents? Had they seen Wren?

The headlights inched closer. Suddenly, Spencer realized who it was. The sky was a dark purple, but she could just make out Andrew Campbell's longish hair.

She gasped, ducking behind her mother's rosebushes. Andrew slowly pulled his Mini up to her mailbox, opened it, slid something in, and neatly closed it again. He drove away.

She waited until he was gone before sprinting out to the curb and wrenching open the mailbox. Andrew had left her a folded-up piece of notepaper.

Hey, Spencer. I didn't know if you were taking any calls. I'm really sorry about Alison. I hope my blanket helped you yesterday. —Andrew

Spencer turned up her driveway, reading and rereading the note. She stared at the slanty boy handwriting. *Blanket? What blanket?*

Then she realized. It was *Andrew* who helped her?

She crumpled up the note in her hands and started sobbing all over again.

33

ROSEWOOD'S FINEST

"Police have reopened the DiLaurentis case, and are in the process of questioning witnesses," a newscaster on the eleven-o'clock news reported. *"The DiLaurentis family, now living in Maryland, will have to face something they've tried to put behind them. Except now, there is closure."*

Newscasters were such drama queens, Hanna thought angrily as she shoved another handful of Cheez-Its in her mouth. Only the news could find a way to make a horrible story worse. The camera stayed focused on the Ali shrine, as they called it, the candles, Beanie Babies, wilted flowers people no doubt just picked out of neighbors' gardens, marshmallow Peeps—Ali's favorite candy—and of course photos.

The camera cut to Alison's mother, whom Hanna hadn't seen in a while. Besides her teary face, Mrs. DiLaurentis looked pretty—with a shaggy haircut and dangly chandelier earrings.

"We've decided to have a service for Alison in Rosewood, which was the only home Ali knew," Mrs. DiLaurentis said in a controlled voice. "We want to thank all of those who helped search for our daughter three years ago for their enduring support."

The newscaster came back on the screen. *"A memorial will be held tomorrow at the Rosewood Abbey and will be open to the public."*

Hanna clicked off the TV. It was Sunday night. She sat on her living room couch, dressed in her rattiest C&C T-shirt and a pair of Calvin Klein boxer briefs she'd pilfered out of Sean's top drawer. Her long brown hair was messy and strawlike around her face and she was pretty sure she had a pimple on her forehead. A huge bowl of Cheez-Its rested in her lap, an empty Klondike wrapper was crumpled up on the coffee table, and a bottle of pinot noir was wedged snugly at her side. She'd been trying all night *not* to eat like this but, well, her willpower just wasn't very strong today.

She clicked the TV back on, wishing she had someone to talk to . . . about the police, about A, and mostly about Alison. Sean was out, for obvious reasons. Her mom— who was on a date right now—was her usual useless self. After the hubbub of activity at the police station yesterday, Wilden told Hanna and her mother to go home; they'd deal with her later, since the police had more important things to attend to at the moment. Neither

Hanna nor her mom knew what was happening at the station, only that it involved a murder.

On the drive home, instead of Ms. Marin reprimanding Hanna for, oh, *stealing a car and driving pissdrunk*, she told Hanna that she "was taking care of it." Hanna didn't have a clue what that meant. Last year, a cop had spoken at a Rosewood Day assembly about how Pennsylvania had a "zero tolerance" rule for drunk drivers under twenty-one. At the time, Hanna had paid attention only because she thought the cop was sort of hot, but now his words haunted her.

Hanna couldn't rely on Mona, either: She was still at that golf tournament in Florida. They'd spoken briefly on the phone, and Mona had admitted the police had called her about Sean's car, but she'd played dumb, saying she'd been at the party the whole time and Hanna had been too. And the lucky bitch: They'd gotten the back of her head on the Wawa surveillance tape, but not her face, since she'd been wearing that disgusting delivery hat. That was yesterday, though, after Hanna got back from the police station. She and Mona hadn't talked today, and they hadn't discussed Alison yet.

And then . . . there was A. Or if A was Alison, would A be gone now? But the police said Alison had been dead for years. . . .

As Hanna scanned the guide feature on TV for what else was on, her eyelids swollen with tears, she considered calling her father—this story might be on the Annapolis-area news, too. Or maybe he'd call her? She picked up the silent phone to make sure it was still working.

She sighed. The problem with being Mona's best friend was that they had no other friends. Watching all this Ali footage made her think of her old group of friends. They'd had their rocky, horrible moments together, but they used to have a lot of fun, too. In a parallel universe, they'd all be together now, remembering Ali and laughing even though they were crying, too. But in this dimension, they'd grown too far apart.

They'd split up for valid reasons, of course—things had started to go rotten way before Ali went missing. In the beginning, when they were doing that charity drive stuff, it was wonderful. But then, after The Jenna Thing happened, things got tense. They were all so afraid that what happened to Jenna could be linked to them. Hanna remembered being jumpy even when she was on the bus and a cop car would pass by them, going in the other direction. Then, that next winter and spring, whole topics were suddenly off-limits. Someone was always saying, "Shhh!" and then they all fell into an uncomfortable silence.

The eleven-o'clock newscasters signed off and *The Simpsons* came on. Hanna picked up her BlackBerry. She still knew Spencer's number by heart, and it probably wouldn't be too late to call. As she dialed the second digit, she cocked her ear, her Tiffany earrings jangling. There was a scratching noise at the door.

Dot, who had been lying by her feet, picked up his head and growled. Hanna took the Cheez-It bowl off her lap and stood.

Was it . . . A?

Knees shaking, Hanna crept into the hall. There were long, dark shadows at the back door, and the scratching noise had grown louder. "Oh my God," Hanna whispered, her chin trembling. *Someone was trying to get in!*

Hanna looked around. There was a round jade paperweight on the little hall table. It had to weigh at least twenty pounds. She heaved it up and took three tentative steps for the kitchen door.

Suddenly, the door burst open. Hanna jumped back. A woman stumbled through the entranceway. Her tasteful, gray pleated skirt was up around her waist. Hanna held up the paperweight, about to throw it.

Then she realized. It was her mom.

Ms. Marin bumped into the telephone table as if she were wasted. Some guy was behind her, trying to unzip her skirt and kiss her at the same time. Hanna's eyes widened.

Darren Wilden. Mr. April.

So *that* was what her mom meant by "taking care of it"?

Hanna's stomach clenched. No doubt she looked a little insane, tenaciously clutching the paperweight. Ms. Marin gave Hanna a very long look, not even bothering to turn away from Wilden.

Her mother's eyes said, *I'm doing this for you.*

34

FANCY MEETING YOU HERE

On Monday morning, instead of sitting in first-period bio, Emily stood next to her parents in the high-ceilinged, marble-floored nave of Rosewood Abbey. She tugged uncomfortably at the black, pleated, too-short Gap skirt she'd found in the back of her closet and tried to smile. Mrs. DiLaurentis stood in the doorway, clad in a cowl-neck black dress, heels, and tiny freshwater pearls. She walked up to Emily and engulfed her in a hug.

"Oh, Emily," Mrs. DiLaurentis sobbed.

"I'm so sorry," Emily whispered back, her own eyes watering. Mrs. DiLaurentis still wore the same perfume—Coco Chanel. It instantly brought back all kinds of memories: A million rides to and from the mall in Mrs. DiLaurentis's Infiniti, sneaking into her bathroom to steal TrimSpa tablets and to experiment with her expensive La Prairie makeup, going through her enormous, walk-in closet and trying on all her sexy size-2 black Dior cocktail dresses.

Other kids from Rosewood streamed around them, trying to find seats in the high-backed wooden pews. Emily hadn't known what to expect at Alison's memorial service. The abbey smelled like incense and wood. Simple cylinder-shaped lamps hung from the ceiling, and the altar was covered with a billion white tulips. Tulips were Alison's favorite flower. Emily remembered Ali helped her mom plant rows of them in their front yard every year.

Alison's mom finally stood back and wiped her eyes. "I want you to sit up in the front, with all of Ali's friends. Is that okay, Kathleen?"

Emily's mom nodded. "Of course."

Emily listened to every click of Mrs. DiLaurentis's heels and the shuffling of her own chunky loafers as they walked down the aisle. Suddenly it hit Emily why she was here again. Ali was *dead*.

Emily clutched Mrs. DiLaurentis's arm. "Oh my God." Her field of vision narrowed, and she heard a *waaaah* noise in her ears, the sign that she was about to faint.

Mrs. DiLaurentis held her upright. "It's okay. Come on. Sit down here."

Dizzily, Emily slid into the pew. "Put your head between your legs," she heard a familiar voice say.

Then another familiar voice snorted. "Say it louder, so *all* the boys can hear."

Emily looked up. Next to her were Aria and Hanna. Aria wore a blue, purple, and fuchsia-striped cotton boat-neck dress, a navy velvet jacket, and cowboy boots. It was so Aria—she was the type who thought wearing some color to funerals celebrated the living. Hanna, on the other hand, wore a skimpy black V-neck dress and black stockings.

"Dear, can you move over?"

Above her, Mrs. DiLaurentis stood with Spencer Hastings, who wore a charcoal suit and ballet flats.

"Hey, guys," Spencer said to all of them, in that buttery voice Emily had missed. She sat down next to Emily.

"So, we meet again," Aria said, smiling.

Silence. Emily peeked at all of them out of the corner of her eye. Aria was fidgeting with a silver ring on her thumb, Hanna was fumbling around in her purse, and Spencer was sitting very still, staring at the altar.

"Poor Ali," Spencer murmured.

The girls sat quietly for a few minutes. Emily wracked her brain for something to say. Her ears filled with the *waaaah* sound again.

She twisted around to scan the crowd for Maya, and her eyes landed square on Ben's. He was sitting in the second-to-last row with the rest of the swimmers. Emily lifted her hand in a tiny wave. Next to this, the party stuff seemed petty.

But instead of waving back, Ben glared at her, his thin mouth in a stubborn, straight line. Then he looked away.

Okay.

Emily swung back around. Rage filled her body. *My old best friend was just found murdered,* she wanted to scream. *And we're in a church, for God's sake! What about forgiveness?*

Then it hit her. She didn't want him to take her back. Not one bit.

Aria tapped her on the leg. "You okay after Saturday morning? I mean, you didn't even know yet, right?"

"No, it was something else, but I'm okay," Emily answered, even though that wasn't true.

"Spencer." Hanna's head popped up. "I, um, I saw you at the mall recently."

Spencer looked at Hanna. "Huh?"

"You were . . . you were going into Kate Spade." Hanna looked down. "I don't know. I was going to say hi. But, um, I'm glad you don't have to order those purses from New York anymore." She put her head down and blushed, as if she'd said too much.

Emily was startled—she hadn't seen Hanna make that expression in years.

Spencer's brow crinkled. Then, a sad, tender look came over her face. She swallowed hard and looked down. "Thanks," she murmured. Her shoulders started to shake and she squeezed her eyes shut. Emily felt her own throat choking up. She'd never actually seen Spencer cry.

Aria put her hand on Spencer's shoulder. "It's okay," she said.

"Sorry," Spencer said, wiping her eyes with her sleeve. "I just . . . " She glanced around at all of them and then started crying even harder.

Emily hugged her. It felt a little awkward, but by the way Spencer squeezed her hand, Emily could tell she appreciated it.

When they sat back, Hanna pulled a tiny silver flask out of her bag and reached over Emily to pass it to Spencer. "Here," she whispered.

Without even smelling it or asking what it was, Spencer took a huge swallow. She winced but said, "Thanks."

She passed the flask back to Hanna, who drank and handed it to Emily. Emily took a sip, which burned in her chest, then passed it to Aria. Before drinking, Aria pulled on Spencer's sleeve.

"This'll make you feel better too." Aria tugged down the shoulder of her dress to reveal a white knitted bra strap. Emily immediately recognized it—Aria had knitted heavy woolen bras for all the girls in seventh grade. "I wore it for old time's sake," Aria whispered. "It's itching like hell."

Spencer sputtered out a laugh. "Oh my God."

"You're such a spaz," Hanna added, grinning.

"I could never wear mine, remember?" Emily chimed in. "My mom thought it was too sexy for school!"

"Yeah." Spencer giggled. "If you can call scratching your boobs all day sexy."

The girls snickered. Suddenly, Aria's cell phone buzzed. She reached into her bag and looked at the phone's screen.

"What?" Aria looked up, realizing they were all staring at her.

Hanna fiddled with her charm bracelet. "Did you, um, just get a text message?"

"Yeah. So?"

"Who was it?"

"It was my mom," Aria answered slowly. "Why?"

Low pipe organ music began to lilt through the church. Behind them, more kids shuffled in quietly. Spencer glanced nervously at Emily. Emily's heart started to pound.

"Never mind," Hanna said. "That was nosy."

Aria licked her lips. "Wait. Seriously. *Why?*"

Hanna's adam's apple rose with a nervous swallow. "I . . . I just thought maybe strange things had been happening to you, too."

Aria's mouth fell open. "Strange is an understatement."

Emily clutched her arms around herself.

"Wait. You guys, too?" Spencer whispered.

Hanna nodded. "Texts?"

"E-mails," Spencer said.

"About . . . stuff from seventh?" Aria whispered.

"Are you guys *serious?*" Emily squeaked.

The friends stared at each other. But before anyone could say anything else, the somber-sounding pipe organ filled the room.

Emily turned around. A bunch of people were walking slowly up the center aisle. It was Ali's mom and dad, her brother, her grandparents, and some others who must've been relatives. Two redheaded boys were the last to come down the aisle; Emily recognized them as Sam and Russell, Ali's cousins. They used to visit Ali's family every summer. Emily hadn't seen them in years, and wondered if they were still as gullible as they used to be.

The family members slid into the front row and waited for the music to stop.

As Emily stared at them, she noticed movement. One of the pimply, redheaded cousins was staring at them. Emily was pretty sure it was the one named Sam—he'd been the geekier of the two. He stared at all the girls and then slowly and flirtatiously raised an eyebrow. Emily quickly looked away.

She felt Hanna jab her in the ribs. "Not it," Hanna whispered to the girls.

Emily looked at her, puzzled, but then Hanna motioned with her eyes to the two gangly cousins.

All the girls caught on at the same time. "Not it," Emily, Spencer, and Aria said at once.

They all giggled. But then Emily paused, considering what "not it" really meant. She'd never thought about it before, but it was kind of mean. When she looked around, she noticed her friends had stopped laughing too. They all exchanged a look.

"I guess it was funnier back then," Hanna said quietly.

Emily sat back. Maybe Ali didn't know everything. Yes, this might have been the worst day of her life, and she was horribly devastated about Ali, and completely freaked about A. But for a moment, she felt okay. Sitting here with her old friends seemed like the tiny beginning of something.

35

JUST YOU WAIT

The organ started up again with its dreary music, and Ali's brother and the others filed out of the church. Spencer, tipsy from a few slugs of whiskey, noticed that her three old friends had stood up and were filing out of the pew, and she figured she should go, too.

Everyone from Rosewood Day hung out at the back of the church, from the lacrosse boys to the video game–obsessed geeks who Ali no doubt would have teased back in seventh. Old Mr. Yew—the one in charge of the Rosewood Day charity drive—stood in the corner, talking quietly to Mr. Kaplan, who taught art. Even Ali's older JV field hockey friends had returned from their respective colleges; they stood in a teary huddle near the door. Spencer scanned the familiar faces, remembering all the people she used to know and didn't anymore. And then, she saw a dog—a seeing-eye dog.

Oh my God.

Spencer grabbed Aria's arm. "By the exit," she hissed.

Aria squinted. "Is that . . . ?"

"Jenna," Hanna murmured.

"And Toby," Spencer added.

Emily turned pale. "What are they doing here?"

Spencer was too stunned to answer. They looked the same but totally different. His hair was long now, and she was . . . gorgeous, with long black hair and wearing big Gucci sunglasses.

Toby, Jenna's brother, caught Spencer staring. A sour, disgusted look settled over his face. Spencer quickly jerked her eyes away.

"I can't believe he showed up," she whispered, too quietly for the others to hear.

By the time the girls reached the heavy wooden doors that led to the church's crumbling stone steps, Toby and Jenna were gone. Spencer squinted in the sunlight of the brilliant, perfectly blue sky. It was one of those lovely early-fall days with no humidity, where you were dying to skip school, lie in a field, and not think about your responsibilities. Why was it always on days like this that something horrible happened?

Someone touched her shoulder and Spencer jumped. It was a blond burly cop. She motioned for Hanna, Aria, and Emily to go on without her.

"Are you Spencer Hastings?" he asked.

She nodded dumbly.

The cop wrung his enormous hands together. "I'm

very sorry for your loss," he said. "You were good friends with Ms. DiLaurentis, right?"

"Thanks. Yeah, I was."

"I'm going to need to talk with you." The cop reached into his pocket. "Here's my card. We're reopening the case. Since you were friends, you might be able to help us. Is it okay if I come by in a couple of days?"

"Um, sure," Spencer stammered. "Whatever I can do."

Zombielike, she caught up with her old friends, who'd gathered under a weeping willow. "What did he want?" Aria asked.

"They want to talk to me, too," Emily said quickly. "It's not a big deal though, is it?"

"I'm sure it's the same old stuff," Hanna said.

"He couldn't be wondering about . . . ," Aria started. She looked nervously to the church's front door, where Toby, Jenna, and her dog had stood.

"No," Emily said quickly. "We couldn't get in trouble for that now, could we?"

They all glanced at each other worriedly.

"Of course not," Hanna finally said.

Spencer looked around at everyone talking quietly on the lawn. She felt sick after seeing Toby, and she hadn't seen Jenna since the accident. But it was a coincidence that the cop had spoken to her right after she'd seen them, right? Spencer quickly pulled out her emergency cigarettes and lit up. She needed something to do with her hands.

I'll tell everyone about The Jenna Thing.

You're just as guilty as I am.

But no one saw me.

Spencer nervously exhaled and scanned the crowd. *There wasn't any proof.* End of story. Unless . . .

"This has been the worst week of my life," Aria said suddenly.

"Mine too." Hanna nodded.

"I guess we can look on the bright side," Emily said, her voice high-pitched and jittery. "It can't get any worse than this."

As they followed the procession out to the gravel parking lot, Spencer stopped. Her old friends stopped too. Spencer wanted to say something to them—not about Ali or A or Jenna or Toby or the police, but instead, more than anything, she wanted to tell them that she'd missed them all these years.

But before she could say it, Aria's phone rang.

"Hang on . . . ," Aria muttered, rooting around in her bag for her phone. "It's probably my mom again."

Then, Spencer's Sidekick vibrated. And rang. And chirped. It wasn't just her phone, but her friends' phones too. The sudden, high-pitched noises sounded even louder against the sober, silent funeral procession. The other mourners shot them dirty looks. Aria held hers up to silence it; Emily struggled to operate her Nokia. Spencer wrenched her phone out of her clutch's pocket.

Hanna read her screen. "I have one new message."

"I do too," Aria whispered.

"Same," Emily echoed.

Spencer saw she did, too. Everyone hit READ. A moment of stunned silence passed.

"Oh my God," Aria whispered.

"It's from . . . ," Hanna squeaked.

Aria murmured, "Do you think she means . . . "

Spencer swallowed hard. In tandem, the girls read their texts out loud. Each said the exact same thing:

I'm still here, bitches. And I know everything. —A

ACKNOWLEDGMENTS

I owe a lot to a great group of people at Alloy Entertainment. I've known them for years and without them, this book could never have happened. Josh Bank, for being hilarious, magnetic, and brilliant . . . and for giving me a chance years ago despite the fact that I so rudely crashed his company Christmas party. Ben Schrank, for encouraging me to do this project in the first place and for his invaluable writing advice. Of course Les Morgenstein, for believing in me. And my fantastic editor, Sara Shandler, for her friendship and dedicated help in shaping this novel.

I'm grateful to Elise Howard and Kristin Marang at HarperCollins for their support, insight, and enthusiasm. And huge thanks to Jennifer Rudolph Walsh at William Morris for all the magical things she made happen.

Thanks also to Doug and Fran Wilkens for a great summer in Pennsylvania. I'm grateful to Colleen

McGarry, for reminding me of our junior high and high school inside jokes, especially those about our fictitious band whose name I won't mention. Thanks to my parents, Bob and Mindy Shepard, for their help with sticky plot points and for encouraging me to be myself, however weird that might be. And I don't know what I'd do without my sister, Ali, who agrees that Icelandic boys are pussies who ride small, gay horses and is okay with a certain character in this book being named after her.

And finally, thanks to my husband, Joel, for being loving, silly, and patient, and also for reading every draft of this book (happily!) and offering good advice—proof that boys might just understand more about girls' inner struggles than we think.

WHAT HAPPENS NEXT . . .

I bet you thought I was Alison, didn't you? Well, sorry, but I'm not. Duh. She's dead.

Nope, I'm very much alive . . . and I'm very, very close. And for a certain clique of four pretty girls, the fun has just started. Why? 'Cause I say so.

Naughty behavior deserves punishment, after all. And Rosewood's finest deserve to know that Aria's been doing some extra-credit smooching with her English teacher, don't they? Not to mention the nasty family secret she's been hiding for years. The girl is a train wreck.

While I'm at it, I really ought to tip Emily's parents off to the reason she's been acting funny lately. Hey there, Mr. and Mrs. Fields, nice weather, huh? And by the way, your daughter likes kissing girls.

Then there's Hanna. Poor Hanna. Just free-falling into dorkdom. She may try to claw her way back to the top,

but don't worry—I'll be there waiting to knock her rap-
idly growing behind back into a pair of stonewashed
mom-jeans.

Oh my god, I almost forgot Spencer. She's a total
mess! After all, her family thinks she's a completely worth-
less skank. That's gotta suck. And just between us, it's
about to get much worse. Spencer's keeping a deep, dark
secret that could pretty much ruin all four of their lives.
But who would tell such an awful secret? Oh, I don't
know. Take a wild guess.

Bingo.

Life's so much fun when you know everything.

Just how do I know so much? You're probably dying to
know, aren't you? Well, relax. All in due time.

Believe me, I'd love to tell you. But what's the fun in that?

I'll be watching. —A

Psssst!
We've got a secret . . .

WANT A TASTE OF *FLAWLESS*, THE SECOND BOOK IN THE PRETTY LITTLE LIARS SERIES? READ AN EXCLUSIVE EXCERPT FROM THE BOOK, AND FIND SCANDALOUS PRETTY LITTLE LIARS GOSSIP, GIVEAWAYS, AND SERIES SECRETS—ONLY AT WWW.PRETTYLITTLELIARSBOOKS.COM. WE KNOW YOU'RE *DYING* TO FIND OUT WHAT HAPPENS NEXT!

Flawless
A PRETTY LITTLE LIARS NOVEL

ARIA, HANNA, EMILY, AND SPENCER THOUGHT THEIR SECRETS WERE SAFE, BUT A ISN'T DONE WITH THEM YET. EVERY CRUMPLED NOTE, WICKED IM, AND VINDICTIVE TEXT MESSAGE A SENDS PROVES THAT SOMEONE HAS THE DIRT TO BURY THEM ALL ALIVE—BUT WHO IS IT? AND WHAT DOES A WANT? ONE THING'S FOR CERTAIN . . . THEIR PRETTY LITTLE LIVES WILL NEVER BE THE SAME AGAIN.

HarperTempest
An Imprint of HarperCollinsPublishers

WWW.HARPERTEEN.COM